THE HAUNTING OF SILVER CREEK LODGE

ALEXANDRIA CLARKE

❀ Created with Vellum

*M*y nose was on fire.

That was the risk of going for a jog when it was thirty-five degrees outside and the air felt as sharp as knives upon inhaling it. But I needed to move. When winter settled in Colorado, so did my seasonal depression, and exercise was one of the surefire ways to combat it.

I'd forgotten to smear petroleum jelly across my face like snowboarders did to protect their skin before they hit the slopes. Usually, I coated my nose, lips, and cheeks with the tacky stuff, but I was in such a rush to get out of the cramped condo and get my blood moving that I'd stupidly forgotten my protective goo. I pulled my scarf over my nose and mouth, but the thick fabric made it difficult to drag enough air into my lungs. I let the scarf fall back to my neck and slowed to a walk. The stinging around my nose lessened.

The suburbs of Denver varied greatly. In some parts of

town, luxury mansions and custom estates sat high on the hills and lorded over the less fortunate locals. In other areas, red rocks and green forests surrounded cozy cabins. Where we lived was popular with the blue-collar crowd and empty nesters. Condos, patio homes, and apartment complexes lined the streets because no one could afford much else. It made for a boring jog—all the buildings blurred into a forgetful background after a while—but when it snowed, the neighborhood descended into a dreamier state.

As I walked at a quick pace to keep my heart rate up without ruining the skin on my face, a few fresh flakes floated from the sky. I'd slept through the first snowfall of the season a few days ago, so I took the time to enjoy the second one, tilting my head back to let the snow settle on my eyelashes before blinking them away. The remnants of the last snowstorm hadn't faded completely. It sat atop chimneys and mailboxes, and a glistening white coat decorated the conjoined roofs of row houses. The street-lights' yellow glow made the slush in the gutter look pleasing rather than dangerous.

I took a deep breath to inhale that fresh snow scent and promptly regretted it. The cold air stabbed me in the back of the throat and made me cough. I cupped my hands around my face, huffed into them, and found relief in the warmth of my breath. It was a brief respite. The cold was adamant tonight.

A twig snapped behind me. I thought nothing of it. This was a quiet neighborhood without much crime. It was probably someone walking their dog.

But there was no sound of a leash or collar jingling. I glanced over my shoulder. No one was there. My heart rate slowed. I kept walking.

Were those footsteps?

I whirled around. The prints of my shoes in the half-melted slush walked alone. I faced front and quickened my pace.

"Relax," I told myself in a low tone. "Nothing is following you. You're safe. You've jogged along this path a hundred times."

Another dead branch crunched.

"Just an owl," I muttered, "or a rabbit."

I started jogging again. The wind picked up, cruelly lashing against my face. The skin beneath my nose stung. Moisture gathered at the corners of my eyes and traced erratic patterns down my cheeks.

A light pattern echoed the soft pad of my feet against the pavement. Intentionally, I performed an awkward step to interrupt the rhythm of my run. I listened hard. The other set of footprints went on smoothly. Someone *was* behind me.

My toes cracked as I picked up more speed. I feared they might freeze and splinter off, but I kept running. The cold was almost unbearable at this pace. I tasted salt as my nose ran into my mouth, but I didn't dare slow to wipe it. My shins vibrated with each fall of my foot, absorbing the impact of my increasing gait. The footsteps kept pace with mine.

My breath felt ragged in my throat, tearing up and down my airway. The condo wasn't far, a half-mile maybe. I could run a half-mile in four minutes...in the summertime.

The footsteps pounded against the sidewalk, loudly, as if my pursuer wanted me to know how close they were to catching up with me. With my last bit of effort, I lengthened my stride. My legs and lungs burned. I couldn't keep this up for long.

As I turned onto my street, my shoes slipped over a patch of invisible ice. I stumbled and almost fell, but I managed to keep myself upright by grabbing hold of the stop sign. I broke into a run again, but the footsteps were closer now. Much closer.

My back rounded as I fatigued. My legs shook with every step. When I caught sight of the condo, I let out a gasp of relief—just a few hundred more yards.

But my pursuer had been holding out, saving their strength for this moment. The footsteps thundered upon the pavement. A shadow grew tall in the streetlights. Panting, I forced one foot after the other. It wasn't enough. I got ready to scream as shadowy arms stretched out and encircled me.

"Boo!"

Instant alleviation flooded my body as my boyfriend, Simon, wrapped his lean arms around me and drew me against the warmth of his body. I spun around and smacked his chest, anger quickly replacing relief.

"Are you crazy?" I said. "Why would you do that? I thought someone was trying to kill me."

His dark brown eyes twinkled with mischief when he opened his jacket and drew me inside the fake sherpa lining. A walking furnace, he warmed me up straight away.

"It's our prank month," he said lightly. "I thought you'd realize it was me."

As per our annual tradition, we spent the month of October playing harmless tricks against each other. We had three strict rules in place: no inducing physical harm, no inconveniencing the other before work, and no fake break-ups. Technically, Simon hadn't broken any guidelines by terrifying me on my jog.

"October is over," I reminded him, my head bouncing against his chest as we walked the rest of the way home. "Halloween is done, and so is our prank month."

He kissed the top of my head. "Sorry, Max. I didn't mean to freak you out. Hot chocolate's on me tonight."

Inside the small condo, we hung our coats in the closet and lined our wet shoes up next to several pairs of different sizes on the rack. Simon shook the snow out of his dark, curly hair. As a teenager, he landed a gig as an Abercrombie model, and though he didn't pursue the career, he hadn't lost the features that made him so picturesque in the first place. Years of competitive swimming had given him broad shoulders and a narrow waist. His square jaw and strong chin caught gentle shadows from the overhead light, and a smattering of freckles decorated his cheeks and dotted his chest. Best of all, he reserved his signature smile for me.

His background was Greek and Irish; mine was Welsh and Italian. We were both a strange combination of contrasting physical traits. I often imagined what our kids might look like. I pictured a daughter with our dark hair, my olive skin, and Simon's cute freckles or a son with Simon's curls and my sea-green eyes. As always, sadness tinged the thought. Kids weren't in our immediate future.

Simon gently stroked my cheek. "Everything all right? You look like you're spiraling."

Whenever I got sucked into deep thoughts, whether creative or depressive, it showed in the blankness of my eyes. Or, so Simon thought.

"I'm fine."

I took his hand and led him upstairs to the conjoined living room and kitchen. Christian and Sienna, our friends who owned the condo, weren't home yet. I turned on the fake fireplace while Simon heated a pot of cocoa for the four of us. I flipped on the fairy lights strung along the loft floor—above which was mine and Simon's makeshift bedroom. We didn't have a door, our own bathroom, or any privacy except for a curtain, but that was the sacrifice you made when you bummed off someone else's rent.

"Are you excited about tomorrow?" Simon asked as I joined him in the kitchen and watched him drop chunks of dark chocolate into the boiling milk. "It's the big day."

"Thrilled," I said wryly. "How I've wished to be legally bound to you from the day we met."

"Our six-year relationship meant nothing," he played along. "Only a piece of paper signed by a court representative will make our love official."

Some other couple might be offended by our bleak outlook on marriage, but neither one of us was particularly traditional. By our definition, we were already married. Sometimes, I forgot we weren't and referred to Simon as my husband. He almost always called me his wife. Were it not for the tax benefits and health insurance breaks, we wouldn't bother at all, but our finances had reached a low enough point to consider marriage as a potential solution to our burdening debt.

"I can't wait to see you in your dress," Simon went on. The enticing smell of melted chocolate rose with the steam from the pot. "Who designed it again? Vera Wang?"

"Target."

He feigned ignorance. "Were they featured at fashion week? I've never heard of that brand."

"What about you?" I shot back. "Is your suit Armani?"

"No, it's from a classic designer," he replied. "Been around for ages. His name is Wal-Mart."

I clapped my palm to my heart. "What luxury! We're so lucky everything is lining up. Can you believe the Plaza Hotel had a spot open for us? Good thing our private jet is gassed up and ready to fly us to New York tomorrow for the ceremony."

"And our honeymoon to Paris is booked, too!" Simon added. "What a dream these next few weeks will be, my darling."

Christian appeared at the top of the steps, balancing two stacked pizzas in one hand and a six-pack of beer in the other. "What the hell are you guys talking about?"

We burst into laughter. I relieved Christian of the pizzas so he wouldn't drop them.

"We were simply appreciating our lavish wedding

details," Simon said, unable to drop a schtick. "Say, did you happen to pick up the champagne for the fountain?"

Christian shot me a confused look. "What does he want?"

"Ignore him." I set the pizzas on the small table squished between the kitchen counter and the living room sofa. "Where's Sienna?"

"Outside. She stepped in dog shit."

"Oh, boy."

Christian clapped his hands together. "Help me with damage control?"

"I'm on it."

I jogged downstairs and went outside without a coat. Sienna was busy scraping the bottom of her boot against the edge of the sidewalk, muttering murderously under her breath. The vicious wind whipped her long blond hair into her face, making the task more difficult than it had to be.

I shivered and hugged myself tightly. "Sienna, use a stick!"

The wind howled.

"What?" she hollered.

"A stick!" I picked up a skinny tree limb and hurried over to her. I held my breath and used the branch to dig the dog crap out of the treads when she presented her boot to me. "There, that's good enough. We'll hose the rest tomorrow when it's warmer."

"What a beautiful way to start your wedding day." She used me as a crutch and hopped inside to keep her poo boot off the floor. When she took it off, she set it upside

8

down and wrinkled her nose. "Why can't people clean up after their dogs? It's not that hard!"

Upstairs, Christian set the table with paper plates, and Simon set aside the hot chocolate to simmer. We all washed our hands and sat down to dinner together. Simon was the only one who didn't take a beer.

"What's the plan for tomorrow?" Sienna asked, daintily cutting her pizza with a knife and fork. "What time are we supposed to be at the courthouse?"

"Two o'clock," I answered.

"What should I wear?"

I shrugged. "Whatever you want. Jeans, if that's comfortable."

She groaned dramatically. "Maxine Finch, we have been through this a hundred times. "As your maid of honor, I am *not* wearing jeans to your wedding! Don't you have any ideas on coordinating colors?"

I piled extra bacon on top of my barbeque chicken pizza. "Nope."

"What about rings?" she asked. "Or flowers? Somewhere to host the reception?"

"Yes!" Simon said. "We have a reception place."

Sienna shifted excitedly. "Great! Where?"

"Hector's."

Sienna's face fell. "You're not serious. You can't have your wedding reception at Hector's Taco Hut!"

"And yet..."

Sienna slouched in her chair and crossed her arms like a five-year-old who was served raw broccoli and nothing else. "This is ridiculous. This is not how a wedding should be done. When Christian and I got married, we had a beautifully decorated hall and a big cake and a champagne fountain!"

"Christian is in charge of the champagne fountain," Simon said.

Christian looked up. "Wait. What?"

"Rings," Sienna said. "Please tell me you at least have rings. They don't have to be gold."

"We're getting them tattooed on," I answered.

She gasped. "No!"

"Can you relax?" I asked. "I'm joking. We're not doing rings. It's archaic."

"It's traditional." She waved her massive engagement ring and matching gold band in front of my face. "Don't you want this on your finger?"

I wrinkled my nose. "Five extra pounds and the weight of the guilt because we bought something from an industry that supports child labor? No, thanks."

Her face dropped. She regarded her ring with a sad look.

"Yours is vintage," Christian informed his wife hurriedly. "You're not contributing to child labor by wearing it."

"It's beautiful," I added. "I didn't mean to devalue your view of weddings. Simon and I have different ideas. That's all."

She stole the biggest chunk of chicken off my pizza. "Excuse me for thinking a wedding should be about more than getting a joint bank account. You're binding yourselves to each other. That has weight, and you're taking it so lightly."

Simon leaned forward and said gently, "Only because we already feel bound to each other. We don't need the government to recognize it for us. We're sure of ourselves and our relationship."

"But the government likes married people better than 'unmarried partners,'" I added. "That's why we're doing this. It's still a celebration, even if it looks different than yours did."

Christian held Sienna's hand over the table and placed a kiss on her ring. "Do you remember how helpful Max and Simon were when *we* got married? It's our job to be supportive of them for theirs."

Sienna tossed her hands into the air, almost upsetting her carefully cut pizza squares. "Fine, have it your way, but I'm bringing a bottle of champagne to Hector's! We are not toasting with margaritas."

"What about tequila shots?" I asked.

THE OFFICIAL CEREMONY was short and sweet. I wore my sparkly, off-white Target dress with floral accents on the sleeves while Simon showed up in a dark-green suit jacket, a white shirt, and black slacks. Sienna was best-dressed out of all us in a beautiful, wine-red, long-sleeved gown, and Christian looked great next to her in a tan suit and red tie.

The magistrate was a stern man with gray hair and a triangular patch of facial hair beneath his lower lip.

"Hello, everyone," he said in a slow monotone as he set our soon-to-be-signed marriage license on the desk. "We are gathered here today to witness the marriage of—" he checked our driver's licenses—"Simon York and Maxine Finch. Witnesses, please state your names."

"Christian Cooper."

"Sienna Cooper."

"Great," said the magistrate. "Simon, Maxine, do you have any vows prepared?"

Warmth spread to the ends of my fingers and toes at the sight of Simon's smile. "Love you."

He grinned. "Love you, too."

"That's it?" Sienna said, unable to contain herself.

Christian shushed his wife.

The magistrate handed us a pen. "Go ahead and sign the license."

Simon scribbled his name then passed the pen to me. I half-expected to feel different as I added my name to the license, but the magistrate grabbed the license before I had time to process the meaning of it.

"By the power vested in me," he said, signing his name, "I now pronounce you husband and wife. You can kiss or whatever, but don't go on forever. This is a small room."

Simon kissed me politely on the lips as Christian and Sienna cheered. We lifted our conjoined fists into the air.

"To Hector's Taco Hut!" Simon proclaimed.

AN HOUR LATER, we'd devoured twenty tacos between the four of us. Hector himself had decided to hook us up with free drinks when we told him we were here to celebrate our brand-new marriage. We powered through two pitchers of margaritas and were currently working on a third.

"To Max and Simon!" Sienna hiccupped as she lifted her glass into the air. "May your marriage be as weird as the two of you!"

"To Sienna's third toast of the evening," I added, clinking my glass against hers. "You might want to lay off the tequila."

She sniffed her drink and wisely set it aside. "I do feel a bit woozy."

"Some fried ice cream should fix that," Christian said, flagging down Hector. "So, what do you two plan on doing next, now that you're officially hitched?"

Simon, bottomless, ate another taco. "That remains to be seen. The handyman jobs are drying up around here. No one wants to hire someone who isn't a certified plumber or whatever. If *someone* would finish her comic book" —he nudged me playfully— "we wouldn't have to worry about money for a few months."

Though I knew Simon wasn't putting any real pressure on me, I couldn't help blushing with embarrassment. When I first started dealing with my fears and anxieties by drawing them, I never expected it to turn into a career. Four years later, IDW bought my material and published it. My series—*Rebel Queen*—was set in a futuristic fantasy world and featured a main character with a dark secret, much like myself. The first two volumes sold well, and the advances were enough for us to live off of, but the cash had long since dried up. I'd been in an artistic rut for a year and a half.

"I won't publish something with a story I'm not passionate about." The excuse was stale and overused. Everyone here had heard it before. "When I come up with something good, I'll let you know."

Sienna, sensing we had broached a touchy subject, asked Simon, "What about you? How's your music going?"

It was his turn to look sullen. "Not great."

"Have you got writer's block, too?" Christian asked.

"No, I have tons of songs," Simon replied. "But I can't make them sound as good as I want them to without the proper equipment. And since they don't sound good, no one's streaming my stuff on Spotify. I need a producer."

Like me, Simon had big artistic dreams. As a guitar and piano-playing singer-songwriter, he had a lot of competition. Unlike me, he hadn't found a way to make those dreams a reality. So far, he hadn't been able to stand out enough to gather followers or make his music profitable. At least he had content, though. He was ahead of me on that front.

Sienna elbowed Christian, and I sensed a plot was afoot. Christian nervously cleared his throat. "So, no idea when the two of you might get your own place?"

My heart sank. Simon and I had a savings account dedicated to our eventual honeymoon, but it was slowly turning into emergency funds as we continued to pull out of it.

"Not that we don't enjoy having you," Christian added

hurriedly. "But the condo's really small, and we're thinking about kids soon—"

"We won't kick you out if you have nowhere to go," Sienna said further. "We just wondered if you might consider moving out now that you're married." She dumped her face in her hands. "Oh, I feel horrible about this."

Simon squeezed my hand under the table. "You have been too kind letting us stay for as long as we have. We'll figure something out."

"I have a proposition for you if you're interested," Christian said. "A buddy of mine was passing through a little town called Silver Creek on his way to Breckenridge for vacation. He saw this old foreclosed ski lodge there. I looked it up. The bank's selling it for dirt cheap. If you bought it, you could live there, fix the place up, and start taking guests. Boom. Instant housing *and* constant income. I could help you buy it."

Christian was a realtor in the Denver area. More than once, he'd offered to help us find an affordable place to live, but the places we liked were never within our budget.

"I don't know much about managing a ski lodge," I said.

"Learn while you make repairs," Christian suggested. "Or fix it up and flip it. The location's perfect. It's right near a bunch of ski trails. Whoever owns the place would get a ton of business from skiers and snowboarders looking for a more intimate adventure."

"It's not a terrible idea," Simon said. "We could dip into our savings to buy it and do the repairs—"

"That's not what that money is for."

"We'd earn it back one way or another," he assured me. "Either by booking guests at the lodge or selling the place for twice the price. We should at least take a look, don't you think?"

"How far is it?" I asked Christian. "This Silver Creek?"

"About a two-hour drive."

"We'll come to visit you," Sienna assured me. "Especially during ski season. I've wanted to practice more, and we could stay at the lodge if you buy it! How cute would that be?"

The thought bloomed in my mind. A beautiful ski lodge we had complete control over. Right by the slopes, so I could learn to snowboard like I'd always wanted. It'd be the perfect place to get away from everything and focus on my next comic book. Above all, it was an investment.

"Okay," I agreed. "We'll have a look at it. *Just* a look."

---

2

*S*ilver Creek, Colorado, was south of Breckinridge, far enough away from any major cities to be labeled in the middle of nowhere. The snow thickened as we drove through the mountains, and it seemed doubtful we would find the little town at all, when all of a sudden, it appeared before us.

Local shops, boutiques, and markets lined Main Street. A roundabout marked the center of town, in the middle of which stood a huge decorative cornucopia. Handmade garlands of red, orange, and yellow leaves hung from the streetlights. Kids and happy couples skated on a temporary ice rink. Locals bustled about, carrying coffee and shopping bags as they enjoyed their Saturday. In the distance, a chair lift took skiers and snowboarders up the nearby mountain.

"Where's the lodge?" I asked eagerly. I hadn't planned on being excited, but the little town was so cute and picturesque, I couldn't help but imagine Simon and me settling down here.

We would walk along this street, buy apples at the market for homemade pie, wave to our neighbors, and chitchat about the ski conditions. Our kids would skate on the rink, happily shouting at Simon and me to join them—

"Another twenty minutes away," Simon answered, popping my happy bubble of the potential future. "It's not technically in town."

We drove past the cheerful locals and into the woods once more. The trees thickened, and the road narrowed. Simon made a sharp right onto a one-lane street and started up a steep incline. I half-expected our ancient car to give up and roll backward, but it made it to the top of the slope. The land evened out, and the trees gave way to the old lodge.

I peered through the windshield. "That's it?"

Simon grimaced. "That's it."

The Silver Creek Lodge did not meet the standards set by the adorable town down the road. For one thing, it was buried deep in the trees. Nature had nearly reclaimed it for its own. Moss and vines grew over the stacked river stones and logs that formed the foundation of the building. Every window was shattered, no doubt due to bored teenagers armed with rocks, and the broken glass was frosted over. The wooden porch steps were busted, as were several of the railing supports. From the front, the Lodge looked no larger than a honeymoon cabin.

"It goes deeper into the woods," Simon said, answering

my unasked question. "Twenty rooms total to rent out. Nineteen, if we decide to take one for ourselves."

"Simon, this place is not livable."

"We haven't seen the inside yet."

"It doesn't even have windows!"

Another car pulled up next to us, and the man inside—a pudgy-faced fellow with round silver glasses and a button nose—waved at us through the window.

"There's Dwayne," Simon said. "Bank representative. He sounded cool over the phone."

"I don't care how cool he sounded," I said. "We're not buying this piece of crap if it's not worth it."

"Give it a chance, Max. Please?"

Were it not for his adorable pout, I would have never gotten out of the car. As it was, he coaxed me from the warmth of heated seats and into the chilly clearing.

"Hey, folks!" Dwayne called, struggling to free himself from the car. His gray suit jacket got stuck in the door. "You must be Simon and Maxine."

"Max," I corrected. "People only call me Maxine if they're mad at me."

"Well, I'm not mad at ya!" Dwayne joked, and I smiled politely. "Are you ready to see this place? It's got great bones."

"Isn't that what realtors say when they want to sell you a piece of crap property?" I asked.

Simon nudged me in the ribs. "She's kidding, Dwayne."

"No, no, I completely get it." Dwayne fumbled with a set of keys as he led us to the front of the Lodge. "It doesn't look like much, but this place is in decent shape for how low it's priced. The last owner kept it well-managed." He stepped awkwardly over the broken steps. "Be careful there."

Simon helped me onto the porch as Dwayne fit the key into the door. "Not much to lock up, is there? What with the broken windows?"

"We have to do it, no matter what condition the property is in." Dwayne shoved the door with his shoulder, and it creaked open. The space beyond was completely dark. "Shall we? I'll go first."

We followed Dwayne inside. He flipped the closest switch on the wall. A massive iron chandelier with eight sconces flickered on. Four of the sconces were burned out, but the other two were bright enough to give us an idea of what the lobby looked like.

Once upon a time, the Lodge was a beautiful place. Exposed beams supported an upside-down, V-shaped ceiling made of dark, rich wooden planks. The same silver rocks that formed the porch outside also framed the huge fireplace. Giant windows looked out on the snowy grounds, tall trees, and godlike mountains. The leather couches, handwoven rugs, and craftsman tables needed love but could be saved from the damage nature and vandals left behind.

That damage, however, was not to be overlooked. The wood floors were warped. Someone had taken a sledgehammer to the check-in desk. The rocks were falling off the fireplace in some spots and needed to be re-cemented. The wiring had been ripped out of several sockets. The snow that had seeped in would be the biggest problem.

Moisture meant mold, and sometimes mold meant tearing the whole damn place down.

"I want an inspector in here," I announced. "I want a list of everything that needs to be done before we can start booking guests. If we don't have the cash to get this place fixed up, there's no point in buying it."

"I can arrange that," Dwayne said. "Would you like to see the rooms? There are eight on the first floor and twelve on the second. There's also a kitchen on the first floor, a dining area, and a recreation room. Out back, some naturally heated pools are fed by nearby hot springs."

The Lodge was bigger on the inside than it looked from the outside. The guest rooms came with a couple of options. Large king suites with hot tubs and kitchenettes were on the first floor. On the second floor were the cheaper rooms with two queen beds and a regular bathroom. The exception was the last room at the very back of the Lodge, which Dwayne opened with a flourish.

"This is the presidential suite," he announced as we stepped in to have a look. "Actually, it's where the owners have always lived, but you could rent it out for honeymoons or other such occasions if you liked. People would pay top dollar for that view."

The presidential suite was more like a loft apartment than a room at the local ski lodge. It spanned the width of the building, and windows made up the entire back wall. A glass door led outside to an equally large balcony with a private hot tub and wood-burning fire pit. From any angle, you could see the mountain tops soaring over the trees. As the sun shined in, it felt like the only room in the Lodge that wasn't dark and depressing.

"We'd definitely take this room," I said to Simon. "I need the sunshine."

He ruffled my hair. "I know you do."

We toured the rest of the Lodge. Though it was in poor shape, it had a lot of potential. I wondered how it had fallen into such disrepair in the first place. Why hadn't the last owner kept up with it?

"What do you think?" Dwayne asked when we returned to the ruined lobby and sitting area. "It's a fixer-upper, I know."

"Do we have to give you an answer right away?" I asked. "I wouldn't mind some time to think about it."

Dwayne checked his watch. "I'm willing to give you until the end of the day to decide if you'd like to make a deal. A little tip, though. If you really want it, offer the auction price. I've got a few other people bidding on this place, but out of everyone, I think the two of you would make the most out of this location."

We followed Dwayne out, and he locked up the house.

"Why don't you look around Silver Creek? Get to know your potential hometown? It might help you make your decision. I'll be waiting on your call. Let's say around six?"

We agreed, Dwayne waved goodbye and drove away. Simon spun me around to look at the Lodge once more.

"It's not so bad," he said.

"It's pretty bad," I countered. "Sure, it's cheap, but the repairs are going to cost a fortune."

"Not necessarily," he said. "I'll do most of the work myself, or I can hire someone local to help."

"What about the materials for the job?"

"I can check construction recycling centers," he offered. "Look for sales. If worse comes to worst, we could start a GoFundMe."

I planted my foot. "No way. I won't beg people for cash."

"It's not begging. It's asking for support." He made a rectangle with his index fingers and thumbs, framed the Lodge in the center, and narrowed his eyes. "If you squint, it almost looks nice."

"Almost," I grumbled.

Simon wrapped his arm around my shoulder. "Come on, it would look great on a postcard. This could be a good adventure for the two of us."

I chewed on my lip. "You have that much faith in your handyman skills?"

"Sure, I've worked construction jobs before."

I shielded my eyes from the sun and considered the Lodge again. "I'm not completely sold."

Simon kissed my temple. "Let's see if the rest of Silver Creek can convince you."

ON THE WAY back into town, we took the long way around through the neighborhood. Cute, cozy cabins lined the streets. Old-fashioned lampposts stood stark against the snowy backdrop. Chimneys puffed wood smoke into the air. I cracked the window to get a good whiff of it. In a few front lawns, I spotted For Sale signs.

"What about one of these houses?" I asked Simon. "They're small. They can't be so expensive."

"They're not," he replied, "but they are out of our budget. We couldn't afford the down payment on one."

In comparison to the cabins, the Lodge was a nightmare. Pouting, I watched as a happy couple played with their young daughter in their front yard.

"Besides," Simon went on, "we don't have a steady enough income to buy a house. That's why we're checking out the Lodge in the first place, remember?"

"No one's going to want to stay at that hellhole."

"They will when we fix it up."

A little farther on, we passed the schools. A combined elementary and middle school was separated from the high school by a deeply sloped, grassy knoll. The snow was hardly an inch deep—dead grass poked through the slush—but that didn't stop the kids from trying to sled on it. Others scraped what they could off the ground, packed it into dirty snowballs, and threw them at opponents. Several teachers were supervising, mostly to keep the younger kids from eating the snow.

Silver Creek was also home to a park with long hiking trails that snaked upward into the hills, a community center with ball courts and a heated indoor pool, and a sweeping golf course that was closed for the season. The Lodge and the closest place to ski were a twenty-minute drive from the center of town.

To get the full effect of Silver Creek's quaint small-town vibes, we parked at the top of Main Street and walked along the main drag of shops and restaurants. Simon caught my gloved hand in his, swinging my arm as he led our stroll. His running commentary, an obvious attempt to convince me to move here, made me smile.

"Oh, look at that soap store," he would say as we passed a shop display. "You love soap! Handmade. All-natural ingredients. Essential oils. Wouldn't it be a delight to have access to such great natural self-care products? They have facemasks, too!"

A few steps later, we came across another gem Simon needed to announce. "An art shop!" He pointed to the massive, hand-painted sign as if I hadn't already noticed it. Peering through the windows, he added, "They have those pens you like. Babe, it's a sign!"

When a familiar Christmas song played on the speakers lining the streets, Simon's eyes went wide. "Do you hear that? They even know your favorite Christmas jingle! Even though it's so weird."

"It's Lou Monte," I reminded him. "And 'Dominick the Donkey' isn't weird. It's a classic Italian-American Christmas song. My mom used to play it all the time at our house. She would swing me around by my arms until I got too dizzy."

He placed one hand around my waist and took me up in a classic dance posture before thoughts of the past swept me into the slushy gutter. As he spun me around the sidewalk, he sang along with the song. He knew every word.

"Santa's got a little friend. His name is Dominick, the cutest

little donkey. You never see him kick. When Santa visits his paisans, with Dominick, he'll be! Because the reindeer can't-a climb the hills of Italy. Hey!"

The next part of the song required imitating a donkey's *hee-haw!* with great enthusiasm, which Simon happily performed. I couldn't stop laughing as he pulled out all the stops and swung me to and fro along with the music. People dodged out of our way as we barreled down the sidewalk, giving us strange looks as we made the world our stage.

"They won't let us move here if they think we're crazy!" I said, grasping Simon's shoulder to keep from slipping on an icy patch.

That only made him sing louder, but when the last verse switched to Italian slang, he made up similar-sounding gibberish that was nowhere close to the original words.

"A café!"

I shoved him through the door, and the bell chimed overhead. As Simon stumbled over the doormat, he finished off the song with a resounding vibrato, but the speakers inside didn't echo the music outside. Simon ended up belting his last *hee-haw!* to a room full of confused coffee drinkers as lo-fi remixed holiday songs played softly in the background.

Everyone turned to look. I patted Simon's chest as his cheeks turned bright red.

"Sorry," he muttered.

The locals went back to their work, though not as

focused as before. As we ordered at the counter, I kept making accidental eye contact with random people. It wasn't my fault. Every other second, I noticed someone glance at us from the corner of their eye. When I looked at them, they pretended to go back to whatever they were doing before.

"This place is weird," I murmured to Simon as we moved past the register to wait for our order. "Why is everyone staring at us?"

"It's because no one knows you," the barista said as she steamed milk. She was tall and lean, with blond hair and blue eyes. She wore a bright-yellow Silver Creek High School Varsity Volleyball sweatshirt beneath her café apron. "We don't get a whole lot of visitors here, not since the Lodge stopped taking bookings a few years ago. Where are you two from anyway?"

"The Denver area," Simon answered.

"Wow, big city people." She expertly arranged a foam heart on top of a cappuccino. "What are you doing all the way out here?"

"Actually, we're thinking about buying the Lodge and fixing it up," Simon said.

The barista's eyes sparkled. "Really? That'd be so cool! That place deserves some new owners. It's been looking pretty pathetic."

"Have you ever been there?" I asked her.

"Nope," she replied. "It's kinda gross, right? But my older sister said it used to be a cool place to hang out when it got too cold on the slopes. When do you think you'll be finished rebuilding it?"

I answered before Simon could. "We're not entirely sure we're going to buy it yet."

"You should!" the barista insisted. She slid the cappuccino across the bar and added a muffin we never ordered. "Free muffins if you give me a discount on chair lift passes."

Simon laughed and took the plate. "You drive a hard bargain. What was your name?"

"Cassie," she said, wiping her hand to shake Simon's. "*Please* buy the place. We need some excitement around here."

"We're thinking about it," he promised. "Nice to meet you."

We sat at the only free table, in the front corner by the door. I didn't take off my coat. Every time someone came inside, a gust of freezing wind and a handful of snow came with them. I hunched my shoulders and sipped my coffee.

"This is a cute place." Simon, on the opposite side of the table, wasn't getting as much backdraft. He shook off his coat and hung it over his chair. As he ran his hands through his damp curls, a table of teenaged girls giggled and stared. Simon, oblivious, squinted at the menu written in chalk above the register. "They have breakfast in the mornings. Farm-fresh eggs. We should try that sometime."

"It is cute," I agreed. "The coffee's good, too."

"There you go," he said. "Good coffee. Good muffin. I'm sensing a pattern."

"You could never sell cars," I commented. "Too heavy-handed. People would think you're trying to rip them off."

He laughed and gently stepped on the toe of my boot. "Can't I be excited about a new opportunity? Admit it; you can picture us living here. It's what you always told me you wanted for us. A small town where everyone knows each other, local businesses, places to take the kids—"

"Minus the kids," I said abruptly.

Simon's grin fell. He reached across the table to tickle my knuckles. "We could adopt, you know. It doesn't matter to me."

Thankfully, someone knocked into my chair, putting an end to the conversation. My coffee sloshed over the lip of my cup as the culprit—an older woman with adorable pink earmuffs and a matching scarf—turned toward us.

"So sorry, dear!" she said, dropping a stack of napkins on the table. "I suppose I was too excited. I overheard you say you might buy the Silver Creek Lodge, and I knew I had to introduce myself. I'm Selma Owens. I run the Silver Creek Book Club."

"That's lovely," Simon said. "What can we do for you?"

"I wanted to tip you in the right direction," Selma replied with a wink. "The Lodge served as our cozy book club spot for years. Ever since it shut down, we've had to gather at the library, and it's not the same. We don't have enough room, and the library doesn't sell booze. You can see why some of us might be put out."

I chuckled. "So, you want us to buy the Lodge and fix

it up so you have a nice place to hold your book club meetings again?"

Selma beamed. "Exactly. We bring in quite the crowd, and my friends are heavy tippers. It would be excellent business for you."

"Thanks for letting us know," Simon said. "I hope we can oblige."

"Just in case." Selma took a bookmark from her coat pocket—printed with her contact information and a cute drawing of an open novel—and placed it on the table. "Give me a call if you get everything sorted. We'd love to have you in town. You're an adorable couple!"

"Did you hear that, babe?" Simon wiggled his eyebrows as Selma left. "We're adorable."

"Everyone thinks *you're* adorable." I jerked my head toward the table of teenaged girls. "You've already got a fan club here."

He rested his elbow over the chair and turned. The spying girls broke into a fresh wave of giggles, blushing as they tried to cover up their blatant staring. Simon faced the front.

"Would it be weird if I went over there and told them to look me up on Spotify?" he asked. "I need more listeners."

"Don't you dare."

As he shrugged and took another bite of his muffin, I caught sight of someone else who'd taken an interest in Simon. A handsome man with salt-and-pepper hair sat in the opposite corner of the café, half-hidden behind an open newspaper. In an expensive blue suit and leather loafers, he was the best-dressed person I'd seen in Silver Creek so far. When his piercing blue eyes caught mine, he folded the newspaper and stood, buttoning his suit coat as he came over.

"Good morning," he said in a pleasantly melodic voice. "I'm Boyce Driscoll, sort of the unofficial Silver Creek mayor. Did I happen to hear you're thinking of buying the Lodge down the road?"

"Apparently, everyone heard," I grumbled.

Simon stepped on my toe. "You did indeed," he told Boyce. "Why?"

"I thought it'd be unfair not to warn you," Boyce said. "That property isn't a good investment. The bank's been trying to get rid of it for a year. No one will buy it."

"I thought it just went up for auction," I replied. "The bank representative said they have multiple officers on it."

"That's what he *said*," Boyce said, chuckling politely. "No doubt to make you more interested in buying it. Trust me. Don't waste your money. Two young kids like you? You need a starter house. Not a money pit."

Simon had gone a bit stiff. "Thanks for letting us know."

"Sure thing." Like Selma, Boyce had something to give us, but instead of pulling a bookmark out of his breast pocket, it was a business card. "Keep in touch. If you have any questions about the town, I'll be happy to take you to lunch."

Since Simon was being weird, I took the card. "Thanks. We'll do that."

. . .

SIMON WAS USUALLY quiet on the drive home. As Silver Creek disappeared in the rearview mirror, I found myself not wanting to leave. I turned off the radio.

"It's almost six," I said. "We have to call Dwayne soon."

He kept his eyes on the road. "Mm-hmm."

"What are we doing to tell him?"

"Sounds like you've already decided we're not going to buy the Lodge."

"Well, Boyce said—"

"One person," Simon said. "Everyone else thought it was a great idea. I think we should do it, but I can't change your mind for you. You call the shots, Max. That's the way it's always been."

"Are you mad?" I asked, surprised. "We haven't discussed anything yet!"

"I'm not mad," he said in a gentler tone, "but you tend to play things safe. We have the money to buy the Lodge and fix it up. Eventually, we'll make that money back. Take the chance with me. Dive in."

"I'm scared it's not going to work out," I admitted.

He held my hand over the center console. "We'll never know until we try. It could go really well. If it doesn't, well, we'll figure something else out. We always have. Whatever happens, we're in this together."

I glanced in the side mirror. The snowy peaks rose in the distance. Though we were miles away, I swore I could see the lights of Silver Creek twinkling behind us.

"Let's do it," I said.

*a*s soon as we closed on the Lodge, we packed our belongings from the condo loft and rented a storage unit closer to Silver Creek to store it all. Until we got the windows fixed and installed new locks at the Lodge, our valuables—like Simon's recording equipment —needed a safe place to live. Sienna and Christian helped wrap our dishes in newspaper and box up my library of books.

"I'm not sure this is a good idea," Sienna said for the twelfth time as she carefully arranged our coffee mugs in a padded box so they wouldn't shatter during the drive. "Are you positive you want to go?"

"Yeah, this lodge doesn't sound move-in ready," Christian added.

"This was your idea," I told them, laughing.

"I know," Sienna pouted. "I got used to having you here. What am I supposed to do when you're two hours away?"

"Call me," I said. "Or come visit. We'll need the extra hands."

Sienna taped the box shut. "I'll wait until you get the windows fixed. Aren't you afraid you'll freeze to death?"

"The big room upstairs is intact," Simon answered, tossing a hastily folded sweater into a suitcase. "First thing on my list is to fix the radiators."

"Radiators? How old is this place?"

"Old." I refolded the sweater and placed it neatly into the suitcase. "Thankfully, it's been remodeled a few times. We won't have to make a ton of updates."

"Starting with the radiators," Christian teased.

"I think radiators are charming," Simon countered. "When I was a kid, we would run in from the snow and put our socks and gloves on the radiator to dry. It was a tradition."

I smiled and squeezed Simon's hand. Like me, he didn't talk much about his childhood. There were too many unhealed wounds to deal with in the past. When he found a happy memory, it was a rare occurrence.

"I like radiators, too." Sienna tweaked Christian's nose. "We're not all snobby realtors."

"Hey, this snobby realtor got this pretty condo for you for half the asking price," he retorted.

Sienna rolled her eyes and looked around the loft. "That's about it. Gosh, what am I supposed to do with all this space?"

"Take up painting," I suggested. "Or pottery. You could reenact the scene from Ghost."

Simon sat behind me, snaked his arms around me, and

guided my hands to tape up another box, singing while he did so. *"Oh, my love, my darling, I've hungered for your touch—"*

I elbowed him in the ribs, and he cut himself off with a dramatized gag. Sienna and Christian cracked up.

Sienna pushed Simon aside and hugged me. "I'm going to miss you."

"What about me?" Simon asked.

"Yeah, yeah. You too."

Christian outstretched his arms to Simon. "Feel the love, brother."

Simon howled in fake anguish and ran into Christian's embrace. "It won't be the same without you!"

A few weeks ago, I hated the idea of moving out of the condo, spending a huge chunk of money, and leaving Sienna and Christian. Now that the money was gone, I felt free. Simon and I were onto the next big adventure, whatever that meant.

As Christian said, the Lodge was nowhere near move-in ready, so we packed the car with an air mattress, heated blankets, battery-powered lanterns, a hot plate, camping utensils, and other leftover gear of Simon's.

"Is it weird I'm sometimes grateful for being homeless back then?" Simon asked as he filled a canteen with fresh water and added it to our bags. "Otherwise, we wouldn't be able to move into the Lodge this quickly."

"You're a regular Jack Kerouac," I said, hopping into the driver's seat. "You ready for this?"

He closed my door for me and kissed me through the window. "You know it."

No matter how many times Simon reminded me to ease up, I kept letting my foot weigh heavy on the gas pedal. I was excited to return to Silver Creek and its picturesque landscape. The Lodge had grown on me, too, mostly because I'd spent way too much time on Pinterest looking for ideas on how to decorate it once we finished the repairs.

Due to my speeding, we made it to Silver Creek fifteen minutes early. I hit the brakes as we approached the town, sending Simon's coffee thermos flying.

"Easy!" He mopped coffee off the dashboard. "What got into your Wheaties?"

I turned onto Main Street, smiling instinctively as the twinkling town greeted us. "I don't want the locals to think I'm a bad driver."

"Don't slam on the brakes then, you nutso."

Twenty minutes later, we arrived at the Lodge, and I remembered how much work we had to do before this place was livable. The trash company had already dropped off an industrial-sized dumpster in the front yard. If only we could pick up the entire building and drop it in the enormous trash can. I didn't let the thought dampen my enthusiasm.

I dangled the key in front of Simon. "Want to do the honors?"

"You betcha."

When we reached the busted porch steps, Simon swept my feet out from under me and scooped me into his arms. "This is a thing married people do, right?" he grunted. "Carry their betrothed over the threshold of their first home together?"

"I'll allow it. Don't slip."

He carefully planted his boots and hauled us both upward. With one hand, he unlocked the door then carried me through. He wrinkled his nose and set me down.

"Does it smell mustier in here than before?" he asked.

I sniffed. "Ugh. Mold."

"We'll get rid of it," he promised. He pulled a pair of heavy-duty work gloves out of his back pocket and handed them to me. "Where should we start?"

I grinned. "With demolition."

ARMED with Simon's power tools, we got straight to work. We ripped up carpets, tore out rotting wallboard, and waged war on old pipes. We unscrewed ugly light fixtures, trashed ruined furniture, and removed termite-eaten doors from their hinges. We knocked out the broken windows in the lobby and covered the gaping holes with heavy black tarp. With every passing hour, the dumpster looked smaller and smaller as we filled it with the guts of the abandoned lodge.

We worked all through the morning and straight through lunch. When a family of roaches crawled out of the cabinet I'd been hammering off the wall, I screamed and fell backward. Simon rushed in from the next room, the light of his headlamp swinging crazily.

"What is it?" he demanded. "What happened? Are you hurt?"

The roaches skittered off.

"Just bugs," I said, wiping the cold sweat from my forehead. "They startled me. I'm light-headed."

Simon lifted me off the floor. "No wonder. It's three o'clock. We haven't eaten in hours. Want to head into town?"

Since we'd temporarily turned off the Lodge's plumbing, we did our best to wipe the dirt, sweat, and construction dust off our faces and hands with baby wipes. Despite this, the same material coating our jackets and pants garnered more curious looks from those out and about in Silver Creek.

"You must be Simon and Maxine!"

We heard this phrase once every five minutes. We couldn't walk one block without a different stranger approaching us to introduce themselves and share their opinion of the Silver Creek Lodge. Though everyone was nice and welcoming, it grew old quickly.

"If one more person tells us what a cute couple we are," I grumbled, linking my arm through Simon's."

"They're excited to have new people in town," he reminded me. "Don't be mad at them."

"I'm not mad. I'm hungry."

"With you, it's the same thing."

We visited the same café as before. This time, I noticed it was called Bourbon and Bites. No mention of coffee at all and no sign of bourbon on the menu. Small towns were weird.

Our friendly neighborhood barista, Cassie, manned the espresso machine. When she spotted us, she beamed. "You're back! And covered in dust. Does this mean you bought the Lodge?"

"It sure does," I said.

She squealed with joy. "That's awesome! Your coffee is on the house today."

"Thanks, Cassie," Simon said. "Hey, you wouldn't happen to know anyone who might be interested in helping us fix up the place, would you? I underestimated how much work needs to be done."

"For free?"

"Course not. Say, fifteen bucks an hour?"

Cassie pursed her lips and scanned the café. She pointed out a tall, skinny kid in his early twenties, eating alone as he scrolled on his phone. "Try Keith. He's always looking for work. He's a lifetime hometowner."

"What does that mean?"

"When you grow up in a small town, you have two options." She held up a finger. "One, get the hell out as soon as possible because you know there's more to see in the world than this tiny corner of the earth. Or two, stay forever because you're too scared you'll never make a name for yourself outside Silver Creek. You know the type: they peak in high school, get married too early, and never find a job they like."

Simon raised an eyebrow. "Judgy, judgy."

Cassie smirked. "As you can probably tell, I can't wait to get out of Silver Creek."

"Didn't you promise free coffee for life if we rebuilt the Lodge?" I reminded her.

"I'm only a sophomore," she said. "You've got two and a half years of free joe. After that, you're on your own. Besides, I found you Keith, didn't I?"

With our food on the grill, Simon and I went to introduce ourselves to our potential part-time employee. As we approached, I got a closer look at Keith. He looked exactly like a boyfriend I'd had in high school: overgrown ashy hair, a shapeless chin, and lopsided shoulders indicative of a varsity baseball career. To confirm, he watched a live baseball game on his phone.

"Nationals fan, huh?" I asked, peering over his shoulder. "Are you from DC?"

He glanced up, startled. "Uh, no. I just like the team."

"Solid. I'm Maxine Finch. Max," I corrected myself. "This is my husband, Simon."

His eyes brightened with recognition. "Oh, you two bought the Lodge up the road, right?"

"That's why we wanted to talk to you," Simon said. "Cassie said you might be interested in some work?"

Keith immediately set aside his phone to give us his full attention. "Absolutely. What do you need? What's the pay?"

"Fifteen an hour," I answered. "It's hard work. Construction. Think you can handle that?"

"Hell yeah." He nodded. "When can I start? Now?"

Simon and I exchanged a look. My arms shook, thinking of how much more trash and debris we had to haul out of the Lodge's lobby, and we hadn't begun to tackle the actual rooms yet.

"We need to eat," I told Keith. "After lunch, we're heading to the store to pick up construction materials and rent a truck. Would you be able to come with us?"

"Sure, I can haul the stuff if you want. Save you some cash." The bell over the door chimed, and Keith's eyes darted around us. "I've got, uh—"

A chorus of deep laughter made me turn around to see what Keith was looking at. A group of older men had come in, all dressed in slick business attire. In the center of the throng was Boyce Driscoll, in the middle of an evidently hilarious joke.

"You've got what?" Simon prompted Keith.

Keith's eyes and attention flickered back to us. "I've got a truck with a huge bed. You don't have to rent one."

"Great, we'll meet after lunch."

Keith leaned around me to watch Boyce and the other men. "Cool, see you then."

As we walked to our table, Simon whispered, "What was that all about?"

"Long lost daddy?" I guessed.

Keith never took his eyes off of Boyce as the older man ordered a latte to go.

"Evil stepfather?" Simon countered.

"That's admiration, not animosity," I said of the look in Keith's eyes.

"You're probably right. Small towns are notorious for drama."

Boyce and his chuckling friends didn't stay long. As

Cassie made their coffee, they chatted with other people in the café. Boyce's deep voice resonated across the room as he held court with the locals.

"I made arrangements to have the sprinklers fixed in your yard," he told one man. "By spring, you'll have beautiful green grass. Can't wait!"

A few minutes later, a little girl around the age of six came in with her mother. When she saw Boyce, she ran over and wrapped herself around his leg. "Mr. D! I love you."

"I love you, too, Katie!" Boyce said. With a flourish, he pulled a lollipop out of his pocket and offered it to her. "Your favorite flavor."

"You'll rot her teeth," the mother said half-heartedly as the child unwrapped the candy and stuck it happily between her lips.

"I can't help it," Boyce said. "How do you say no to a cute little face like that?"

"Mommy, I want a donut!"

"Like this." The woman faced her child. "No."

Everyone shared a chuckle as Cassie handed the last of Boyce's friends his coffee order. As the group passed us on their way out, Boyce caught my eye. He nodded politely but didn't say anything.

"That guy's weird," Simon said. "He's like Mr. Monopoly."

"Minus the mustache."

"Did you notice that ugly mansion we drive past on the way to the Lodge?" he asked me.

"What mansion?"

Simon picked the tomatoes off his sandwich. "It's hidden in the trees. The place is enormous. I looked up the address. That's where Boyce lives. Apparently, he designed and built the manor himself. The town uses it to host events and stuff."

"That's nice of him."

"Hmph."

"You're doing it again," I warned him. "Judging people before you get to know them. Remember when you first met Christian? You called him a supercilious frat boy with a superiority complex and a crush on Jesus."

"To be fair, we met him because he was canvassing for his church."

"We met him because Sienna wanted me to meet her boyfriend," I corrected him. "Pretty sure you made up that whole church canvassing thing in your head."

"I did not."

"Mm-hmm."

As PLANNED, we regrouped with Keith after lunch and headed to the hardware store. We mostly bought a ton of wood to temporarily board up the windows until we gutted the rest of the Lodge. Keith's truck came in handy. Were it not for him, we would've had to bungee the materials to the surf rack of our crossover. Instead, we stacked it in the bed of his truck.

"You know how to get there?" Simon asked Keith as we finished up.

"Yeah, I partied there with a few friends—" Keith cut

himself off as Simon shot him a sharp look. "I didn't break anything, though. It was like that when we got there."

"Weird kid," Simon muttered once we were in our own car. "Think he knows what he's doing?"

"Give him a few days to get used to us," I advised. "We can't afford professional help, and Keith's all we got so far."

In the following hour, Keith proved his worth. Despite his skinny build, he had enough strength to hold a board over the window holes and drill it in place without any help. Once we got the Lodge sealed against the elements, the space heater didn't have to work so hard to keep us warm.

Keith worked hard and didn't complain. When a huge splinter pierced his palm through the glove, he yanked the piece of wood out, slapped a Band-Aid on the hole, and went on without his work. After we finished the windows, he hauled more garbage to the dumpster without being asked, then helped Simon take down an entire wall to make the lobby bigger. Keith had an instinct for what needed to be done next.

"I'd get rid of that insulation," he recommended, indicating the ugly pink fluff inside the walls that helped keep in the heat. "It's probably what's stinking up the place with that musty smell."

Careful not to spread the splintery fiberglass pieces across the floor, Keith yanked the insulation out of the walls and packed it into heavy-duty trash bags. With that completed, he took a sledgehammer to the ugly check-in desk at my request. We watched in awe as he swung the hammer over his head with relative ease and smashed the desk into manageable pieces.

"I take it back," Simon whispered in my ear. "He can stay."

WHEN IT GOT TOO dark to continue safely, Keith and Simon worked on cleaning up while I ordered pizzas from the locally recommended parlor.

"Two large sausage and onions," I said into the phone, gazing at the view behind the Lodge. Steam rose off the hot springs. I was tempted to dive in. I hadn't felt properly warm in hours. "That'll do it, thanks."

As I hung up, an unfamiliar guitar melody floated through the icy air. Confused, I peeked into the hallway. I didn't think Simon had brought his guitar with him.

"Babe, is that you?" I called.

The tune went on without an answer. I followed the sound, but when I reached the lobby, it faded out. Keith and Simon were outside, sitting on a part of the porch that hadn't fallen to bits yet. I went out to join them, beer in hand.

"You're twenty-one, right?" I asked Keith, withholding the bottle.

"This past May," he said. "Wanna see my driver's license?"

"I trust you." I handed him the beer. "You deserve it after all the work you did. Did you keep track of your hours?"

He expertly popped the lid off by angling it against the porch railing. "Three?"

"Dude, you've been here for at least four and a half," Simon rectified.

"I know, but I didn't want to seem like I was over-shooting."

We all laughed, and I decided I liked Keith. I swallowed my sip of beer as quickly as possible, wishing it were hot chocolate as the cold liquid ran down my throat. "How long have you been in Silver Creek, Keith?"

"Since birth," he answered. "My great grandparents opened the first school here when the town was settled, so we're Silver Creek originals."

"Wow. You must know a lot about the Lodge then?"

He shrugged. "About as much as everyone else. Why?"

"Did you know the previous owner?"

"Earl? Sure, he was a good guy. Kinda weird, though." He caught the look on my face and explained further. "Earl used to be a real townie. He went to every event, volunteered all the time, made friends with everyone in town. Then his wife died, and he became a complete recluse. That's when he stopped taking reservations at the Lodge and let the place go. We barely saw him after that."

"How long ago was it?"

"Almost ten years."

Simon stomped his feet to warm them up. "So, what happened to Earl?"

"He passed away," Keith replied. "Old age. That's why this place went up for sale."

"Uh... Where exactly did Earl die?" I asked.

"In his room, I guess."

"In the Lodge?" Simon asked.

"Where else? There's the pizza guy. I got this. He's a buddy of mine."

Keith leaped to his feet and bounded across the yard to meet the car driving up. Simon looked over his shoulder at the Lodge.

"Should we bother to ask which room was Earl's?" he said.

"I have a feeling it's the one we intend to sleep in."

Simon lifted his beer in a toast. "To Earl. May he rest in peace."

KEITH LEFT ONCE the pizza was gone, and Simon and I were officially alone for our first night at the Lodge. We set up camp in the presidential suite.

"I'm not sleeping on that mattress," I said of the stained king bed by the window. "Who knows what kind of critters have been living in there?"

"Rats, most likely." Simon, ever prepared, set up a portable generator to power the space heater. He unfolded the air mattress and began blowing it up with his mouth. I marveled at the strength of his lungs.

While he did that, I set up the bathroom. We had nothing but bottled water to wash with and no way of warming it up unless we wanted to waste time with the hot plate. I quickly dowsed myself with cold water, cleaning what I could and drying off immediately. Shivering, I changed into flannel pajamas and wool socks.

Simon had made up the bed and plugged the heated blankets into the generator. I snuggled underneath the covers, trying to ignore my lackluster surroundings. Simon washed up in the bathroom and returned without a shirt.

"Excuse me, sir. It is illegal to look that good half-naked when I'm too cold to take advantage of you," I said in a serious tone.

He lowered himself to the air mattress in a push-up position, intentionally showing off his arms as he hovered over me. "I can think of a few ways to warm you up."

His cold nose pressed into my cheek as his lips met mine. I grasped his broad shoulders and pulled him closer, grateful both for the heat of his body and the warmth it was generating in mine. My skin tingled as he dipped his hand beneath the blankets and traced the outline of my waist. His breath warmed my neck as I lost mine.

"I love you, Max," he whispered.

"I love—"

A horrible screech rent the air, echoing from the nearby road—tires skidding across the icy pavement. *Crash!* Metal against wood.

Simon rolled off me, shot to his feet, and went to look out the front window. I wasn't far behind him. Outside, a plume of smoke rose from the trees.

"Shit," he said, hurrying to put on his winter coat and boots. "Someone crashed their car. Call 9-1-1."

4

*W*e ran down to the road. Around the bend, just out of sight of the Lodge, we found a smoking wreck of a car. By the looks of it, the driver had taken the turn too quickly, lost control, and plowed into a tree. The front was completely smashed in, the airbags were deployed, and the front windshield was totally shattered. There was no sign of a driver.

"Hello?" Simon shouted through the woods. "Is anyone there? We called emergency services!"

I had already put the request in and described our location, but since Silver Creek didn't have a police department, it would be a few minutes before an ambulance arrived from the next town over.

I pointed into the darkness of the trees beyond the front of the car. "Over there. They could've been ejected from the car if they weren't wearing a seat belt."

We tramped through the wilderness. Sharp, thorny branches nicked the skin of my hands. I'd been in too much of a hurry to put gloves on. In the darkness, I misstepped and sprawled forward, careening into Simon's back. He steadied me and kept one arm around my shoulders to guide me.

"See anything?" he asked, squinting through the poorly lit forest.

I turned on my phone light, but it was no match for the shadows of the trees. "Nothing. What happened to the driver?"

"Maybe they were okay?" Simon suggested. "Maybe they got out and headed down the road for help. Should we check that way?"

We turned around and walked back up the slope toward the car. As we did so, the crushed driver's side door rocketed open, and someone fell out.

"Simon, look!"

It was a woman. She scrambled to her feet, gasping for air. When she looked up, my stomach plummeted. Blood coated her face. She waved at us.

"Help," she pleaded. "Help me." Then she collapsed.

Simon and I leaped up to the road. The woman wasn't completely unconscious. She was breathing, at least. The blood was due to a huge gash from where her forehead had hit the windshield during the collision.

"Don't touch her," I warned Simon. "We're supposed to wait for the ambulance so they can stabilize her neck."

She gasped sharply and came to, scaring the crap out of me. "No!" she said. "Can't stay here. He's chasing me. Help—hide me—"

"Miss, we can't move you," I told her. "Stay still. We have to make sure you're not badly injured."

The woman's hands shot up, seized the collar of my jacket, and yanked me toward her. Breathless, I found myself staring into obsidian eyes. Flecks of gray in them caught the moonlight overhead. I couldn't look away.

"He's behind me," the woman whispered, her face mere inches from mine. "Please help me. Hide me."

"Who's behind you?" Simon went to the back to look farther down the road. "There's no one there."

I pried the woman's cold hands off my coat. "You hear that? No one's there. You're safe."

"No, please!" She flung her arms around me and buried her face in my neck, making me acutely aware of her sticky warm blood against my skin. "Help me!"

"Okay," I said softly, and Simon stared at us, aghast. "Just relax. We'll make sure you're safe. Simon, can you help me?"

"I thought you wanted to wait for the paramedics."

"Well, I changed my mind," I snapped. "Can you help or not?"

Without another word, he helped me lift the woman to her feet. With our help, she was able to walk up the road to the Lodge.

"You got her?" Simon asked, helping us up the porch. "I'm going to stay out here and wait for the ambulance."

The woman draped herself more heavily on my shoulder, but I managed to move her into the lobby. I laid her on one of the leather couches that we intended to save and covered her with a clean blanket. She trembled violently, eyes squeezed shut as if trying to keep out a scary image.

I flipped on the camp lamp. In the light, I got a real look at her. She was extraordinarily beautiful with smooth pale skin and long dark hair that settled in voluminous waves around her shoulders. The angles and dimples of her cheeks made her seem like she belonged in an earlier era. And those eyes—so deep in color they looked like an entrance to another universe.

"Stay with me," I murmured, squeezing her hand as her tremors began to subside. "Don't fall asleep. If you have a concussion, you have to stay awake."

She struggled to keep her eyes open. "Thank you."

The cut on her forehead was ugly but not deep—head wounds bled more than others. I was more concerned about bruising in her brain or other internal injuries. With a gentle hand, I wiped the blood from her face and neck with a clean washcloth.

A few minutes later, sirens echoed outside.

"Max!" Simon called.

I ran outside as a firetruck emerged from the narrow road, knocking dead branches from the trees overhead. An ambulance followed shortly behind, and a team of paramedics sprang out. Their leader, a stout man with blond hair, approached us.

"Where's the crash?" he said.

"You didn't see it?" I asked. "You would've passed it on your way here."

He threw a confused look over his shoulder. "We didn't see anything."

"Do you have eyes?" I demanded.

"Relax, babe," Simon said. To the paramedic, he replied, "I'll show you."

"Where's the driver?" the paramedic asked. "Did you find them?"

"She's inside," I answered.

He lifted a wary eyebrow, no doubt, because we disobeyed general common sense by moving her away from the crash site.

"It's freezing," I said. "I didn't want her to die of pneumonia. Are you going to help her or chide me?"

The paramedic signaled to his team. "Check the woods for others. Meet back here."

"She's in the lobby," I said, leading Simon and the paramedic inside. "I'm worried she hit her head hard against the—"

As we cleared the hallway and turned the corner, I stopped talking. The leather couch was empty. The woman was gone.

The paramedic crossed his arms. "You two know it's illegal to make an emergency call when there is no emergency, right?"

"She was right here!" I checked the closest rooms for any sign of the woman. "I left her on the couch."

"No injured driver. No crash that I can see," the paramedic said. "Admit it, you're either pulling my leg, or the two of you are hitting some pretty good drugs right now."

Simon's shoulders rose like the hackles of a dog. "Sir, I can assure you we are not addicts. There *was* a crash and

53

an injured driver. If my wife says she was on the couch, she was on the damn couch."

The paramedic took a step back. "I'm going to join my team, do a sweep of the woods. If we find anything, we'll let you know."

He stepped out, but Simon's posture remained stiff. I laid a hand on the middle of his back.

"Hey, he said it offhand," I told him. "He didn't mean anything by it. He doesn't know how you grew up."

"That's a shitty thing to assume of someone," Simon spat.

"I know, baby. It was a stupid comment."

He tucked me into his side and pressed his cheek against my hair. "How could they have missed the crash? It's right on the side of the road."

"It's dark out, and the smoke's gone," I said. "Maybe they drove past it. More importantly, where did that woman go?"

Simon reluctantly detached himself from me. "I'm going to help them look. Apparently, they need someone with twenty-twenty vision."

I hugged myself in Simon's absence, watching through the open door as the paramedics disappeared into the woods. When a floorboard creaked behind me, I jumped and whirled around.

The woman swayed in the center of the room as if she'd been there the entire time. "Sorry to startle you," she said, gazing vacantly past me. "I don't feel well."

I rushed toward her and slipped my arms under hers

as she fell. Carefully, I lugged her back to the couch. "Why did you run? You need to let the paramedics look at you."

Her long lashes fluttered. "I can't let them find me. Please. I'll be okay. I promise."

As she grasped my forearms, I had every intention of calling the paramedics back inside. Despite her protests, she was exhibiting signs of serious injuries. But as she pulled me closer, her strength stalwart, and I gazed into her eyes, assurance washed over me.

"You'll be fine," I said. "I won't call the paramedics back, but you have to tell me your name."

"Lily," she whispered. "I'm Lily."

"I'm Maxine."

"Max," she said before I had the chance to tell her I preferred my nickname. "Thank you for taking me inside."

"Of course. What happened to you out there?"

Lily's cheeks slowly regained a bit of pink. "I got lost. The roads are confusing."

"It's one way up to the Lodge," I said. "All you would have had to do was turn around. Did you mean to come up here?" Her eyes flickered toward mine again, locking me in like a weird gravitational pull. I resisted. "You said someone was chasing you."

"He's gone," she said. "It's fine. I got lost in the woods, and my car hit a patch of ice."

I recalled the wrecked car on the lonely road. "You need new tires. Yours had no tread left on them."

"I can't afford it," Lily murmured. She began to drift

off, sleep pulling her down swiftly. "Don't let them find me, please. Don't let them…"

She released my arms and sank into unconsciousness. The clouds in my head cleared. Confused, I arranged her head on the pillow and backed away. Something about Lily was strange.

"You'll never believe this," Simon said, returning from outside. He shook the snow off his shoulders. "The car's gone. It's like it never happened. The paramedics think we're crazy. Where's the girl?"

"On the couch, asleep. Her name is Lily."

He peered around the corner, brows scrunched. "Did she say where she disappeared to?"

"I think she hid because she's scared of the police," I answered. "She adamantly insisted she didn't need to see them."

"That's stupid." Simon took out his phone. "I'll get a doctor in here."

"No!" I smacked the phone out of his hand. It clattered to the floor.

"What the hell, Max?" He picked it up and showed me the cracked screen. "What was that for? I can't afford to fix this right now."

"I—I'm sorry," I said, genuinely bewildered by my behavior. "I don't know what came over me."

He pocketed the phone, staring at me with equal confusion. "It's okay. We had a long day. What do we do with her then?"

"Let her sleep," I suggested.

"Max, she can't stay here."

I watched Lily doze, her chest moving to the subtle sound of her breath. "Why not? She's not bothering us?"

"For one thing, this place isn't livable yet," Simon replied. "We're practically camping upstairs."

"Maybe she doesn't mind camping."

"We don't have insurance," he went on. "This is a construction zone. If something falls on her head, she could sue us. We don't have the money for a lawsuit. We'd be homeless."

"She won't sue us."

"You don't know that."

"It's one night," I insisted. "She's scared, hurt, and alone. Who knows what might happen to her if we send her away? What if she has nowhere to go?"

Simon sighed. "That's not our responsibility."

I looped my arm around his waist and leaned my head against his chest. "Tell me the story about you and your brother again. The one I like."

"Why?" he asked warily.

"Because I asked you to."

He guided me to a big armchair across from Lily's sofa. We wrapped up in a thick blanket and sat together.

"You know the beginning," Simon said quietly, playing with my hair. "My parents cared more about drugs than their kids. They used to send us out to pick it up for them. Morphine, codeine, whatever they could get their hands on. Drug dealers knew Casey and me from the time we were eight years old. As long as we had money, they handed over the goods. Didn't care that we were kids." He held me tighter, the skin around his mouth tightening.

"Anyway, Casey and I got sick of it and ran away when we were fourteen. That first night was the hardest. Dad had broken my nose, and Casey had fractured his wrist defending me. We were in bad shape."

I gently ran the pads of my fingers along the inside of his arm, just to remind him things were different now. He was safe here with me.

"It was the middle of the night," he went. "We were in a strange neighborhood, way nicer than we were used to. All of a sudden, a porch light comes on, and this guy steps out of his house. I thought he was going to call the police."

"But?"

"But instead, he called out to us," Simon said. "I remember his exact words. 'Get in here, boys. My wife's a doctor. She'll fix you up.'"

"And you almost ran."

"Almost." Lost in the past, his eyes glazed over. "I was sure it was a trick. Casey automatically trusted him—Saul —though. We staggered inside, and Saul woke up his wife. We explained what happened as she set my nose and Casey's wrist. They fed us and let us sleep in their son's old bedroom."

"If it weren't for them, what do you think might have happened to you?" I asked.

"I don't want to know," Simon replied. "My nose definitely would have healed crooked, and I wouldn't have gotten those modeling opportunities in high school. It was freezing that night, too. We might have died if Saul hadn't taken us in."

I took his chin and turned his face toward Lily.

"Ah," he said. "I get it."

"One night," I said again. "It won't hurt to let her stay. We'll figure out what to do tomorrow, along with everything else."

He took my face between his palms and laid the gentlest kiss on my lips. "You are beautiful in every way. You know that, right?"

I flipped my hair over my shoulder. "Oh, I know."

He studied Lily. "We should move her. It's too cold for her to stay in here. Can you wake her? I'll fix up one of the rooms."

Were it not for Lily's health, I wouldn't have moved off his lap. The warmth of his grip was too alluring to give up so easily. As it was, I climbed out of the chair. Simon headed upstairs to gather materials while I tended to our unexpected guest.

"Lily?" I softly shook her shoulder. "Can you wake up?"

She let out a quiet moan and rolled toward me. "Yes, Max?"

A rush of affection—the kind I usually associated with Simon—came over me as I caught sight of those deep, dark eyes again. "Can you stand? We're going to set up one of the rooms for you so you won't be so cold out here."

"Can I run a bath?"

"The water's not on," I said apologetically. "We have to replace the pipes first. I have some baby wipes, though."

She took my hand as she stood, swaying slightly.

Simon appeared at the bottom of the stairs with a blanket, pillow, and the extra portable heater we'd brought along. "Hi. I'm Simon. We didn't officially meet."

Lily smiled demurely. "Yes, I'm Lily. I'm so sorry to impose on you like this, but I am grateful to you and your lovely wife."

Simon, to my shock, blushed. He wasn't so easy flattered normally.

"It's nothing," he said. "Sorry about the state of the place. We literally just started fixing it up today. It's not meant to look like this."

Lily gazed upward to the exposed beams. "I think it's beautiful."

Simon cleared his throat. "Um, follow me? One of the rooms on the first floor isn't in terrible shape. We'll put you in there for now."

Together, we escorted Lily to one of the king suites not destroyed by the elements midway down the hall. Simon stripped the bed and flipped the mattress over to the clean side while I set up the portable heater.

"It's not much," I said as Lily looked around. Embarrassment made my cheeks flush. I hadn't intended our first guest to have such a dirty, dingy welcome. "I hope you'll be comfortable."

"You might get some visitors," Simon warned her. "We haven't bombed the place for bugs yet, and I'm sure there are some rats around."

"Rats don't scare me," Lily said. Standing without help exhausted her. Her bones sagged toward the floor. "I'll go to bed if you don't mind."

Simon and I quickly finished up and excused

ourselves. Outside her door, Simon paused. "She looks sick," he whispered.

"She was in a car accident," I reminded him. "It's probably stress."

"No, she looks *sick*," he said again with more emphasis. "I've never seen anyone that pale. Do you think she has a pre-existing condition?"

"If it was something she was worried about, I'm sure she would have told us." Worry gnawed at my stomach. "Maybe she's hungry. Do we have any leftover pizza?"

"A few slices."

"I'll bring her some."

WHILE SIMON WENT to bed for the second time, I crafted a miniature oven out of aluminum foil and our hot plate to warm up the pizza. I also warmed a cup of water and dropped a teabag in it. From my suitcase, I drew a sweater and pajama pants. Lily looked to be about my size, and she shouldn't have to sleep in dirty clothes.

When I went downstairs to Lily's room and knocked, no answer came. "Lily?" I called, tapping on the door again. "It's Max. I brought you something to eat."

Anxiety riddled holes in my head as the silence remained. I swallowed hard and let myself into the room.

The bed was empty. Lily was nowhere to be seen.

"Not again," I muttered. "Where does she go?"

As I set the pizza on the side table and the clothes on the bed, trickling water caught my attention. The bathroom door was cracked open. I inched toward it without realizing I was holding my breath and peeked in.

A candle glowed on the edge of the bathtub, where Lily washed in hot, steamy water. She looked up as if she sensed my presence, and her black eyes connected with mine. My breath left my lungs.

"Sorry!" I yelped, turning away. "I didn't mean to spy."

A light chuckle emanated from the bathroom. Water rushed as Lily got out of the bath and emerged with one of our towels wrapped around her. Steam rose from her delicate shoulders.

"I don't mind," she said, lightly touching my hand. Her fingers were warm from the bath. "I like visitors."

"The water's turned off," I said robotically. "How did you draw a bath?"

She shrugged. "I turned the knobs. Hot water."

"Huh. Maybe there are two water sources."

"Perhaps." She spotted the pizza and the cup of tea. "Is that for me? How kind of you."

I cleared my throat. "I thought you might be hungry after such a crazy day. I also brought some clothes of mine for you to wear."

She caressed the soft fabric of my sweater. "That's so sweet of you." Without preamble, she dropped the towel.

Surprised, I performed a quick about-face to give her privacy. "Um, anyway. I hope you'll be comfortable."

"You said that already," she replied in a teasing tone. "You can face front again."

In my forest green sweater and billowy silver pajama pants, she looked like a nymph who'd arrived at the Lodge from out of the woods. I was sure I didn't look so ethereal in the same outfit.

"I meant it," I said, teasing back. "You're our first official guest here at Silver Creek Lodge. I want it to be special."

"It already is."

A blush crept up my neck. "I'll leave you to it. See you in the morning."

"Good night, Max."

5

*S*unlight touched my cheeks. I pulled the sheets over my head and reached to the other side of the mattress to find it empty. Simon had gotten up already. The bed was cold. The heated blanket had automatically shut off to prevent a fire hazard. The portable warmer had run out of battery power, too.

I put on my winter coat and cozy slippers before getting out of bed. In the bathroom, I jiggled my legs to stay warm while I did my business. The cold was no joke. We needed to get the electricity up and running before the winter grew worse.

Simon was in the kitchen downstairs, doing his best to make breakfast with our limited supply of food and materials. By the sound of his constant muttered swearing, it wasn't going so well.

"Stupid stove," he said murderously as he held a match beneath a propane camping stove. Unlike the hot plate upstairs, the stove didn't need a generator to work. "Why —won't—you—light? Ouch!"

The match had burned down to his finger. He dropped it on the floor and stepped on it, sucking on his wounded appendage.

"It's finicky," I reminded him, stepping forward to help. I lit a match and held it under the propane stove's lucky spot. A second later, it caught, and I turned up the dial to keep it burning. "There you go."

"You have fire magic," Simon said and stiffened when he realized what had come out of his mouth, but I didn't react. He filled a kettle with water and set it on the stove. "I was trying to surprise you with coffee, but you beat me to it."

I picked up the can of instant coffee, lifted the lid, and sniffed it. "Are you sure this stuff's going to do the trick?"

"It's got caffeine," he said. "That's all we need to get going, right?"

"It also has to be drinkable," I added. I looked around. "Have you seen Lily this morning?"

"Nope. Quiet as a mouse. I think she's still sleeping."

We ate cold bagels and cured ham for breakfast—items that wouldn't go bad without refrigeration. The instant coffee wasn't terrible, though I stirred in twice the recommended amount.

"Let's tackle the wiring today," Simon proposed. "I'm not sure I can handle another night like the last one. The temperature's dropping more each day. We won't last two weeks out here if we don't get the heat fixed."

"And the water," I added. "I am in dire need of a hot bath."

He jerked his head toward the back. "Got those hot springs out there if you're desperate."

"Not quite there yet."

Simon chuckled. "I'll call Keith. See if he's up for a twelve-hour day. Do you want to check on our guest?"

"Sure. Hand me the instant coffee."

WITH ANOTHER OFFERING of food in hand, I made my way to Lily's room. Once again, she didn't answer when I knocked. I was starting to think this was how things were going to be with her.

I inched the door open with my elbow. "Lily? It's me, Max. Do you want some breakfast?"

The blanket was pulled back, but Lily was gone again. I sighed. Perhaps one time, she might actually be around when I called for her. I went to put her breakfast on the table, but there was no room. The pizza and tea from last night were still there, completely untouched. I swapped her uneaten dinner for the fresh bagel and coffee.

"Maybe she's vegan," Simon suggested when I showed him the uneaten pizza, "and she didn't want to be rude."

"I'll ask when she gets back," I said. "Where do you think she went?"

"To take care of herself, I hope," he replied, refilling his cup. "Or to talk to the police. It doesn't make sense. Her car can't have disappeared like that. Someone must have

THE HAUNTING OF SILVER CREEK LODGE

stolen it and sold the scraps. I can't believe they managed it in such a short amount of time."

"Poor Lily."

Simon warmed his nose in the steam rising from his cup. "Keith's on his way. We're going to map out the wiring in the Lodge, then head to the hardware store to get what we need. It'll be a long day, but we should we able to get this place lit and heated by tonight."

"Heat!" I said. "What a dream!"

He laughed and hugged me. "Don't worry, baby. I won't let you freeze. Do you want to come with us?"

"That depends. Do you need my help?"

"Keith and I can handle the work," Simon answered. "If you'd like to check out the town today, you're free to go."

I lifted my hands. "Yes, sir."

"Are you going to work on your comic book?"

My art supplies and writing journals were piled in a box upstairs. I hadn't put it in storage in the hopes that I'd come up with a decent story idea while renovating the Lodge.

"I guess I could," I said without feeling.

"You can do it. I believe in you."

A horn honked outside.

"That's Keith." Simon put on his coat and kissed my forehead. "See you in a bit, baby. Don't get into any trouble."

"I won't."

I waved to Keith from the porch as Simon traversed the snowy front yard and hopped into the truck. Keith, as bright-eyed and bushy-tailed as he was yesterday, waved back and shot me a huge smile.

In the lobby, I knelt in front of the hearth, stuck my head into the unlit fireplace, and looked up. The situation wasn't as bad as I expected. The chimney was relatively clean and showed no signs of water damage. I could get a fire going to warm up the lobby without lugging the portable heater down here.

A pile of wood was stacked in the corner of the room, leftover from the last owner. I arranged a few logs in the fireplace and got the matches from the kitchen. As I struck one and leaned in to place it, a memory flashed in my head.

Everything burning. Skin peeling off bones.

With a gasp, I shook the match to extinguish it and sat back on my hands. I stared into the unlit fireplace, my breath quickly making its way in and out of my chest.

The back of my neck prickled. Was someone—something—watching me? Frozen in place, locked in the fire, I couldn't turn around.

I squeezed my eyes shut, forcing the fiery images out of my head. Darkness was better than that damned inferno from fifteen years ago. My ears roared. I thought of rushing rapids, thundering waterfalls, and intense rainstorms, anything to put out the flames.

Slowly, the bad memories faded. My head cleared, and my breathing slowed. I kept my eyes closed, grounding myself in the present moment. My hands flattened against the wood floor, the cold seeping through my coat. Simon's warm breath tickling my ear.

But Simon wasn't home.

My eyes flew open, and I spun around. The lobby was empty. I let out a long breath. The condensation hovered briefly in the cold air. I hugged myself and bowed my head.

"Max? Are you okay?"

Startled, I looked up quickly to find Lily standing where no one had been the previous second. She still wore my clothes, and the sight of her warmed me. She looked better than last night, not so pale and sickly. Her cheeks were pink, and her eyes had a bit of light in them.

"Yeah," I said. "I, uh, was having a moment."

"A moment?"

"Like a panic attack? It's a long story." I hurried away from the fireplace. "Have you been here all morning? I brought you breakfast, but you weren't in your room."

She was a few inches taller than me. I hadn't noticed yesterday since exhaustion had made her slump. She smiled and reached out. I held my breath as she tucked a wayward strand of hair behind my ear. Bumps rose on my arms.

"You think of everything," she said kindly. "You don't have to serve me. I had breakfast after I visited the doctor."

"You went to the doctor?" I asked. "What did they say?"

"I'm fine," she said, lifting her shoulders. "They didn't find anything wrong. They did say this would leave a scar, though." She touched the bandaged wound on her forehead. "Scars build character, right?"

"You don't need any more character," I said without thinking.

"I'm not sure that's supposed to be a compliment," she laughed.

"It definitely is."

She noticed the burned match on the floor. "Do you need help starting a fire?"

"No," I answered hastily. "That's okay."

"Are you sure? I happen to be a bit of a fire whisperer."

My body buzzed with fear. "Really, it's okay. I can get the portable heater. That chimney doesn't look like it's in the best shape."

She cast a weird look over me. "Are you sure you're okay?"

"I have a complicated history with fire."

"Ah." As if sensing the true meaning behind those words, she immediately changed the subject. "What are you working on today? You and Simon are renovating this place, right?"

"Yes, ma'am," I said, relieved to have something to talk about. "We bought it with our honeymoon money. I'd like to get it up and running in six months. We're doing the electricity today. Well, Simon and Keith are. I'll probably supervise."

Lily smiled. "Are you an expert on electricity?"

"Hardly," I answered. "This is more Simon's thing. I'll help out when I can, but I think he secretly hopes I'll take the downtime to write my second book."

She swayed unexpectedly and put a hand to her head. "Sorry. I'm still a little woozy." She moved to the couch and patted the empty space beside her. "So, you're a novelist?"

"A comic book artist actually." I sat next to her, feeling that instinctive connection again. "I write and illustrate all of my stories by myself."

"That's amazing. Can I see your stuff?"

I rolled my eyes at myself. "There's nothing to see right now. I'm in a rut. Do you want to see stuff from my older books? It's kind of nerdy."

"I like nerdy."

I pulled up the pages on my phone. My first few volumes were released digitally as well as in print. As I scrolled through to show Lily, pride filled me. Sometimes, I forgot how much I liked my work.

"My main character is loosely based on Queen Isabella," I explained. "She was called the she-wolf of France or the Rebel Queen."

"Why's that?" Lily asked.

"Because she killed her husband, the King of England."

Lily's eyes widened. "That'll do it."

"The same sort of thing happens in volume one of my comics," I went on excitedly. "But the queen has a good reason for killing her husband."

Lily leaned against my shoulder to examine my brightly-colored drawings. "Something tells me this isn't set in 14th century England."

"Definitely not," I agreed. "It's set in a high-tech fantasy world where humans and animals have evolved to form new species."

She pointed to one of my favorite pages in the book,

an intricate portrait of the Queen halfway through a transformation. The Queen bared wolf-like fangs as claws ripped out of her skin and fur grew along her spine.

"The she-wolf?" Lily questioned.

"She's a changeling," I said. "Swapped at birth. In this world, humans consider themselves pure. They would kill her if they knew she was a half-breed."

"Let me guess," she said. "The King finds out and threatens to tell everyone. That's why she murders him."

"Wow, you're good at this. Any chance you want to help me plot out my new book? I have zero ideas."

Lily grinned. "I'm not much of a storyteller, but I have faith in you. Why are you in a rut?" She leaned in. "Are you secretly a she-wolf?"

Her breath tickled my cheek. The warmth of it washed over me. Something felt good about being this close to Lily. She radiated positive energy. I found myself drawing even closer to her. For the first time, I noticed her scent. Pleasantly musky and tangy, like pine and iron.

The rumble of Keith's truck pulled us apart. Whatever spell had settled over the room vanished as the boys' voices approached the house and they stomped their boots on the creaky porch.

"You two look cozy," Simon said when he noticed the two of us on the couch. He huffed into his hands and rubbed them together. "Keeping warm?"

"So far," I said. "Keith, this is Lily. Lily, this is Keith. He's helping us fix up the place."

Keith peered intensely at Lily as he took her hand. "You look familiar. Have we met?"

"I don't believe so," she replied.

"Did you go to Silver Creek High School?"

"A long time ago."

"That must be it," Keith said confidently. "I must have seen you at a football game or something."

From the amusement on Lily's face, I got the feeling she had never attended a Silver Creek High football game in her life. "Or something," she said.

"What are you girls up to?" Simon asked.

"We're plotting Max's next comic book," Lily answered.

"Really?"

I took hold of Simon's wrist. "Don't get too excited. We haven't pitched any ideas yet. We'll see what happens."

He looped his pinky in mine. "We'll leave you to it then. Keith, you ready to make some light?"

Keith nodded. "Let's do it."

As they went on their way, Keith glanced over his shoulder and smiled at Lily. She smirked back.

"You've never seen him before, have you?"

"Not once," she replied. She got comfy on the couch again. "So, are we going to do this or what?"

My stomach rumbled. "I'm dying for some food first. All I had was a stale bagel. Do you want to go into town with me? We could go to the cafe, get breakfast—"

"No, thanks." Lily examined her nails with automatic detachment.

The air between us grew colder, maybe because we weren't sitting close anymore.

"Oh, okay," I said, trying to keep myself from sounding

so obviously disappointed. "Maybe some other time then. They have really good coffee."

She didn't look up. "I'm not much of a coffee drinker."

"They have tea, too. Do you like matcha?"

Lily wrinkled her nose.

"You know what?" I said. "I'm not really in the mood to go out in the snow. Maybe I'll order some food for here."

Lily brightened immediately. "That's a great idea. I love gray days like these. It makes me want to stay inside and cozy up with a great book."

"Me, too." I took out my phone. "What's a good place to eat around here? Somewhere that delivers."

"I'm not sure. I'm not well acquainted with the area."

"I thought you went to high school here."

She yawned and stretched. Subtle shadows beneath her eyes made themselves known when the light hit her face at the right angle. She hadn't completely recovered from yesterday's crash. "I haven't been back since I graduated," she said. "The town's changed."

Somehow, I doubted that. The market on Main Street proudly displayed a sign with the year of its grand opening: 1922. Silver Creek was the type of place that changed very slowly, if at all.

Without Lily's help, I ended up Yelping the various restaurants in town and decided on a place that served different homemade soups and sandwiches each day. As I ordered online, I asked Lily, "Would you like something?"

"I ate already," she said as she had earlier that day.

"You might be hungry later."

"I'm fine." She stood. "I think I'm due for a nap. Yesterday really took it out of me."

She did look woozy and pale again. The bags under her eyes had deepened. As she walked off, she brushed her fingers across the tops of my shoulders. A shiver went through me.

WITH LILY SLEEPING and the boys hard at work, I had no excuse not to pull out my journals to start the outline of my next book. Upstairs in the presidential suite, I wiped the dust from a luxurious leather armchair and dragged it over to the wall of windows that looked out on the mountainside. I curled up with my writing materials, a fresh cup of instant coffee, and a layer of blankets to stay as warm as possible. Determined, I uncapped my pen and flipped to a clean page in my journal.

Half an hour later, I chucked the stupid journal from the chair. It bounced off the window and landed pages down on the floor like a dove with a broken wing. I threw the pen, too. It rolled under the old king bed in the corner of the room.

I let my head fall back and glared at the ceiling. This kept happening. Every time I sat down to concentrate, my brain emptied itself of anything remotely creative. I forgot about my characters' arcs, the progress they had made in the first two volumes, and the important plot points. I couldn't connect the dots. Nothing measured up to the story I'd already told.

I knew logically what needed to happen in volume

three. The last book had ended with a cliffhanger: the Rebel Queen's lover had discovered what she was. With her secret revealed yet again, the Queen had to make a choice. Kill her lover or trust him enough to keep her true identity quiet? The problem was I couldn't decide what the Queen should do.

I let out a long breath and gazed at the mountainside, wishing for inspiration to whiz by like one of the skiers or snowboarders in the distance. When it didn't, I gave up. It did me no good to sit here and do nothing.

The Lodge was a piece of Silver Creek history. The people who had stayed here must have left things behind. I wandered out of the presidential suite and into the hall, letting the aura of the old building wash over me. There was always something creepy about abandoned buildings. The dark corners, outdated decor, and looming shadows were a recipe for unease. I felt it in my bones, a shiver of uncertainty.

It was dark. When had night fallen? The Lodge was quiet—no hammering or construction. I flipped a light switch, but the sconces along the corridor remained unlit. Simon and Keith must not have gotten around to wiring the second floor yet.

I meandered through the hall. The doors to the rooms were shut, though I remembered leaving them open to promote airflow. I grasped a handle—it was cold as ice— and entered the room next to ours.

It was small, one of the cheaper rooms to rent in the Lodge. Dusty white sheets covered the old furniture. The small window above the bed looked to the left side of the

Lodge. The woods there were strangely barren except for one tall, narrow tree that grew close enough to hop onto its branches from the roof. The clouds parted, and the moon shone through. Something heavy swung from the tree on a length of rope.

I blinked, and it was gone.

Like a scared mouse, I skittered out of the room. A soft light glowed at the end of the hallway. I tiptoed barefoot across the musty rug toward the railing that kept those on the second floor from tumbling into the lobby. A voice murmured below, calling me forward.

I looked over the railing. There was Simon, wearing his favorite pair of pajama pants. No shirt or shoes. He must have been freezing. While I watched, he pried up floorboards with a crowbar. Was that part of our renovation plan?

"Somewhere," he muttered, his voice floating up to the second floor. "Around here." He reached into the ground, his arm disappearing up to his shoulder, ear flat against the floor as he groped for something buried beneath the lodge. "Where are you?"

Something creaked overhead. One of the massive beams supporting the roof had a huge crack in it. The pressure was too much. As I watched, the wood splintered and threatened to break.

"Simon!" I called, though my voice sounded muddy and warped. "Get out of the way! The beam's going to fall!"

He didn't listen but pried up the next floorboard and kept searching. The beam cracked. A scream ripped from my throat as it split in two and fell from the ceiling. The sharp, splintered ends turned downward, hurtling toward Simon. With a sickening crunch, the beams pierced his back and legs—

I woke with a yelp. The cold nipped at my skin from all sides. I was lying on top of the bed, the covers flat beneath me. Darkness pressed against my eyes. The curtains were drawn, blocking out the moonlight.

Holding my breath, I reached toward the other side of the bed. My fingers connected with warm skin, and I let out a sigh of relief. It was a dream. Simon was right here next to me.

Without opening my eyes, I crawled on top of him, squared my hips over his, and took comfort in his closeness. A brief mumble—he sounded different—emanated from the pillows. Beneath the covers, hands moved up my thighs. A shiver rolled down my spine as I leaned over him and opened my eyes.

"Oh my God!"

I scrambled off the bed, stumbling across the freezing floor. It wasn't Simon next to me. It was Lily, her dark eyes glowing in the darkness as she sat up to look at me.

6

"*Y*ou did *what?*"

I busied myself with the coffee maker, refusing to look Simon in the eye. "I must have been sleepwalking. I have no idea how I ended up in her room."

"You also somehow ended up on top of her," he whispered. "What the heck, Max?"

"I thought she was you!" I replied hotly. "I had a nightmare that you were working in the lobby and a beam fell on you. Can you blame me?"

He ran a hand through his hair. "We feel completely different. For one thing, Lily has boobs."

"I didn't exactly feel up her chest, but if you need confirmation, yes, she has boobs."

"This isn't funny."

I set the coffee maker aside and looked at him. "No, it's embarrassing. For Lily and me. Think about how she feels. I told her she would be safe here, and the next night, I'm practically molesting her."

Simon chewed his bottom lip. "You *really* couldn't tell it was her instead of me?"

"I was dead tired," I answered. "And half-asleep. She could have been a bear and I wouldn't have noticed."

"Thanks," he grumbled.

I plugged in the coffee machine. The red light came on to indicate it was working. "Did you rewire the entire lodge yesterday?"

"Yeah, don't you remember Keith singing 'Hallelujah' when we tested the lights?"

I wracked my brain, but the memory wouldn't come. "No. Yesterday was kind of a blur."

That was an understatement. I couldn't remember anything after working on my comic book in the presidential suite. Maybe I'd fallen asleep in that chair—

"Was I awake?" I asked Simon. "While Keith was singing?"

He shot me a confused look. "Of course you were. We were all in the lobby together. You harmonized with him."

My stomach dropped like I'd swallowed a rock. Why was I blanking?

"Good morning," a small voice said.

Just as quickly, my stomach shot into my throat as Lily shuffled into the kitchen. She was still wearing my sweater from the day before, her hands tucked inside the sleeves to keep them warm.

"Um, hi," I said. "The electricity's on. Would you like a fresh cup of coffee?"

"No, thank you," she said.

Simon eyeballed Lily with poorly hidden animosity. "Did you sleep well?"

Her gaze flickered to me. "I slept extraordinarily well."

Simon's lips tightened. "Mm-hmm."

I rested a hand on Simon's arm. "Can you check the heating units? I smelled something burning this morning. There might be something stuck in there."

"It's probably just dust," he said and shot Lily another warning look before leaving the kitchen.

"I am so sorry," I said to Lily as soon as he was gone.

She waved off my apology. "It's fine. I bet he's always grumpy in the morning."

"Not just for Simon," I went on. "For last night. I've never sleepwalked before in my life. I didn't mean—"

Lily held up a slender ivory hand. "Please forget about it. You startled me. That's all. We can pretend it never happened if you want."

For whatever reason, a tinge of disappointment settled in my chest. "Right. Totally. That sounds good." I filled a coffee filter and stuck it in the pot. "Do you need some other clothes to wear? I have a ton in boxes I haven't unpacked."

She leaned against the counter, close enough for her woodsy scent to wash over me. "That would be great if it's not a complete inconvenience. I haven't figured out what I'm going to do."

"Stay as long as you like," I heard myself saying. The phrase was sure to incite another bickering match with

Simon later. The insurance issue weighed heavily on him. "Well, Simon might—"

She laid a hand over mine. "Don't worry about Simon."

Automatically reassured, I smiled. "You're right. We'll work it out. Let me grab those clothes for you."

UPSTAIRS, Lily and I combed through my boxes. When she came across something she liked, she held it up for me to confirm.

"What about this?" she said, lifting a sequined red dress with a low cut back and a thigh slit out of a box.

"Do you have somewhere to wear it?" I asked.

She shrugged and ran her fingers across the sequins. "I like how it feels. Where did you wear it?"

"To my best friend's wedding," I replied. "It was a Monte Carlo theme."

"Was she upset you upstaged her?"

I laughed. "I definitely did not upstage her."

Lily's eyes caught mine. "You certainly did."

Simon popped his head into the bedroom, and I dragged my gaze away from Lily's. "Hey babe, can we get some help out here? Keith and I are tackling some of the downstairs rooms, but it'd go a lot faster with another person." He noticed the clothes strewn everywhere. "That is, if you're finished playing dress-up."

"She'll be down in a minute," Lily said. "We're almost done."

"Uh-huh. Great." He vanished again.

Lily giggled. "Is he always so straight-laced? Does he ever smile?"

"He's a big goof most of the time," I said, folding a pair of pants Lily had chosen and adding them to her pile. Most of the clothes I'd agreed to let her borrow were things I didn't wear anymore. "I don't know what's gotten into him today."

"And yesterday," Lily added.

I handed Lily an empty box to put her new clothes in, then dusted my hands and stood. "I should get downstairs. Let me know if you need anything else."

"Sure. Don't let your husband get you down."

BUT WITHOUT LILY AROUND, Simon was his usual happy-go-lucky self. Keith's optimistic attitude and amazing work ethic also elevated the mood. As we tackled the guest rooms on the first floor, we laughed and joked. Keith, it turned out, had also been a theater kid as well as a baseball player, so he had a musical number at the ready for any occasion. He often burst into song without warning.

"*A spoonful of sugar makes the medicine go down,*" he sang, ripping ugly flowery wallpaper off with his bare hands with a ferocity Mary Poppins would balk at. "*The medicine go down, the medicine go do-wn!*"

"Pick a different song," hollered Simon. "If that gets stuck in my head, I'll kill you."

"*It's a small world after all—*"

Simon and I howled in protest, and Keith laughed

raucously. The room we were working in was half the size of the other guest rooms, so it was close quarters for three people, especially when one of them was belting show tunes at the top of his lungs. We were all sweating, despite the cold outside, and the boys were starting to smell pretty ripe. I was ready to get the wallpaper off as quickly as possible.

With a satisfying rip, I tore through a good chunk of the ugly stuff. When I went back for seconds, my hand thumped against the bare wall. A solid thunk resonated through the room. Both Simon and Keith stopped what they were doing and looked over.

"What was that?" Simon asked.

I formed a fist and hit the fleshy part of my hand against the wall again. *Thunk.*

"Sounds solid," Keith said. "Maybe a stud?

Simon rapped his knuckles against the wall, his ear tilted toward the sound. Experimentally, he knocked around the area, establishing how much was solid behind the wallboard. It was much larger than a narrow stud.

"What do you think is back there?" Keith asked.

"Only one way to find out." Simon grabbed the sledge-hammer and raised it over his shoulder. "Everyone step back."

Keith and I moved away, and Simon swung. The sledgehammer made short work of the drywall. Once Simon loosened it up, Keith and I stepped forward to help rip it off. As we peeled the rest of it off, we revealed—

"A door," Keith said.

"A safe," Simon corrected.

To be fair, the only thing visible to us was the huge iron plate with the spinning lock in the middle. Simon grabbed hold of it and pulled. To no one's surprise, it remained firmly shut.

"Worth a shot," Simon said, dusting the rust off his hands.

"Wait here," said Keith, and he ran out of the room.

I spun the dial on the lock. "What are the chances there's a pile of money in there that officially belongs to us now that we've bought the place?"

Simon chuckled. "Slim to none, though it's good to dream."

Keith came back, panting a little. "I checked outside. The exterior of the building juts out there, farther than the other bigger rooms. That safe must be huge. I bet if you got the blueprints, you could figure out the dimensions."

"Somehow, I doubt a hidden safe is going to be included on the official blueprints," I commented. "Whoever built this thing did not want it to be found."

"Well, we're not going to get in there anytime soon," Simon said. "I don't know anything about safe cracking. We'll have to hire someone."

"When we can afford it," I added.

He sighed. "It's a mystery for now."

WE FINISHED DEMOLISHING the small guest room. As Keith and Simon carried the debris to the dumpster outside, I examined the safe again. Maybe it was the storyteller in me, but I had to know what was inside. Something pulled me toward the door, like a magnetic force. I placed my palm flat against the metal.

Energy pulsed through me, real or imagined, and I yanked off my hand. Though the metal was cool to the touch, my palm was angry and red as if I'd laid it on a hot stovetop. What was behind that door?

Simon came in. "Max? We've got visitors."

I scrunched my nose and hid my hand behind my back. "Who?"

"Boyce Driscoll and some other guys from town," Simon replied. "Keith says they've got money and they like to invest. He recommended we give them a tour in case they're interested in the Lodge."

"I'm coming."

Boyce stood out front, his hands on his hips as he looked over the Lodge's exterior and chatted happily with his company. He'd brought the same group of men I'd seen with him in the cafe the previous day. Like before, they all wore expensive clothes and shoes. No normal person would come up to a half-derelict lodge covered with snow in Italian leather loafers, but the businessmen of Silver Creek considered this appropriate attire.

Keith lingered at Boyce's side, staring at the older man with sparkling eyes and rapt attention. Whenever there was a slight pause in the conversation, Keith interjected.

"This place was a real charmer back in the day," Boyce was saying to his friends. "I'd like to see Silver Creek bring in more tourism revenue from those ski slopes. We're so close but not reaping any of the benefits."

"The Lodge could be ready by next ski season," Keith proposed hastily. "Earlier even, especially if you invest. If we got a few more workers in here to help out—"

"Keith," I called from the porch. "That's enough, thank you."

The younger man had enough decency to look bashful as he stepped away from Boyce. Boyce spread his arms wide.

"There's the woman of the house," he said cheerfully. "We were hoping you would be here. We require the warmth of your hospitality. It's quite a trek up here!"

"Hospitality is easier to offer when you know you're expecting someone," I replied with equal amounts of snark and teasing. "Surprise visits make for cold rooms, hastily made coffee, and a lack of enjoyable snacks."

"Luckily, Silver Creek folk know this about surprise visits." Boyce returned to his large shiny SUV and reached through the window. "We brought fresh coffee and donuts. Can I offer you a double chocolate? They're my favorite."

"Sure. Come on in, boys."

Boyce and his friends stomped out their loafers and filed into the Lodge. Keith brought up the rear, smiling from ear to ear. As they formed a loose circle in the lobby, Boyce handed off the boxes of donuts and coffee to Keith.

"Why don't you set those up somewhere, kiddo?" Boyce asked. "And grab some napkins while you're at it."

"Sure thing, Boyce. I mean, Mr. Driscoll. I mean, sir." Keith, bright-red, hurried off.

The men gazed around the gutted lobby with prying

eyes. Boyce ran his finger across the top of the mantle and pulled away a thick layer of dust.

"You two don't waste any time, do you?" he asked. "I was in here less than a week ago. I can't believe how much you've done already."

Simon draped his arm around my shoulders and drew me close. "You were here? What for?"

"Oh, I threw my hat in the ring to buy the place," Boyce said casually. "The Lodge is vital to Silver Creek's success as a community. Anyway, we're not here to talk business! We'll do that some other time. Let me introduce you to some of my friends. This is Mike Nichols," he said, gesturing to the man closest to him. "He manages the bank. That's Henry Paramount—his family's in the movie business…"

There was not a chance in hell I'd remember who was who, not when all of Boyce's friends looked so similar in face and stature. One thing I did notice was that each of them seemed to have a large stake in Silver Creek, one way or another. They were bankers, business owners, small-town political figures, and lawyers.

"We like to think we're the town's caretakers," Boyce said, once he'd finished introducing everyone. "We put on charity fundraisers and do our best to make sure everyone is comfortable in Silver Creek. That includes you two!"

"Uh, thanks," Simon said.

Boyce clapped Simon on the back and separated him from me. "That's not all. My buddies and I would like to invite you, Simon, to join us for a meeting."

Simon raised an eyebrow. "A meeting?"

"Yes, for the Gentlemen's Club of Silver Creek!" he announced grandly. "It's a way for all of us boys to get together and talk about the community. We go skiing, take trips together, go out for drinks—"

"I don't drink," Simon said shortly.

"You can order a Coke," Boyce replied. "We won't judge you for it as long as you come out with the boys every once in a while. What do you say?"

Keith, who had finished setting up the donuts and coffee on the sofa like it was a buffet table, stood behind Boyce's shoulder and nodded emphatically at Simon.

"I'll let you know," Simon said. "We've got a lot of work to do here, and I've been exhausted in the evenings."

Boyce patted Simon's back. "Of course! The work you're doing is outstanding. I can't wait to see this place when it's finished. Do you mind if we have a look around?"

"It's not safe," I said, reading the look on Simon's face. I gave Boyce an apologetic grimace. "Too many construction hazards. But I promise to invite you back when it's not such a demolition zone."

Boyce gave me a thumbs-up. "Good looking out, Maxine. You're always one step ahead. All right, then. Let's go, boys! Leave this beautiful couple to their work."

"See ya, Boyce!" Keith called. "Let me know about the next meeting."

Boyce waved above his head without looking back at Keith. Leaving the donuts untouched, the men shuffled out in a single-file line behind their leader. A minute later, they fired up their army of Cadillacs and were gone.

"Gentlemen's Club?" I scoffed. "Don't they know it's sexist to exclude women?"

"It's not sexist," Keith argued. "The Gentlemen's Club of Silver Creek is historical. They practically built the town."

"Do they allow women to join?"

"No, but—"

"Then, it's sexist."

Keith crossed his arms. "Not everyone is invited to join. Only people Boyce thinks would be an asset to Silver Creek. Simon should be over the moon that he got asked to a meeting." He turned to Simon. "You're going to go, right?"

Simon wrinkled his nose. "I'm not sure. Max has a point, and I don't fit in with Boyce's boys."

"It doesn't matter if you fit in," Keith said. "You were *invited*. You have to go."

Simon playfully pushed Keith. "What's up with you and Boyce, man? Why do you worship the ground he walks on?"

Keith blushed. "I don't! But if you want to be someone in Silver Creek, you get in with the Gentlemen's Club. That's how it works. Everyone respects them."

"I'll think about it," Simon said. "Happy?"

"For now," Keith answered.

Crash!

I hit the floor, curling into a ball and covering my head with my arms as something shattered overhead. All I could think about was my nightmare, the broken beam splitting Simon in two.

Simon, however, was perfectly fine. So was Keith. The beams were all in place.

"Are you okay?" Keith said, helping me up from the floor. "That scared me, too, but not enough to hit the deck."

"Sounded like broken glass," added Simon. "Isn't Lily up there?"

"I'll go check on her," I volunteered, eager to get out from under the beams. "Be back in a minute."

As Simon and Keith got back to work, I went upstairs to investigate the sound. When I reached the presidential suite, I saw the broken lamp first. Then I saw Lily, sprawled across the floor.

"Lily!" I rushed toward her. When I turned her over, her face had a green tint to it. "What happened? What's wrong?"

"I'm so sorry," she gasped. "I stood up too quickly. The head rush—I stumbled and knocked the lamp over."

"Don't worry about it," I said, propping her head onto my knee. "We're getting rid of all this old stuff anyway. You don't look good. Are you sure the doctor said nothing was wrong?"

As she rested against my leg, the ugly green faded a bit from her skin. "He said not to overdo it. I was arranging your things. I guess I shouldn't have been so keen—" She broke into a coughing fit, her whole body convulsing.

"There's fluid in your lungs," I said. "I can hear it. You

must have bronchitis or something. Come on, let's get you to bed."

As I lifted her from the floor, I remembered we'd gutted Lily's room on the first floor already. There was nowhere for her to sleep except our air mattress.

"No, I can't," she said, as I pulled back the covers. "What about Simon?"

"Simon can deal with it until I find another place for you to sleep." I piled the pillows behind her so she was propped up. "Try to stay elevated. Otherwise, all that stuff is going to drain into your throat. I'll make you some soup."

"Really, you don't have to—"

"I'm making soup. End of discussion."

WITH SOME CAJOLING, Simon got the old industrial stove to work. I sent Keith to the grocery store with a list of things I needed to make chicken and vegetable soup. When he returned, I invited him to stay for dinner.

"I appreciate it, but I can't tonight," he said. "I promised my mom I'd help her reupholster her couch."

"Do you ever stop working?" Simon asked.

"Not really. See you guys tomorrow."

Once Keith was gone, Simon came up behind me, framing my waist with his arms. "Alone at last," he said, nuzzling my neck. "What do you want to do about it?"

"We're not alone," I said, stepping out of his grasp to cut celery. "Lily's upstairs."

I could hear the disappointment in his tone as he said, "Oh. What happened up there anyway?"

"She fell and knocked over a lamp. She's sick, so I put her to bed."

"Upstairs?"

"Hm-hmm."

"In our bed?" he pressed.

"Where else?" I questioned. "The first floor is a disaster. She can't stay down here."

Simon huffed and moved away from me. "She shouldn't be here at all, Max. This isn't a homeless shelter. Shouldn't she have moved on by now?"

I set a pot on the stove and threw the chopped celery in. "Are we arguing about this again? I told her she could stay as long as she needed."

"What? *Why?*"

"Because she obviously needs our help." The celery done, I moved on to the carrots. "Don't scold me, Simon. I know what I'm doing."

"You don't know anything about this girl," he countered, stepping closer to me. "She could be a grifter, running a scam! She could be psychotic, planning to kill us in our sleep, and you've let her into our bed!"

"Don't be ridiculous."

His chest bumped my elbow as I scraped carrots into the pot from the cutting board. "We've always been a team, Max. We've always made decisions together. All of a sudden, you're pulling away. It doesn't make sense. What do you know about Lily that I don't?"

"Yes, we're a team," I shot back. "When you're being reasonable. But for the past two days, you've been an ass!"

I rotated the dial to turn on the burner. Flames exploded from the stove, licking the side of the pot and grazing my bare skin.

This was hell. Fire burned everything around me. The walls were made of flame. The heat was so intense, my bones could feel it. I saw my mother, crawling across embers as she tried to reach me. Her hair was blackened, most of it gone. She coughed, and a cloud of ash came out. I opened my mouth to scream.

"Max. Max, look at me!"

A sharp slap across my cheek brought me back to my senses, and I found myself standing in the kitchen of the Lodge. Simon had shut off the stove. Everything was fine.

Sobbing, I collapsed against Simon's chest.

7

*I*n the morning, Lily and I rested next to each other on the old leather couch in the lobby, sharing a blanket, while Simon made eggs and bacon for breakfast. The miniature explosion last night had been due to a minor problem with the gas line. Though Simon fixed it, I couldn't venture into the kitchen without seeing another fire in my head.

Lily looked no better than she had yesterday. To make matters worse, I had picked up the same phlegmy cough. Whatever she had, she'd passed to me. I didn't care. It gave me an excuse not to work on my comic book or the Lodge construction. After my episode last night, all my energy and motivation were gone.

Lily rested her head on my shoulder. The contact was the only thing that made me feel better. Maybe I missed having a best girl friend. Without Sienna around, Lily was the closest substitute.

"Alrighty, breakfast is served," Simon announced, too

loudly, as he emerged from the kitchen, balancing plates like a circus performer. With his foot, he dragged a foldout table to the couch and set the meal in front of us. "Bacon, eggs, coffee, and leftover donuts from yesterday. You two should be feeling better in no time."

Despite our recent spats, Simon hadn't dropped the ball. After fixing the stove, he cleaned the room next to ours from top to bottom. Then he inspected every mattress in the Lodge, picked the best-looking one, and dragged it in for Lily. Once we were alone, he helped me take a bath. Then he held me all night long, even after I fell asleep. When I woke up, his arms were still around me.

"Aren't you hungry?" Simon asked when neither one of us attempted to eat.

"A little," I said.

"Not much," answered Lily at the same time.

Simon used a plastic fork to make plates for us. "You need to eat something. Both of you. You can't fight off whatever virus you have without some food in you. Here." He handed Lily her meal. "It'll make you feel better. I promise."

Once he'd served both of us, he returned to the kitchen to clean up.

"I changed my mind about him," Lily said. "He's one of the good ones."

"I know." Poking one hand out of the blankets like a T-Rex, I started to feed myself. "He only gets grumpy when we don't communicate well."

Lily considered her plate. "Do you think he'll be offended if I don't eat this?"

"Probably." The eggs were delicious. Simon had a knack for getting the whites crispy without drying out the yolk. "You should try to eat a little. Simon's right about that."

She flicked a piece of bacon back onto the serving plate. "There. Now he'll think I've had some. Don't tell him, okay?"

AFTER BREAKFAST and a heavy dose of decongestants, I felt good enough to help with the Lodge. While Keith and Simon continued gutting the first floor, I started clearing crap from the second. To make things easy for me, Simon placed a big plastic garbage can directly under the overhang of the second-floor corridor. All I had to do was chuck junk over the railing and into the can. When it was full, either Simon or Keith emptied it in the dumpster, and I started all over again.

The work itself was gross yet cathartic. Dust and dead bugs coated everything. I worked one room at a time, tossing old linens, moldy pillows, and broken furniture into the garbage below. Sometimes, I found lost items from past guests: a necklace with a gold Virgin Mary pendant, a tobacco pipe, and a dog-eared copy of *Cat's Cradle* by Kurt Vonnegut.

I gave Lily strict orders to stay in her room and rest. Thankfully, she took my advice. I heard nothing from her for the rest of the morning, which hopefully meant she was catching up on some much-needed sleep. Every so often, I got the feeling that someone was watching me. I suspected Lily, but when I glanced over my shoulder, no one was there.

The fifth or sixth time this happened, I caught a quick glimpse of an unfamiliar man as he strolled past the open door of the room I was working in. I quickly stood.

"Hey!" I called, heading out. "You can't be in here—"

But the corridor was empty.

"Max?" Keith called from the first floor. "Did you need something?"

I peered over the railing to see Keith. "Did you see a man come down the stairs?"

Keith looked confused. "No, why?"

"I could've sworn…" I wiped sweat from my forehead. "Maybe I'm getting sicker. Where's Simon?"

"He's trying to squish down the stuff in the dumpster," Keith replied. "It needs to be emptied soon. Come down. I'll make you some tea. Simon said, you don't like using the stove."

I smiled. "Thanks, Keith."

I KEPT MY DISTANCE, standing on the opposite side of the kitchen as Keith heated the kettle. He made sure to thoroughly wash the construction dust from his arms and hands so the debris didn't end up in my tea.

"I got an exciting call this morning," Keith announced. By the way he bounced on his toes, he'd been waiting to share this information for a while. "Boyce officially invited me to tonight's meeting with the Gentlemen's Club."

"Wow," I intoned. "That's great."

"I know you think it's kind of snobby," he went on. "I guess it is, in a way. But Boyce is a good guy. I'm glad Simon agreed to tag along. It'll be good for the two of you—"

"Simon's going with you?"

Keith browsed our tea selection. "He didn't tell you? We're going together. Boyce invited both of us. The bar has a private room reserved just for the Gentlemen's Club. Isn't that cool? I hope Boyce brings his cigars. Did you know he rolls them himself? Who does that?" As Keith prattled on, I stewed in slow-burning anger.

Something about this whole Gentlemen's Club thing rubbed me the wrong way. It was elitist and exclusionary, not just toward women, but toward the rest of the people in Silver Creek who didn't have as much money or influence as Boyce and his friends.

Simon came in, taking off his heavy work gloves. "Okay, I shoved enough of it down to finish today's work, but we're going to have to empty it tomorrow—oh, hey, baby." He smiled sweetly. "I didn't realize you were in here. Do you want some lunch? I can make—"

"When were you going to tell me that you were going out with the Gentlemen's Club tonight?" I demanded.

The kettle whistled. Keith removed it from the stove and backed out of the room. "I'll leave you guys to it. *Sorry*," he mouthed to Simon before disappearing."

Simon calmly washed his hands and poured a cup of

hot water into a clean mug. "I just told Keith I'd go with him ten minutes ago. I was going to tell you as soon as I saw you."

"I shouldn't have had to hear it from him. I should have heard it from my husband."

"I don't get why this is such a big deal."

"You should have discussed it with me first."

"Why?" he asked. "You didn't discuss anything with me before you invited Lily to stay for as long as she wanted."

Fury made me shake from head to toe. "That was different."

"But this is somehow worse?" He abandoned his tea-making to face me. "The only reason I agreed to go was that Keith wouldn't stop bothering me about it. I said yes to shut him up. Why are you acting like a jealous bitch?"

My mouth dropped. "What did you call me?"

"You heard me. Ever since you started hanging out with Lily, things have been weird between us. I've seen the way she looks at me. I know she doesn't like me."

"That's not true!"

"Whatever." He dunked a tea bag into the hot water and handed me the mug. "Drink this. Maybe it'll help with your bad mood."

I knocked his hand aside. "Forget it. You always make it too weak. I'm going into town."

"You're sick," he shouted after me as I stomped out of the kitchen.

"I'm fine!"

. . .

After twenty minutes walking up and down Main Street, determined to shop or find something fun to do without Simon, my runny nose and itchy throat encouraged me to seek shelter in the cafe. I struggled to open the door against the blustery wind. Thankfully, Cassie, the friendly barista, took pity on me and helped out. As I came inside, she dusted snowflakes off my shoulders and rubbed my arms to warm me up.

"Lovely out, isn't it?" she said brightly. "I wouldn't want to be stuck on the hiking trails right now."

The snowfall had picked up since I'd left the Lodge. It whirled past the windows in great gusts, piling along the curbs and settling on stagnant windshields. My first thought was of Simon at the inn. Would the subpar heater keep him warm enough?

"No, I wouldn't, either," I told Cassie.

"Coffee?" she offered.

"Tea, please," I said. "I'm fending off a cold."

"You got it. Take that booth by the kitchen. It's the warmest seat in the house."

The table she pointed to seated four, but the hot air coming out of the nearby kitchen coaxed me into the booth. I shook off my coat my shoulders and hung it up to dry. Cassie dropped off the tea and a bowl of bright-orange soup.

"Roasted carrot, sweet potato, and turmeric," she announced. "It'll chase whatever's got you down right out of there."

"Thanks, Cassie."

"No worries. By the way—" She leaned down and pointed across the cafe. "You've got a fan."

I glanced toward the other side of the room. A little girl, maybe ten or twelve, sat at the counter, her feet dangling far above the floor. She had straight blond hair and familiar blue eyes, but I hadn't seen her in town before. She whipped her head away and stared down at her book when I looked at her. A moment later, she snuck another peek at me.

"A fan of what?" I asked.

"I'll let her tell you," Cassie said with a wink.

The girl continued to spy on me throughout the hour. Eventually, I forgot she was there and focused on soothing my cold with the rich, creamy soup. I ate slowly, savoring the taste and the way the pureed sweet potatoes coated my throat with a protective layer.

I forgot about last night's freak-out, the fire, and my spat with Simon. I let it all drain from my thoughts as if my brain were a large sieve, keeping only the pleasant aroma of coffee and fresh pastries inside. A Christmas song played softly overhead. Since it was a weekday, the cafe wasn't as busy as it normally was. Every few minutes, someone would come in and order a coffee to go, but that was the only disruption from my calming lunch.

The soup finished, I wrapped my hands around my mug, closed my eyes, and inhaled the scent of the warm tea. I hadn't specified what kind I wanted. Cassie automatically supplied chamomile and peppermint sweetened with honey, the best combination to fight a cold.

The worst way to fight a cold, or any illness for that

matter, was opening your eyes to find a child standing silently two feet away from you, staring intently at your face. I nearly jumped out of my skin.

"Hello," I said cautiously to the blond girl. "Can I help you?"

She had a yellowing bruise along her cheekbone. "Are you Maxine Finch?"

"Yes, why?"

The girl drew something from behind her back. My comic book, *Rebel Queen, Volume One.* She pointed to my name on the front cover. "This Maxine Finch?"

I lifted my chin. "You betcha."

"Wow." The little girl hugged the comic book to her chest and gazed at me with sparkling eyes. "I can't believe you're here. I can't believe it's you! Can I hug you?"

"Well, I'm getting sick, so I don't know if you want to, but—*oh!*"

She threw her arms around my neck anyway and gave me a hard squeeze. She lingered a moment too long before pulling away. "Sorry, but I can't believe it's you."

"You said that already," I said, smiling.

She blushed.

"What's your name?" I asked.

"Bubbles," she replied. "Well, that's not my real name, but it's what everyone calls me because when I was two, I drank from a bottle of bubbles and sneezed them out through my nose."

I couldn't help it. I burst out laughing, and Bubbles smirked, pleased by my amusement. I wiped my streaming eyes on a spare napkin. "Wow, that is some nickname. How did you find *Rebel Queen*?"

"In the library," Bubbles answered. "There's barely ever new comic books there. We get hand-me-downs from other places, but I saw *RQ* in there and knew I had to read it."

"*RQ*?"

"It's what your fans call the series," she explained. "Didn't you know that already?"

"I've never met any fans."

Her mouth dropped. "You're kidding. Why not?"

"I didn't do any press tours," I said. "*Rebel Queen—RQ* was a bit of a sleeper hit, popular enough for my agent to want me to keep writing. Not popular enough for them to send me to conventions or anything like that."

Bubbles bounced on her toes. "Wait, wait, wait. Did I hear that right? You're writing more!"

"Um, well—"

"Because the cliffhanger in volume two is driving me crazy!" Without my invitation, she slid into the booth and placed the comic book between us. The Queen stared up at me with bold eyes. "What's the Queen going to do now that her lover knows her secret? Is she going to kill him? She can't kill him, right? She loves him!"

I remembered some of the panels I'd drawn in volume two. They weren't intended for Bubbles's demographic. "Aren't you a little young to be reading my stuff?"

"I'm really mature for my age," she replied. "I get the themes and everything. Especially the big ones."

I grinned. "Really? What are the big themes?"

"Not being afraid to be yourself even when everyone might hate you," she said automatically. "Refusing to hide even though you're different than everyone else. Feeling obligated to stick around for your blood family when they don't support or love you. Finding a family in other people who really matter."

I was speechless. How old was this kid again?

"I guess the Queen is still learning those things," Bubbles went on. "Otherwise, she would have told her lover the secret. She wouldn't have let him find out on his own. She's ashamed of herself, don't you think?"

I swallowed the lump in my throat. "Yes, I would say so."

Bubbles drummed her fingers on the table and gazed into the distance. "I get that. It's hard to feel like you don't belong where you grew up. What do you think is going to happen to her?" Her eyes brightened. "Wait, you're the writer! You *know* what's going to happen to her! Can you tell me? Oh, please tell me! Please, please, please!"

"Whoa, easy," I said. "I haven't written volume three yet."

"Why not?" she demanded harshly. "It's been three years since volume two came out!"

Small bits of tea leaves had settled on the bottom of my mug. I whisked them around with a spoon. "To be honest, I don't know what's going to happen, either. I've had trouble deciding what the Queen should do."

"Be with her lover," Bubbles said automatically. "First of all, it would divert expectations. Everyone *expects* the Queen to kill him, right? She's never trusted anyone before, not even her previous partners. She's always been betrayed, but this time it's different. He loves her regardless of her secret, not *in spite* of it. It's different, you see."

"What grade are you in?"

"Ninth," she said. "I skipped third and fifth."

"So, you're a genius."

"I just read a lot," Bubbles replied. "It's easier to read then deal with real life, don't you think?"

"That's why I started drawing comics in the first place," I admitted. "But real life eventually catches up to you."

"Eventually," Bubbles said. "But I'm going to enjoy fantasy life while I'm a kid. It won't be long before I have to worry about money and jobs and all that."

"You *are* mature for your age."

"I try to appreciate the present," she said. "The Queen is teaching me that. I guess you are, too."

I sat against the booth, looking over the girl. "I'm starting to think I need to take my own advice."

"Let's talk," said Bubbles. She held up two fingers to Cassie. A few minutes later, the barista brought over two steaming mugs of a frothy white substance, each garnished with peppermint splinters and chocolate-dipped tuiles.

"Two Bubbles Specials," Cassie announced. "With extra peppermint."

Bubbles let out a squeal of delight as she pulled the drink toward her and took a long sip. When she pulled away, the stuff coated her nose. She licked her lips. "Ahh. I invented this drink!"

I sniffed mine. "Is this hot chocolate?"

"White hot chocolate," Bubbles corrected. "With peppermint! It makes me happy. That's how you should do your work. Write what makes you happy!"

"It's not so simple."

"What are you scared of?" she asked bluntly.

"Who said I was scared?"

Bubbles shrugged. "If you can't figure out to write, it's for a reason. Maybe you're afraid people won't like it if the Queen makes the wrong decision. They might blame you." She took a crunchy bite of a tuile. "Or maybe something's happening in your real life that's making you question the Queen's decisions."

"Are you a therapist, too?"

"I'm good at perceiving people," she said. "That's all. Drink your drink."

I took a sip of my Bubbles Special. It was the most delicious thing I'd tasted in a long time. Maybe Bubbles was right. Maybe I had to remind myself why I liked writing and drawing in the first place.

By THE TIME I returned to the Lodge, Simon and Keith had finished their work for the day, washed up, and were on their way out to their first official meeting with the Gentlemen's Club of Silver Creek.

Simon kept his head down as he brushed past me. "See you later," he mumbled.

"Simon—" I started, but he was already halfway across the front yard.

I watched as he hopped into Keith's truck, and they drove off.

"Everything okay?"

I turned to face Lily, who'd been lingering near the foot of the stairs without my noticing. "It will be. I was a jerk to him earlier."

"Why?"

I gnawed on my lip, wondering that myself. "I guess I'm blaming him for things that aren't his fault."

Lily came down the stairs. "Do you usually get along better?"

"We never fight," I said. "This is out of the box for us."

"Seems a little unrealistic," she replied. "A couple that doesn't fight."

Cold seeped under the door and into the entrance. I drew the blanket from the couch around my shoulders and sat down in the lobby. "We have miscommunications. We get upset with each other, but we don't yell or scream or shout insults. We always come back together, but this feels different."

She sat next to me and rested her hand on my knee. "Did something happen last night? I heard you scream, and you've looked off all day."

My throat closed up. Did I want to talk about this with someone I barely knew? I thought of Bubbles. *Maybe you're scared.* I was definitely scared. Maybe opening up to someone who wasn't Simon could help.

"When I was a kid," I began, "my house caught fire—gas leak. The whole place went up in flames in a few minutes flat. My best friend was sleeping over. She died that night, along with both of my parents. I was the only one who got out."

Lily didn't speak. She gently rested her forehead against mine. Somehow, that was all I needed. Throughout my life, I'd heard every sentiment in the book. *Sorry for your loss. God, that's terrible. You're so strong.* I didn't need sentiments anymore. I needed a single person to be there for me. Usually, it was Simon, but Lily was doing a decent job in his stead.

"Everything's going to be okay," she said softly, cupping the back of my neck. "That's all you need to know."

Sometimes, I believed that.

8

*N*ovember passed in a haze of construction. Slowly but surely, we made progress on the Lodge. We emptied the dumpster twice more until there was no more debris inside. The Lodge was completely gutted. No carpets, no walls, no bathtubs or sinks. Even the presidential suite was stripped to its bones. The place looked more depressing than it had when we first bought it, but at least it was a blank slate now.

Living in the Lodge when it had next to no amenities was a huge challenge. We'd been showering in the locker rooms of the local gym in town, mostly eating out, and sleeping in one of the rooms on the ground floor while we replaced the flooring upstairs. Without a real place to call home, I couldn't kick my cold. It lived in my chest like it paid rent. At night, a hacking cough kept me up, no matter how much syrup I chugged. Black circles grew beneath my eyes, getting bigger as my insomnia got worse. Half the time, the world seemed foggy around me.

Simon and I didn't talk. We were polite, cordial, but things were different between us. He and Keith disappeared two or three times a week to meet with the Gentlemen's Club. Neither one of them bothered to share the contents of the meetings. Keith's cheerful whistling always increased the day after a meeting, but Simon didn't seem affected. Sometimes, he came home smelling like cigar smoke and whiskey, but I dared not question if he had partaken in such vices.

When I felt well enough, I helped work on the Lodge. When I didn't, I either tried to get some more sleep or mentally mapped out volume three of *Rebel Queen.* On the upside of things, Bubbles's advice somewhat worked. After we had talked, I found myself sketching the Queen on random bits of material, like old two-by-fours or foam takeout containers. The quick sketches came naturally, and other than transferring them to an actual drawing book, I didn't push myself to do much more.

For Thanksgiving, Keith invited us to dinner at his mother's house. Lily politely declined, but Simon and I had no reason not to accept. We weren't accustomed to celebrating holidays with other people. Christian and Sienna usually traveled to see their families, leaving us on our own.

The house was in the neighborhood we'd driven through upon our arrival in Silver Creek, where I wished we'd been able to purchase a place to live. It was the smallest one on the block with pale pink shutters and a matching door. The windowsill flowers were dead for the year, but the mounds of pure white snow made up for the lack of decoration. Simon parked on the curb but didn't get out of the car.

"Do you have extra medicine?" he asked me. "Extra tissues in case you get sniffly in there?"

A slight warmth spread through me. Was he worried?

"It's rude to sniffle all through a meal," he added, rifling through the glove box. "I'll shove some extras into my pockets. We don't want Keith's mother to think we're animals. Are you ready?"

"Mm-hmm."

Keith's mother opened the front door before we made it all the way up the sidewalk. She was an older woman for having a son in his early twenties, with tightly curled gray hair and a pink apron around her waist.

"Welcome!" she said, beaming as we stepped over the threshold. "Oh, it's so nice to meet Keith's friends finally! He's been talking nonstop about the two of you for a month. I'm Loretta—Keith, get down here!" she hollered up the stairs.

The house smelled like fresh herbs and roasted potatoes, wafting out from the kitchen toward the back. The living and dining areas were cramped into one room. The table was set for four with embroidered cloth napkins, pretty ceramic plates, and tall white candles. Pictures of Keith from every school year lined the wall up the steps. He had not always been such a gangly kid. In second and third grade particularly, he resembled a round meatball.

"Don't look at those!" Keith joked from the top of the stairs. He wore a green sweater that clashed with his blue plaid pants. Were it not for the red-and-white fuzzy socks, he'd looked like he was trying to emulate Boyce's style and failing. As he came down, he covered as many school pictures with his arms as possible. "Mom won't take them down."

"Of course not!" Loretta said, offended. "You're my best boy."

"I'm your *only* boy." He kissed his mother on the cheek before shaking Simon's hand and giving me a quick hug. "Come in, you guys! We've got the football game on, and Mom's making enough food to serve a hundred."

"Is it just the four of us?" I asked as I unwound my scarf.

Loretta took our coats and hung them in the closet. "Yes, I'm afraid Keith's father is no longer with us. It's been the two of us for a while now. Sorry, it's probably not the big party you were expecting."

"This is great," Simon said with the soft smile he hadn't shown to me in weeks. "I prefer smaller gatherings. It smells delicious. You must know what you're doing."

Loretta's face turned pink. "You are a charmer, aren't you? And so handsome. Look at these beautiful cheeks."

She cupped Simon's jaw with her hand. He looked startled. Unlike Loretta, who subtly pulled away when she saw Simon's reaction, I knew why. Simon wasn't used to familial affection. He had never had it before.

"You, too, darling," Loretta added, turning her attention to me. "No wonder Keith has a little crush on you. You are a thing of beauty."

"Mom!" Keith hissed. "*Really?* I don't know what she's talking about, Max. She's going a bit nuts in her old age.'

Loretta smacked Keith's shoulder with an oven mitt. "Hush, you. Why don't you make yourself useful and check the turkey?"

"As long as you don't tell more lies about me," he called over his shoulder as he went into the kitchen.

Loretta checked to make sure Keith was out of earshot before saying, "I can't thank you two enough. I've been worried about Keith since he graduated from high school. He's been a bit aimless for the past few years, and I thought he might be getting depressed, but ever since he started working on that old lodge, my boy's been happy as a clam."

"He's a hard worker," Simon said. "If it weren't for him, we would be way behind our schedule. He's good at what he does, too. I wish I could pay him more."

"He's making more than he usually does in town," Loretta said. "He even mentioned getting an apartment. I don't want him to go, but I do think he should exercise more independence—"

"Stop talking about me," Keith ordered, emerging from the kitchen.

His mother tugged his earlobe. "We were just saying what a good boy you are."

Keith puffed out his chest. "I'm a man, Ma!" We all laughed, and Keith returned to his usual posture. "The turkey isn't quite up to temperature. I'd give it another half hour or so. Does anyone want some cheese and crackers? A glass of wine?"

"Water for me, please," Simon said.

Before I could answer, a coughing fit overcame me. I

turned away and hid my mouth in the crook of my elbow. Moisture streamed from my eyes as I fought to control my breath.

"You poor thing!" Loretta patted my back with the right amount of force to coax whatever clogged my lungs up and out. "I know exactly what you need to get rid of that cough."

A few minutes later, I was wrapped in a handmade quilt and propped up on the comfy pink sofa with a hot toddy in hand. I had been instructed not to move until dinner was ready.

Loretta sat near my feet, nursing straight whiskey. She squeezed my toes beneath the blanket as if she'd known me for my entire life. "Feeling a little better? I have vapor rub upstairs if you need it. That was the only thing that stopped Keith's coughing when he was little."

"I'm all right," I said truthfully. The warmth of whiskey, lemon, and honey on my throat and the blanket around my neck eased the soreness in my chest. "Thank you so much. I haven't been so well taken care of in years."

It was, in no way, a slight against Simon. Even so, I saw him cast a furtive look in my direction.

"My mom passed away," I explained to Loretta hurriedly, more for Simon's benefit than anything else. I didn't want another argument when we got home. "Keith's lucky to have you."

"He sure is," she said, loudly enough for Keith to hear her. She chuckled to herself and patted my knee. "No one can replace your mother, but I'm happy to fill in. You can drop by any time you like. Whatever you need, I'm here for you."

My chin trembled. "That's so nice of you."

She looked over her shoulder. Keith and Simon had wandered into the next room, absorbed in a private conversation. "Like I said, Keith's been a different man since the two of you came to town. I owe you."

"You don't owe us anything," I assured her.

"Believe me, I do," she insisted in a low whisper. "Keith had no drive after his father left us. He was sixteen, and he felt abandoned. His grades tanked, he acted out, and he lost his chance at an athletic scholarship. I wanted him to get out of Silver Creek, at least for a little while, but he wouldn't go. He claims he doesn't want to leave me alone. Then the stalking situation happened—"

I sat up a little straighter. "Stalking situation. What do you mean?"

"It was a misunderstanding," Loretta said hurriedly. "Keith took a liking to a man in town. Boyce Driscoll. Everyone knows him. Have you met him?"

"Oh, yeah," I said, my tone darkening as I thought about Simon and the Gentlemen's Club. "I know Boyce."

"After Keith's father left, Boyce caught wind of it," Loretta explained. "He came by and offered to take Keith to a ball game in the big city. Keith was ecstatic. He had a great time. Boyce bought him a hat and Dippin' Dots, the whole shebang."

"But?" I pressed.

"It was a one-time thing," she answered. "Boyce did it to cheer up Keith, but then Keith started following him around like a puppy dog. I didn't think it was a problem at first. Then the school called to tell me Keith had been skipping classes. I confronted Boyce, thinking it was his fault for luring Keith out of class, but he told me my son was a nuisance. Interrupting meetings, butting in where he wasn't invited, et cetera."

She checked once more to make sure Keith wasn't listening in, but the boys weren't even inside anymore. I caught a glimpse of them walking around the front of the house, pointing to something on the roof.

"I read Keith the riot act," Loretta went on. "Told him I wouldn't accept this kind of behavior. I grounded him for the rest of the school year, but it didn't make a difference. I couldn't *force* him to go to class. I had a job of my own to do. He didn't stop chasing Boyce around, either. Rather, he did it in secret. It all came to a head when Boyce had Keith arrested for stalking and trespassing."

I watched Keith through the window, chatting happily with Simon. I had a hard time believing this was the same kid who gave his mother hell. "Trespassing where?"

"First, at Boyce's house," Loretta said, sighing. "Then, up at your lodge. This was four years ago," she added quickly. "He's learned his lesson since then."

My brow furrowed. "He followed Boyce up to the Lodge?"

"That's what the police report said."

"But someone else owned the Lodge then," I said. "A man named Earl. How could Keith have been arrested for trespassing at a public space?"

Loretta took another long sip of whiskey. "By that

time, Earl had long since closed the Lodge to public access. It was private property, with a sign and everything. Keith wasn't supposed to be there."

"But Boyce had permission?"

"*That* has puzzled me to this day," she replied. "The feud between Earl and Boyce was infamous in Silver Creek. Those two men hated each other, and no one in town could figure out why. It's one of the reasons Earl stopped showing up in town. He didn't want to face Boyce, so he stayed at home in the woods. I don't understand why Earl would have had Keith arrested that night but not Boyce." She shrugged. "I guess I'll never find out. Ooh, hush. The boys are coming back inside."

The back door slammed at the same time the oven alarm went off. Simon and Keith's voices floated into the front room.

"You can fix that yourself," Simon was saying. "All you need are some new shingles and a nail gun. You won't have to replace the whole roof."

"That is music to my ears!" Loretta sang, leaping off the couch. "I don't have the money to replace that old roof. Let's see if that turkey's ready to be carved, shall we?"

As Simon went into the kitchen, Keith helped me up from the couch.

"Did Mom tell you any horror stories about me?" he asked with a smile.

I smiled back. "Of course not."

. . .

THOUGH LORETTA'S food was delicious, the richness of the homemade meal got to me later as we were driving home to the Lodge. My stomach tossed and turned, full of turkey, mashed potatoes, and pumpkin pie. My skin was burning up. I pressed my forehead against the car window, relishing the cool glass against my skin.

Simon kept looking at me from the corner of his eyes. He thought I hadn't noticed, but he'd been doing it all through dinner too.

"Do I look that awful?" I asked weakly.

"You, uh, don't look great. I think we should take you to the doctor tomorrow."

The car lurched over a bump in the road. I squeezed my eyes closed, concentrating on keeping the contents of my stomach where they belonged. "We can't afford a hit to our health insurance."

"Then what's the point of having health insurance?"

"What were you and Keith talking about?" I said, eager to change the subject. I hated doctors. I'd spent too much time in sterile offices after the fire. "You were outside for a while."

"His mother's house mostly," Simon answered. "It's old, and Simon's worried it will need more fixing than he can provide in the next few years. I offered to help with the roof."

"That was nice of you." It helped the nausea to keep my eyes on a tree in the distance and follow it until we passed it. "I had an interesting chat with Loretta, too."

"Oh?"

"Did Keith ever mention being arrested to you?"

Simon hesitated.

"You knew already," I said flatly.

"He told me the first week he was working for us," he admitted. "He said it didn't feel right not sharing it with me, but he also asked me not to tell you. He wants you to think well of him."

"He got arrested for stalking and trespassing," I reminded him.

"He was going through a hard time with his dad," Simon replied. "I get parent stuff. You should, too."

"So, you want to be his Daddy now?"

Simon's lips tightened. "Please don't pick another fight with me. I'm sick of bickering with you. It's every day."

I crossed my arms and slumped down, automatically grumpy. I didn't want to fight, either, but irritation grew into anger, and anger grew into rage. More and more, I noticed how little patience I had. The distance between Simon and me was my fault. I gathered my pride, stuffed it in a mental packing box, and taped it shut.

"I'm sorry," I said softly. "I don't feel well."

He reached across the car to rest his hand on my thigh. His palm felt too warm. "Which is why I want to take you to the doctor. I don't care how much it costs. We can get you some meds and nip whatever this is in the bud."

"I don't want to go to the doctor."

He tried to hide his hurt as I moved my leg out from under his hand. I wanted to tell him it wasn't his fault. The moist heat beneath his palm was making me uncomfortable, not his touch. Before I could say anything, we turned up the unpaved road to the Lodge, and I closed my mouth out of fear something other than words might come out of it.

I couldn't get out of the car on my own. My head spun, and the world went with it. I waited for Simon to come around to my side and pull me out. I hung heavily off his shoulder as he helped me up the porch and into the Lodge.

I felt worse as I stepped over the welcome mat. With the new heaters installed, the Lodge was quite warm. It sent a fresh wave of nausea through me. The darkness pressed in on me, squeezing my lungs. I sensed, rather than saw, a presence to my left, and when I turned toward it, two glowing orbs met my gaze like an animal's reflective eyes in the night.

Simon flipped on the light over the entrance. I blinked. It was only Lily, sitting in the lobby, and her eyes looked perfectly normal.

"How was it?" she asked. Then she noticed how terrible I looked. "Whoa, did they feed you poison?"

Lily got up to help, but Simon turned his body to separate us.

"I got this," he said. "She needs to get in bed."

"Can I do anything?" Lily asked.

"No," he replied shortly.

Lily's mouth turned downward as Simon carried me out of her sight. I didn't have the strength to tell him he'd been rude to her. When he set me on the air mattress in our makeshift bedroom, I tumbled limply onto the pillow and lost myself in a world of darkness.

. . .

I AWOKE SOMETIME LATER, feeling better. Simon slept soundly next to me. His hand rested on my stomach as if he'd gone to sleep while monitoring my breath. I gently moved away and slid out from under the blankets.

Though it was warm in the room, cool air swept around my feet, almost beckoning me into the corridor. I stepped into my slippers, took one last look at Simon sleeping peacefully, and left the room.

The magnetic pull—I'd felt it two or three times in the Lodge—took me toward the stairs. My feet barely made a sound as I climbed to the second floor. The hair on the back of my neck rose as I faced the long corridor. All the rooms were closed, except for one. Moonlight spilled into the hallway from the open door.

I walked toward it. As I got closer, a voice whispered in my ear, but I couldn't make sense of the words. It seemed to be speaking inside my head.

I turned into the empty room, the one before the presidential suite. I went to the window. It was open. The gap was big enough for someone to climb out onto the roof. I fit one leg through, ducked, and pulled the other leg out behind me.

The wind should have bothered me. It lapped against my exposed face and neck like a sharp whip. My dry lips burned, but I paid it no mind. My focus was on the tree near the edge of the roof, silhouetted against the dark woods.

The roof was slick with ice and new snow. With every step, it threatened to slide out from under my feet and pitch me over the edge. I didn't care. I had to reach the tree.

Close-up, it became obvious the tree was dead. The branches were white and gray. The bark peeled away from the trunk like dead skin. The air was completely still. The wind had stopped. Nothing moved—not an animal in the woods, nor a snowflake in the air. It was silent.

Swiftly, a body dropped from a higher branch in the tree. Frozen with horror, I watched the rope pull taught. *Snap!* The victim's neck broke.

I couldn't move. My feet wouldn't lift from the roof. The body spun slowly. Long, dark hair. Milky, pale skin. Finally, I saw the face.

Lily.

A scream pierced the air. Then another one. They came one after the next with hardly a breath in between.

"Max!" At the window behind me, Simon struggled to get out onto the roof, but his body was too large to fit through. "Max, what the hell are you doing? Stop screaming!"

It was then I realized the horrific sounds that filled the forest were coming out of my mouth. I turned back toward the tree. Lily's body was gone. She was nowhere. Not up in the tree or on the ground below.

But I couldn't stop screaming.

"Max, please!" Simon's voice rang with panic. "Watch the edge!"

My toes were hanging off the roof. I looked down. The

ground was not too far away. I could easily jump if I wanted.

"Don't you dare!" Simon shouted. Then he vanished from the window, just like Lily's body.

I stared at the ground. I wiggled my toes. One step forward would take me tumbling off the edge of the roof. When was the last time I'd felt real pain? In that burning house, for certain, when the skin on my legs and torso began to crisp. The scars had faded, but they would never disappear. This was my life. Full of fire and doubt. Just as I thought everything was coming together, it all burned away.

I lifted one foot from the roof—I could move them now—and dangled it in the open air, just to see what it would feel like. I lifted my chin to the sky and let the returned breeze whisk my hair from my neck. God, it was good to be free. I shifted my weight forward and stepped off.

"Max, no!"

It was too late. I tumbled toward the ground. For a moment that lasted forever, I fell into oblivion. I fell into darkness. I fell into the world beyond this one.

Then Simon caught me.

9

*S*imon fell under my weight. We tumbled into a snowbank, but he kept his arms wound tightly around me. As soon as I pressed my face against the warmth of his neck, the veil lifted from the world. Whatever spell that had entrapped me on the roof was broken.

Simon sobbed into my shoulder. He made no attempt to lift us from the deep pile of snow. He wore no coat or boots. He was barefoot. But his haste had saved my life or at least saved me from a major injury.

The shadow of the dead tree loomed over us. I looked high into its branches, but there was no sign of Lily's body. The roof seemed farther away from the ground than when I stood on it.

"Why?" Simon whispered, his voice thick. "Why would you do something like that?"

"I didn't do anything," I answered truthfully. My head felt clearer than it had in days. The nausea from earlier had passed. For once, I felt like myself. Better than myself.

Simon clasped my face between his palms and forced me to look at him. "You stepped off the roof."

"I slipped," I heard myself say.

"I saw you, Max," he said with the tiniest hint of fury. "I saw you lift your foot and step forward. You didn't slip."

I shook my head and smiled. "You're being silly. Why would I intentionally jump off the roof?"

"You tell me."

I smoothed his curls away from his forehead and ran the pads of my fingers down his face. It was the first intimate gesture we'd shared in weeks. "Baby, you're imagining things. I slipped and fell. That's all."

The lines around his eyes and mouth softened as I continued to stroke his cheeks. He closed his eyes, relaxed, but when his hand slipped and landed in the snow, it brought him back to reality. He grabbed my hand in his icy one, trapping it against his chest.

"Don't tell me I imagined that," he growled. He drew me roughly toward him and stood up, showing no effort in lifting me from the ground. His back was covered in snow. It fell off in big chunks as he carried me to the front of the Lodge and inside. Unceremoniously, he dumped me onto the couch and covered me with the blanket. "Don't tell me what I did and didn't see," he went on in the same rough tone. He vanished into the kitchen, and I heard him put on the kettle. "I'm taking you to the doctor's tomorrow. I don't care how much it costs. We're going. End of story."

"You can't make me."

"Yes, I can," he roared.

I blanched, hiding beneath the safety of the blanket as he appeared in the doorway between the lobby and the kitchen. His chest heaved as he stared at me, gripping an empty mug so hard I thought it might explode under the pressure. I had never seen him so angry.

Even as I thought it, his rage faded. The longer he looked at me, the more he deflated. His shoulders lowered. His contorted expression relaxed. All at once, the anger morphed into sadness. Or was it fear?

"Don't you understand?" he whispered. "You're all I've got left." His defeat made me reply with the words he wanted to hear.

"All right," I said. "I'll go to the doctor tomorrow. Just don't call 9-1-1."

SIMON HELD me for the rest of the night. His breathing never slowed or evened out. Every once in a while, he shook himself awake. My heart sank. He was afraid to go to sleep, lest I end up on the roof again.

In the morning, he called the primary care doctor in Silver Creek and made an emergency appointment. An hour later, he loaded me into the car like a sick dog and drove me to town.

"I feel fine," I reported, once we were in a private exam room.

Dr. Alvarez was a whole head shorter than me. She had a severe haircut that stopped right at her chin and forearms strong enough to strangle an ox. While she listened to our story from the night before, Simon paced the room with his arms crossed.

"She's been ill," he cut in. "A bad head cold. Probably bronchitis, but she wouldn't let me bring her here until now."

Dr. Alvarez smiled warmly at me. "Not a fan of doctors, I presume?"

"After hours being poked and prodded by them as a kid, it got old quickly," I explained. "Not that I have anything against you personally."

"Don't worry. I'm not offended." Her gaze slid between me, sitting quietly on the exam table, and Simon, who refused to remain still. "Why don't we start with an easy question. What brought you in today?"

Simon opened his mouth.

"I fell off the roof of the house," I said before Simon could tell his version of events.

"She *stepped* off," he revised anyway, finally coming to a stop. "I watched her do it. She was standing on the roof in the middle of the night, screaming her head off like someone was attacking her—"

"Why don't we let Maxine describe her experience?" Dr. Alvarez said, firm but not rude. "She's the patient here."

Simon shut up and resumed pacing. Dr. Alvarez turned to me and waited.

"I don't really remember what happened," I said. That was partially true. The time between waking up in bed and landing in Simon's arms outside was blurry, like a thin fog laid over my memories. "I think I might have

THE HAUNTING OF SILVER CREEK LODGE

been sleepwalking. I don't know how I ended up on the roof."

That was a lie. Though the details were hazy, I recalled the gust of cold wind at my feet, pulling me upstairs and into that specific room. I could see myself ducking through the open window and stepping outside.

"Why were you screaming?" Dr. Alvarez asked.

"I wasn't."

"Yes, you were," Simon said. "It woke me up. They probably heard you all the way in town."

"Simon, why don't you wait outside?" the doctor suggested. "I'd like to talk to Maxine alone."

Simon glared at her. I thought he might refuse, but he grabbed his coat and stalked out. It was just Dr. Alvarez and me. When she leaned forward and made eye contact with me, I sensed what the next conversation would be about.

"How is your home life, Maxine?" she said. "Do you feel safe? Taken care of?"

"This has nothing to do with Simon," I replied automatically. "He gets mad when he's worried. That's all."

Something like pity formed in Dr. Alvarez's eyes. "I've worked with a lot of women who have told me the exact same thing."

"I'm not abused," I said brusquely.

"Okay, let's try something else." She rolled her chair back and folded her hands in her lap, popping the bubble of forced intimacy she'd created with her previous question. "Your husband said he woke up to the sound of your screams and found you standing on the roof. He said you intentionally stepped off. You said you weren't screaming and that you fell off the roof. One of those versions is true. We need to figure out which one."

I knew which was true. The fresh soreness in my throat was evidence enough of our harrowing night. But I couldn't tell Dr. Alvarez why I'd been so horrified. Or could I?

"It won't make sense," I said.

"Try me."

I swallowed my nerves. "I saw something."

"You saw what?" she prompted quietly.

"A woman," I answered, daring not to reveal the victim's identity. "She was hanging from the tree. Dead. I heard her neck snap. I don't know what came over me. I wanted to be free, and the edge of the roof was right there…"

Dr. Alvarez studied me for a long time before speaking again. "Maxine, have you witnessed any trauma in your life? Have you lost anyone before?"

"A house fire killed my parents and my childhood best friend," I said, shaking. "I have scars on my legs and stomach from where I was burned."

"Have you ever had problems with post traumatic stress disorder before?"

I shook my head. "Not really. Not like this. I used to have panic attacks, but they don't happen as much anymore."

The doctor drew my paperwork toward her and skimmed through it. "You recently moved to Silver Creek, correct? That's why I haven't seen you before."

"Yes, we bought the ski lodge, and we're working on renovating it."

"Do you flip houses and such for a living?" she asked. "Have you done this before?"

"No, we decided on it out of necessity," I answered. "We didn't have a lot of money, and we were staying with friends who wanted to start a family. Buying the Lodge and fixing it up seemed like the only logical choice."

Dr. Alvarez set aside the paperwork. "Here's what I'm thinking. You've just gone through a lot of big changes in your life. You've taken on this huge challenge of renovating the Lodge. Both you and your husband are under a lot of stress. You're probably not getting a lot of sleep—"

I laughed humorlessly. "Yeah, we're sharing a double air mattress."

"Exactly," she continued. "You're in a new, unfamiliar place. One that doesn't feel anything like home. The weather is particularly bad this year. My best guess is the stress is piling up on you. You have underlying trauma you haven't addressed, and the combination is triggering these episodes."

Every part of me wanted to tell her she was wrong. PTSD didn't explain the feeling that captured me while I'd been walking around the house last night. It didn't account for the strange magnetic pull that led me upstairs and through the window, nor for the whispers in my head or the shadows without bodies.

"What am I supposed to do about it?" I asked.

"Talking to a professional is a good start," Dr. Alvarez

replied. "I can refer you to a friend of mine. He's a certi-fied psychiatrist—"

I shook my head vigorously. "No, I don't want to go to therapy. I can't talk about this. Not yet, anyway."

She sighed. "In that case, I can give you something to take the edge off."

"That's it? You want me to take a pill."

"I can also give you some exercises to practice on your own that will help with your anxiety," she said. "Breathing techniques to relax and focus on reality, rather than the pictures your brain shows you."

"Can I do that instead of the pills?"

Dr. Alvarez rubbed her palms against her thighs. "I can't force you to fill a prescription, but in instances like this, I highly advise you take some course of action. A suicide attempt—"

"I did not attempt suicide," I said hotly.

She was quiet for a moment while I recaptured my dignity. "Whatever you call it, it endangered your physical health. Normally, I would refer you to a mental health facility, but if you refuse treatment, no one can turn over that decision for you."

"I refuse treatment."

"Do you want to keep feeling like this?" she asked. "Do you want to stay empty and emotionless? Or feel terrified when nothing is wrong? Do you want your husband to live in a constant state of fear because you won't take steps to help yourself?"

When she mentioned Simon, I remembered the look on his face last night. He was scared out of his mind. The panicked yelling, the way he tried to force himself through the tiny window to reach me, how he'd run into the snowy yard without a shirt or shoes.

"Okay. I'll take the pills."

SIMON MANAGED to contain himself until we left the office and got into the car. When he started the ignition but didn't put it in drive, I knew it was coming.

"Well?" he demanded. "What did you tell her? What did she say?"

"She says I have PTSD," I replied simply. "That trauma and stress are piling up on me. She gave me this." I waved the prescription. "Are you happy?"

He snatched the prescription and read it. "Antidepressants?"

"Mm-hmm."

He set the prescription onto the center console, where he could keep an eye on it and reversed out of the parking space. "We're going to pick it up now."

At a red light near the center of town, his phone rang. He dug it out of his pocket and hit the speakerphone button.

"Hello?" he said.

"Hey, Simon. It's Keith. Where are you?"

"We're in town," Simon said. "I had to take Max to the doctor."

"Is she okay?"

Simon glanced over at me as if trying to decide the answer. "Yes, she'll be fine. What's up?"

"Uh, I guess you forgot," Keith said. "We made an appointment for Boyce to tour the Lodge today. So you could talk about investment opportunities with him?"

I glared at Simon. He hadn't told me about any of this.

"Shit, is he there now?" Simon asked, pointedly avoiding my gaze.

"Yeah, he's waiting outside. Should I let him in?"

"Not without a hard hat." Simon switched his turn signal and pulled into the opposite lane. "I'm on my way home now. Keep him busy for twenty minutes."

"Can do."

Simon hung up and looked over at me. "Don't be mad."

I let out a short, derisive laugh.

"We're running out of money," Simon said tersely, his knuckles turning white as he gripped the steering wheel tighter. "We've burned through three-quarters of our budget already, and we haven't bought any materials for the second floor yet."

"This is why I was hesitant to buy the Lodge in the first place," I reminded him. "It's a money pit. We'll go bankrupt and have nothing to show for it."

"Not if Boyce invests," Simon said. "He's loaded, Max. He casually offered twenty-five thousand dollars at the last Gentlemen's Club meeting. That was his *first* offer."

I gaped at him. "Twenty-five thousand?"

"Do you know what we could do with that money?" He glanced over his shoulder to check his blind spot and moved over another lane. "We could finish the Lodge in no time. He offered to help with marketing, too, so we'd pull a profit our first year in business."

"So, this is what you talk about at those meetings, huh?"

"It's mostly business," Simon said. "The guys in that club are all working to better Silver Creek. Now that we're a part of it, they want us to succeed, too. Why is that such a bad thing?"

I gazed through the window, pondering Simon's question. Wealthy men wanted to give us money so we didn't fail miserably in a doomed project. If it was such a great idea, why did it open a pit of doubt in my stomach?

WE WERE quiet for the rest of the drive. When we pulled into the Lodge's parking lot, the sun bounced off the shiny windows of Boyce's black Cadillac and into my eyes. The brightness made me sneeze.

"I have to get in there," Simon said, hurriedly unbuckling his seatbelt. "Are you okay on your own?"

I wondered if he was just desperate to get away from me. "I'll be fine."

Simon rushed inside, but I took my time getting out of the car. For once, it wasn't snowing, so I dawdled in the front yard. To make myself look busy, I pulled dead weeds from the flowerpots and tossed them into the dumpster. When my hands were dirty and numb from the cold, I gathered my courage and went inside.

Simon and Boyce were coming down the stairs as I walked in. They were deep in conversation about the state of the Lodge, so much so that Boyce barely noticed me. All I got was a polite nod and smile as they passed.

"The presidential suite has promise," Boyce was saying. "People would pay hundreds of dollars a night to stay there. That is, if you make it worthwhile. I think you should upgrade that bathroom. We'll get you a double-wide tub with jets and a dual-sink counter. It'll be the ultimate honeymoon suite, especially with that view off the private balcony. You'll have a waitlist a mile long."

Simon nodded, eating up Boyce's words as if they were gourmet chocolate truffles. "I like that idea. We thought about living in the presidential suite ourselves, but it seems stupid to waste that space."

"I suggest you build yourselves a cabin elsewhere on the property," Boyce said as they headed down the first-floor hallway. "It's important to separate work from home. You need your own space."

Simon grimaced. "I'm not sure we have the funds to build an entire cabin from the ground up."

"We'll talk finances in a few minutes," Boyce said, confidence oozing out of his pores. "For now, let's see we can do about improving these ground-floor suites."

Like a nosey ghost, I followed twenty steps behind Simon and Boyce as they explored rooms on the first floor. Simon would pitch his ideas—the ones we came up with together—and Boyce would immediately shoot them down to suggest something more expensive. Simon agreed to almost everything, never once checking with me to see if I liked the changes.

When they reached the last room on the first floor, the one half the size of its counterparts, Boyce took a startled step back. The locked safe was the prime focus of the room. It was hard to visualize any future guests staying there with a huge metal door smack in the middle of the back wall.

"My God," Boyce said. "What is that?"

"No idea," Simon answered. "We can't open it. Even the local locksmith gave it a shot."

I braced myself as Boyce approached the safe and laid a hand on smooth metal. He showed no sign of feeling the pulse of energy I did when I went near the safe. As a matter of fact, he looked more worried than anything else.

"This is inconvenient indeed," he muttered, eyebrows knitted together as he ran his hand over the safe's dial.

"We'll get rid of it," Simon proposed. "If we can work out finances, I'll get a construction crew in here to remove the safe and widen this room. I was going to work around it, but if we have the money—"

"No, no, no," Boyce said. "This is a delicate procedure. We can't go ripping this thing out all willy-nilly. It could bring the whole building down. No, you'll have to leave it."

"Leave it?" Simon's nose wrinkled. "Forever? I wanted to get rid of it eventually."

"I'm no architect," said Boyce, "but I believe this part of the building is supporting a great deal of the presidential suite above it. You can't remove the safe without risking collapse. Then you'd be in a whole mess of trouble, one I don't think I could afford to get you out of."

Simon nodded. "Got it. We'll leave it then. What do we do with this room, though?"

"Make it a storage closet," Boyce suggested. "You won't

be able to keep guests here. It's much too small, and there isn't even a bathroom."

"Should I wall up the safe?"

Boyce regarded the metal door, curiosity growing in his beady eyes. "No, leave an access point. It may come in handy later."

AN HOUR LATER, Boyce was satisfied with his tour of the Lodge and the grounds. While he put on his coat and hat, he fed Simon more hope. "I see a lot of potential," Boyce said, buttoning his wool pea coat. "If you're willing to take my suggestions into account, I'd love to invest."

Simon made a triumphant fist but refrained from raising it in the air like a first-place athlete. "Thank you so much, Boyce. You have no idea what this means to us."

"I'm happy to help out our newest locals," Boyce said. "I want this place to succeed as much as you do. I'll talk to my business partners and see what we can afford to put up. Keep in mind, I'll want updates as you work. I like to know how my money is being spent."

"We'll update you every day if you want," Simon promised.

Boyce chuckled as he tugged on his gloves. "You kids are so eager to please. That's refreshing. We need more people like you in Silver Creek." He tipped his hat to me. "Maxine, it was lovely to see you again. I hope you're feeling better."

"Thank you, Boyce."

He shook Simon's hand. "We'll talk soon. I'll take you

to lunch, and we'll hammer out the finer details." He turned to leave but stopped himself. "Oh, and Simon? The Club is heading out to the slopes tomorrow. Can I interest you in joining us?"

Simon shifted his stance. "I don't really ski."

"Neither does Keith," Boyce said with thinly hidden amusement. "Have you ever done it before?"

"Two or three times when I was a kid."

"That's all the experience you need," Boyce replied. "Don't worry about equipment. We'll get you set up. I know a guy who can help you out. Plan on being there, okay? I don't like excuses."

"You got it."

I held the door for Boyce as he walked out. He looked down at me and smiled. "Thank you, Maxine. Enjoy the rest of your day."

Simon lightly rested his arm across my shoulders as we watched Boyce remote start his fancy car and get into the front seat. He waved through the windshield.

"I don't know if this is a good idea," I muttered, teeth clenched in a smile that didn't feel genuine as we waved back. "You heard him. If he invests, he wants a say in what we do with the Lodge."

"So what?" Simon said. "He has good ideas. He can make this place into the number one tourist destination in Silver Creek. That means more money for us."

"Money that he'll have a claim to. He's basically offering to be our landlord."

Simon rolled his eyes. "You were worried about

139

money, so I'm fixing the problem. Now you don't like the way I'm fixing it?"

"No, I—"

"We still own the Lodge, Max," he said. "Boyce can't take that away from us. The profits are ours. So what if we have to host the Gentlemen's Club or other community events every once in a while? What's the harm in that?"

"I didn't say I didn't want to host events."

He rubbed his eyes, and his voice grew softer. "I don't want to argue about this anymore. After my lunch with Boyce, we can discuss his official offer. But just so you know, I plan on telling him yes."

"Aren't you forgetting something?" I demanded. "We bought this lodge with *my* savings. My publications are what got us here."

"I contributed!"

"Not much," I reminded him.

He glared at me. "So we're doing this? Arguing about every nickel and dime?"

"If that's what it takes to have a say here." I couldn't read his expression before he turned away from me.

"You always have a say, Max," he murmured, so softly. "That's what worries me."

10

Since we weren't talking, I didn't bother to remind Simon about picking up my antide-pressants. I'd go to the pharmacy alone, while he was out skiing with Boyce and the rest of the Gentlemen's Club.

As if to clarify we were in a fight, Simon slept on the couch in the lobby. I woke to a cold bed and an empty heart. I alternated between getting mad at Simon for the decisions he made without me and missing him terribly. The back and forth was starting to get to me.

When I persuaded myself to come out from under the covers, I found Simon huddled beneath a small throw blanket that didn't cover his entire body. His bare feet poked off the end of the couch. I fetched another blanket from our room and laid it on top of him, but he woke up abruptly.

"What time is it?" he mumbled, bleary with exhaustion. "I'm supposed to meet Boyce at the slopes at nine."

"It's eight-thirty," I told him.

He threw off the new blanket, nearly whipping me with it as he rolled off the couch. "Shit, I'm going to be late. Can you get my snow pants? They're on the radiator in the entranceway."

"They're not there," I called to him a moment later.

"Where did you put them?" he hollered back.

"I didn't touch them!"

He stumbled into the room, trying to lace his snow boots and zip his coat at the same time. He wore jeans instead. "If you didn't touch them, where did they go? I left them to dry there."

"It's not my job to watch over your clothes."

"Some would beg to differ, considering your role as a wife," he snapped back. Right after the words came out of his mouth, the rage dropped out of his expression. "I am so sorry. That was an awful thing to say. You know you mean more to me than—"

"Here," I said shortly, shoving his winter hat at him. "Stay warm."

He leaned in, aiming to kiss me on the cheek, but I turned my head. Chagrined, he stepped past me. On the porch, as I was about to close the door behind him, he said, "I love you."

The door snapped shut before I could reply. I stood in the hallway until I heard the car start up and rumble out of the front yard. Then I let out a long sigh.

"Good morning, Max."

Lily, as was her habit, had appeared at the bottom of the staircase as if she'd just woken up and was on her way down for breakfast when she happened to eavesdrop on mine and Simon's fights. I hadn't seen her in person since my hallucination last night.

"Lily!"

I ran up the steps and threw my arms around her, hugging her tightly to me. I inhaled deeply, taking in her familiar metallic and musky scents. At once, the empty part of my head—where my emotions normally sat— began to fill.

"You're okay," I said, squeezing her shoulders as if to make sure she was really there.

"That remains to be seen," she teased. "Are *you* okay?"

She led me to the couch, and we sat in the warm spot Simon had recently vacated. I held the blanket up to my nose. Like Lily, he had a very specific smell—cinnamon and fresh snow—but I couldn't catch it like I usually did. The blanket smelled of nothing but dust.

"I miss him," I muttered, kneading the blanket.

"Simon? He hasn't even been gone for five minutes."

"No, I miss the old him, the old us," I clarified. "We never used to fight like this. I don't know what's happening between us, and it scares me."

Lily wore a look of guilt. "It's not you."

"It's him?" I guessed. "That's selfish, don't you think? Relationships should be about both people."

"No, it's not you *or* him," Lily said, though that didn't make things any clearer. "It's the situation. It's this place."

"The Lodge?"

"Yes."

"Well, yeah. Of course it is." I wiped a stray tear before it could roll down my cheek. "It's a lot of stress. Financially, physically, and emotionally. This whole thing with Boyce—"

"That's not what I meant, either—wait, what thing with Boyce?" she asked.

"He wants to invest in the Lodge," I told her. "We estimated how much this place was going to cost us to renovate before we bought it. Naturally, we lowballed ourselves. Boyce is willing to give up thousands of dollars, but I don't think it's a good idea to let someone as powerful as Boyce have such a huge impact on our main source of income."

"I agree with you one hundred percent," she said firmly.

My chin wobbled. "You do?"

"Yes," she said. "I know everyone in town loves Boyce, and he does a lot of Silver Creek, but it's important to have boundaries. If you don't trust him not to be overbearing, go with your gut. Besides, I know things about Boyce that would send shivers down your spine."

Just the phrase itself made me wriggle in discomfort. "Like what?"

Lily's eyes darkened if that was even possible. She seemed far away when she answered. "Let's just say he's not who the town thinks he is."

"I'd already guessed that," I said. "No one with that much money and so willing to part with it is innocent. He has to have an agenda with the Lodge, right?"

She nodded emphatically. "He definitely has an agenda, and it's not helping you and Simon become successful business owners."

"That settles it then," I said. "I'm telling Simon I don't want him to invest."

"Beware an argument," Lily warned. "Simon isn't going to take it well, especially if Boyce is getting on his good side. Free money is hard to turn down."

"But it's not really free," I pointed out.

"Simon doesn't understand that." She tugged a piece of paper out of my pajama pants. "What's this? You're taking antidepressants?"

The emptiness returned, this time accompanied by the weight of dread in my lower abdomen. "Not yet. The doctor prescribed them yesterday, but I haven't had the chance to pick them up."

Lily gripped the prescription so tightly it wrinkled in her grasp. "What do you need them for?"

In my head, I saw her body drop from the tree again. Swinging from the branch with dead eyes and a broken neck. I drove the image from my head.

"Ever since we got to the Lodge, I've seen strange things," I admitted. "People in the hallways that aren't really there. Shadows on the walls that don't match the things in a room. I feel whispers on the back of my neck I can't understand."

The pink blush around Lily's cheeks went white. "Have these things happened to you before? Outside the Lodge?"

"Not like this or to such an extent," I said. "I'd have flashbacks of the fire, but I've never seen..."

I trailed off, staring absentmindedly into the distance. Part of me didn't want to tell Lily what horrific images had been presented to me last night. It would only scare her.

"You've never seen what?" came the inevitable question.

I looked her in the eyes to remind myself she was okay. She wasn't hanging from the tree outside. She was sitting right here in front of me, alive and well.

"I was sleepwalking again last night," I began. "Somehow, I ended up on the roof outside one of the rooms on the second floor. There's a tree near the Lodge. It's dead and decaying. Something drew me toward it like a magnetic force. When I was close enough, a body dropped from the branches." My lower lip trembled. "Your body."

If this surprised or shocked Lily, she didn't show it. "I'm sorry you had to go through that. It must have been terrible." She paused to reread the medication script. "But I don't think you should take these pills."

"I don't want to," I said, "but this stuff is negatively impacting my relationship with Simon. If I don't get it under control—"

"It's not you," Lily said, yet again.

"No offense, but I'm pretty sure it is." I took the prescription back from her. "No one else is having hallucinations of dead people."

Lily gnawed on her lower lip, much like the quiet girl at a slumber party who knows something she shouldn't. "I don't think you should take it."

I sighed and tucked the paper into my pocket. "I'm still deciding. I think I'll go for a walk. I need to clear my head."

. . .

THE SNOW SHOWED no signs of letting up, but I didn't let that stop me from getting outside. If Simon could go off with his new friends, I could certainly leave the house for a quick stroll through the woods. I bundled up in several layers, including a scarf to wrap around my nose and mouth and two pairs of socks. I chose my waterproof boots with the sherpa lining to keep my feet as warm as possible. It had been over a month since my last jog, and I missed the clarity that exercise brought.

Behind the Lodge, a myriad of hiking trails led to different parts of Silver Creek. One led to the slopes if you wanted to walk that far. Another led into the center of town, again if you up for a forty-five-minute walk. In the summer, it would be a lovely hike, but with the snow up to my shins, I decided to stick to shorter paths.

The air was different in the woods. Cleaner. The trees acted as natural purifiers, blocking out exhaust smells from the road and food smells from the restaurants in town. It was quiet, too. Most of the animals were gone, though I did spot a white fox before it bounded off to its den. The only sound was the crunch of my boots through the snow. I reveled in it, feeling peaceful for the first time in days.

As the effort of hiking set in, my legs burning from lifting them so high with each step, the barrage of thoughts leaked from my head. I thought of nothing but the next tree or bend in the path. It was like being under-water. The whole world was put on mute, and for the time I was in the forest, I was separate from everything else. Lily was right. I didn't need antidepressants. I needed to get away from the Lodge and all the problems it represented for me, including my relationship with Simon.

Before long, I heard voices and glanced up to see the nearby ski spot not far off through the trees. It was my first glimpse of it, and it flooded me with jealousy. It was a collection of cozy, cabin-like buildings: one with a restaurant and café for skiers and snowboarders to warm up, one to rent, buy, or maintenance gear, and one with locker rooms and saunas to warm and clean up after your day in the snow. It was everything I wanted the Silver Creek Lodge to be, but we were so far from this level of comfort, it seemed impossible to ever get there.

Somewhere on that slope, Simon skied with Keith, Boyce, and the other members of the Gentlemen's Club. I imagined him scooting along the snow, far behind the others. Bless his heart, Simon had never been an expert skier. He was too timid, unable to trust himself enough to gain the speed that made it easier to balance. On one of our first dates, I'd taken him to the bunny slopes near my old apartment, and it was a solid twenty minutes before he managed to stand up.

A smile touched my lips as the memories came and went. It should have been Simon and me out there on the slopes for the first time. I promised myself to redo our first date once the Lodge was completed. It would be a celebration of our new adventure *and* to remind us why we ended up married in the first place.

Behind the cabin rentals, a quarrel broke out. A group

of five kids surrounded someone smaller than them. They shoved the kid in the middle like a hot potato, passing her from one person to the next. I squinted and recognized the victim. Bubbles—the fan I'd met in the cafe. I headed over.

"Don't spread lies about my mom!" one of the bigger kids was shouting as he pushed Bubbles across the circle.

Bubbles bounced easily off someone else. "Then tell your mom to stop being such a slut."

I raised an eyebrow. That was not the kind of language I'd ever expected to come out of Bubbles's mouth. The first time I'd met her, she had been so polite. Pushy, but polite.

"You're dead now," said the other kid. He pulled back his fist.

"Hey—" I shouted, surging forward.

It was too late. Bubbles turned to the side, and the punch landed square on her right ear. I yanked the larger kid away as she tumbled to the ground.

"That's enough," I growled, stepping into the center of the circle. "Get out of here before I call your parents."

"She started it!" the other kid claimed.

"I'm ending it," I replied dangerously. "Go."

The kids exchanged dubious glances before taking my advice. Once they were out of sight, I helped Bubbles up and wiped off the snow from her coat and pants. Like the other kids, she was decked out in designer products. Her boots alone probably cost more than my entire outfit.

"Let me see," I ordered, taking her chin to turn her head so I could look at her ear. It was bright red and bleeding, but upon closer inspection, an older scab had opened up. The bruise there was at least a day old, fully formed, and purple. "This isn't from today's fight. What happened to you?"

Bubbles pulled her chin out of my grasp. "It's nothing. What are you doing here?"

"It's not nothing." I held her by the sleeves of her coat. "Why were you provoking those kids? Do you pick fights on purpose?"

"No," she answered stubbornly.

Thankfully, I had a travel pack of tissues in my pocket. I took one out, folded it over, and used it to blot the blood on her ear. "You can't say stuff like that. It won't make you any friends."

"I don't want friends," she said, her lip quivering.

"From what you said at the cafe, I would have thought differently," I told her. I got her a fresh tissue. "Keep that on your ear and put pressure on it. It should stop bleeding soon."

She did as I said, looking me up and down. "Did you walk here from the Lodge?"

I looked behind me, where my footsteps led out of the woods. "I guess I did. I didn't realize how far I'd gone."

"I saw your guy on the slopes," she said.

I brightened. "Simon? Did he look okay?"

"He's like a newborn doe. Even Keith was doing better than him."

I couldn't help but laugh. "Yeah, he's not the best skier."

Bubbles wrinkled her nose and looked up at the slope.

"What's he doing with Boyce Driscoll? You guys planning something for the town?"

"He might give us some money to finish the Lodge," I said. This time around, it didn't sound like such a horrible idea coming out of my mouth. Apparently, being sick and cooped up inside affect more than my mental health. It affected my judgment, too. "How do you know Boyce?"

"He's the unofficial mayor of Silver Creek," she said, echoing Boyce's own words when he first introduced himself to us. "Everyone knows him."

"Right, I keep forgetting. Let me see that ear again."

This time, Bubbles turned voluntarily for me to inspect the injury.

"It stopped bleeding," I reported, collecting the soiled tissues from her. "Go to first aid, and get a bandage for it. You don't want it getting infected. And stop picking fights. No one ever benefits from having a chip on their shoulder."

"I don't have a chip on my shoulder," she replied. "I'm just trying to get by."

"Aren't we all, kid."

WHEN BUBBLES DISAPPEARED, I considered sticking around the ski resort to see if I could catch up with Simon when he finally made it to the bottom of the slope. The hot chocolate was enticing, and all I wanted was to greet Simon with a steaming mug of the stuff when he stumbled in from the cold.

Because this was a business thing with the Gentlemen's Club, I got a hot chocolate to-go and forced myself to march home the way I had come. I didn't look back at the slope. I didn't want to see Simon and Boyce chatting and laughing with the ease that hadn't come to *my* relationship with Simon in weeks.

The return hike to the Lodge felt much longer than the first one. Despite my warm boots and fuzzy socks, my feet were frozen. The petroleum jelly I'd smeared across my face before I'd left the Lodge had all rubbed off. My face was dry, cold, and burning in the wind. At last, I spotted our new home through the trees. Almost at once, dread dropped a weight on my shoulders. I didn't want to go inside.

Steam rose from the surface of the hot springs. Delaying my inevitable return to the Lodge, I knelt near the biggest pool, plucked off my glove, and tentatively dipped my cold fingers in the water. I moaned with relief. Though the drastic temperature change almost burned my skin, I couldn't help but want to submerge my entire body in the pool.

I glanced around. The woods were thick here, and with Simon and Keith gone, there was no one around the Lodge to spy on me. Before sense changed my mind, I stripped off my coat, boots, and many layers until I was bare. Then I slid into the hot pool.

A joyous yelp made its way out of my throat and echoed through the woods. I laughed without holding back, letting myself feel the full shock of the hot water against my skin. The pool was a clear, natural green. I skimmed my hands over the surface, enjoying the feel of ripples beneath my fingers. With my bare feet, I explored the shape of the rocks below and found one shaped perfectly to sit in. I cleared a patch of snow from the ground behind me, reclined, and let my head rest back.

It was heaven. I wondered why I hadn't come out here before. I couldn't remember the last time I'd felt so relaxed. The minutes ticked by without notice, and I remained in the pool until the skin on my fingers and toes shriveled.

An hour or so later, a cloud passed over the sun, and the breeze picked up. Not even the warm water could stop the goose bumps rising on my neck and scalp. Reluctantly, I opened my eyes and considered my options for getting out of the pool. I hadn't thought to go inside and get a towel before jumping in. All I had to dry off with were my clothes. It was going to be freezing run to the Lodge's back door. I counted to three, braced myself, and lifted myself from the deep pool.

Something grasped my ankle and pulled. I glanced over my shoulder and screamed. Deathly white fingers had emerged from the pool, wrapped tightly around my foot. When I pulled harder to get away, another hand appeared and clawed at my calf. Desperate, I grabbed for anything on shore that might serve as a handhold, but it was all snow. The fingers pulled me deeper. I struggled to keep hold of the bank, but with a final yank, my head dipped underwater.

The hot springs had gone cold. Every bone in my body was frozen from the inside out. Before, I'd been able to stand on the rocks below. Now I couldn't see the bottom of the pool. I kicked for the surface, desperate to break through for a fresh breath, but it was all darkness.

Something rose before me. A white face in the darkness. Dead. Always dead. A scream ripped from my throat and rose in innocent bubbles. The hands reached out to encircle me. I backpedaled and hit the wall of the pool behind me. A sharp rock dug into my back, and the pain seemed to awake reality. A beam of sunlight struck the water, and without another look at the corpse, I struck hard for the surface.

I exploded from the water, yelling for my life. Without worry of the cold, I scrambled out of the pool and onto the snowy bank. Naked and shivering, I huddled in a ball, unable to move.

"Max?"

Lily rushed out of the Lodge and ran over to me, but I pushed myself away from her.

"Why?" I asked her, my voice hoarse and shrill. I pointed to the pool, which showed no signs of harboring bodies and endless darkness beneath its steaming, peaceful surface. "Tell me *why* I keep seeing you like that!"

Lily's lower lip wobbled. Here came the secret she'd been holding on to all this time.

"Because I'm dead," she said.

11

*L*ily picked up my coat from the ground and wrapped it around me. She made me step into my boots and led me to the house, guiding me with a firm arm. All the while, I gaped, unable to find appropriate words to join together in a sentence.

She ran me a hot bath in the single bathroom we'd finished renovating and waited politely outside the door while I warmed up from my adventures outside. When I finished, she brought me a set of clothes—a cozy sweater and sweatpants—to get dressed. After I pulled on a fresh pair of fuzzy socks, I ventured out of the bathroom and found her tending to a pot of soup on the new kitchen stove.

"Did you say...?" I began, but the absurdity of the thought in my head stopped me from completing the question.

"I said I was dead," she replied, stirring the canned soup to keep it from sticking to the bottom of the pan.

"But you're here," I said stupidly. "You're talking to me, walking around the Lodge, warming up soup. You can't be dead."

Lily's familiar smirk appeared. "You're taking it better than I thought you would, to be honest."

I hoisted myself onto the counter. "That's because I don't believe you." I reached out and touched her shoulder. She was solid. "How can I touch a dead person?"

"It's hard to explain," she said. "Even I don't know all the details."

"You never eat," I remembered suddenly. "All the times I've brought you food or offered to buy you lunch. You always refused."

"Dead people don't eat," she replied matter-of-factly.

"You don't leave the Lodge, either." I stared at her, open-mouthed. "I've never seen you off the property."

The soup bubbled and popped, plopping over the edge of the pot and spraying the counter with a mess. Lily wiped it away with a dishtowel. "This lodge is special. Or cursed, depending on the way you look at things. I can't leave here. Believe me, I've tried, but I don't always have control over what happens to me here. Every time I've gotten close to stepping over the border of the property, everything goes black and I—" She cut herself off, and her grip on the wooden spoon tightened. "Let's just say I have to relive a moment that I don't like to think about."

"How did you die?" I asked. "Is that insensitive of me? I'm sorry, I just don't understand how this could be happening."

"I got into—"

My phone rang, interrupting her reply. I glanced at the screen and ignored the call. "Don't worry. It's only Simon. He's probably calling to tell me Boyce's new offer. Keep going."

Lily took a single mug—we didn't have any soup bowls yet—from the pantry and spooned soup into it. "I got into a car accident. I don't remember much about it. It was snowing that night. I was in a hurry. I think I was in trouble for some reason. Anyway, I saw the road for the Lodge and turned that way. The pavement was covered in ice. I hit a patch of it, lost control of the car, and rammed into a tree."

"That's how we found you." I steadied myself with a deep breath as I recalled our first night at the Lodge. The smoke billowing out of the woods as we ran down to find Lily's car mangled on the road. "That gash on your head. I knew it wasn't superficial. You died from it, didn't you?"

She shrugged, indifferent to the details of her death. "I guess so."

"The paramedics thought we were lying!" I gasped as everything began to make sense. "Your car disappeared before they could find it. *You* disappeared before they could take you to the hospital because you were already dead!"

"I'm sorry," Lily said as she handed me the mug of soup and a piece of cheesy toast. "I put you through so much strife that first night, and my presence is only stressing you out more. If I could leave, I would, but I don't have that option."

I blew across the hot soup to cool it off. "Why not? Why are you still here?"

She leaned against the counter and shrugged. "All I know is anyone who dies on this property doesn't leave. I'm not the only one here."

"But why don't the others come out like you do?"

"I'm one of the newest," Lily explained. "I died more recently than most of the others, so my spirit—or whatever you call this version of me—is stronger. You've seen some of the others too. You just didn't realize it."

"The man in the halls," I recalled. "I've seen him walking around. Who is he?"

Lily shook her head. "I can't tell you because it's not my secret. They have to trust you enough to reveal themselves. They've started to, but you're stuck."

"I'm...what?"

She pointed through the window at the hot springs, and I shuddered at the sight of them. "The face you saw in the pool. It was mine, right?"

"Yes."

"But I wasn't the person who died in the pool," she explained. "It was someone else, but you saw me because I'm the only spirit you're familiar with in this house. If you look for the others—really *look* for them—you'll start to see what really happened."

Absentmindedly, I ran my finger around the lip of the soup mug, but I was too distracted to drink from it. "The night I went out to the roof. The woman hanging from the tree. That wasn't you, either?"

"Nope. Someone else. Like I said, if you focus on

discovering them, they'll let you see them." She ran her hand through her hair, sending a waft of musk and iron toward me. I finally realized what I smelled: blood and dirt. "You're different than most people who have passed through here. Most don't notice us at all."

"Simon and Keith can see you, too," I pointed out.

"Because I'm fresh," she reminded me. "As the years pass, they'll forget about me. They'll think I finally moved on. I have a feeling you'll always be able to see me, though."

"Why me?" I asked. "Why am I different?"

"There's an energy on this property," Lily said. "It's strongest in the Lodge, but it extends outside, too. It's what keeps us all here and stops us from crossing over to whatever comes next. Some people are more in tune with that energy than others. They sense it better."

"Why is that?"

"I have a guess," she answered. "You're a good piece of evidence for it. I think people who have had a close brush with death are more likely to sense the Lodge's energy. You almost died in a fire when you were a kid."

At last, I tasted the soup, needing the comfort of something familiar as we talked about difficult things. It was much too salty, but it grounded me in reality. "This energy. Is that what also makes you... solid?"

She nodded. "I can touch and hold things, but people are different. If you notice, I've never tried to shake Keith's hand. I'd probably sink through him."

"You don't touch Simon, either."

"Simon doesn't like me," she said.

"It's not that—"

"Oh, it is," she assured me. "He might not know *why* he doesn't like me, but he's definitely sensed that I'm different. Deep down, he knows I'm not like you and him."

"You mean alive?"

To my surprise, she barked out a laugh. "Exactly."

I chuckled with her. "You know what? I'm actually relieved."

She lifted an eyebrow. "Relieved? That's shocking. I thought you'd be running for your life by now."

I tried the soup again. As I adjusted to the sodium levels, it wasn't so bad, and it helped to get some food into my empty stomach. "It makes sense, aside from the incredulity of the situation. I knew I wasn't crazy or hallucinating. I knew something was going on that I couldn't explain."

"So, are you going to fill that new prescription?" she asked.

"I don't see why I should," I answered. "They won't stop me from seeing the others, will they?"

"I'm afraid not."

I set aside the soup and laced my fingers together. "Will it always be so horrifying? Do they have to keep showing me how they died?"

Lily rinsed my dish in the sink. For a dead person, she was very helpful. "It's what they know best, the memory freshest in their heads. Hell, it's what defines who we are in this space."

"I can't live like that," I admitted. "I can't constantly be confronted with those types of images. It'll drive me crazy. I won't be able to stay here."

"The more you learn about the people who died here, the more you'll see of them," Lily explained. "It's a trade-off. They'll stop showing you how they died, but they'll want more of your attention. They'll feel more comfortable to show themselves to you."

"Do they look healthy when they do?"

"As healthy as they were while they were alive."

"Then I think I'd prefer that," I said.

She filled the rinsed mug with fresh coffee and handed it back to me. "They will, too. It's exhausting reliving your death over and over again."

My phone rang again, identifying Simon as the caller. I switched it to silent and turned it over. If Simon wanted to talk, he'd have to come home and do it in person.

"What happens next?" I asked Lily. "You're all trapped here for a reason, right? Am I supposed to help you move on?"

Lily smiled sadly. "I'm not sure you can. No one's ever figured out why the Lodge is like this."

"Then what am I supposed to do?"

"Do what you can," Lily said. "We need someone to protect us."

My eyebrows came together. "Protect you from what?"

Lily's gaze drifted off as if she could see something in the distance that I couldn't. "Everything," she said softly.

For an hour or more, Lily and I talked. I asked the same

questions over and over again, hoping for clearer answers with each repetition, but Lily could only give me so much. The history of the Lodge and its so-called "energy" was a mystery.

"I'm going to find out what's happening here," I said confidently.

We were cuddled on the couch, sharing a blanket. I marveled at the warmth that came off of Lily's skin as if she were no different than me. The fact that she was dead no longer disturbed me.

"I want to know why the Lodge is like this."

"Good luck," Lily said. "You'll be the first one to do it."

An engine growled, and Keith's truck pulled into the front yard.

"They're back." I lifted my head from Lily's shoulder and pulled the curtain away to look outside. "Where's Simon?"

My heart rushed as Keith got out of the truck alone and rushed toward the house. I leaped up from the couch and answered the front door before he could knock.

"Where's Simon?" I asked again, this time demanding an answer.

"That's what I've come to tell you," Keith said, breathless. "He had an accident on the ski slope. The doctors are saying he'll probably be fine, but—"

"Doctors?"

"Yes, ma'am. It was a pretty bad fall. We took him straight to the hospital." Keith nervously kneaded his hat between his fingers. "I've been trying to call you from his phone to let you know what was happening, but you weren't answering. He's in surgery—"

I grabbed my coat from the hook by the door and pushed past Keith. "Take me there. Now."

SINCE SILVER CREEK didn't have a hospital, Simon had been airlifted to one in Breckenridge. By the time we arrived, he was out of surgery but not awake. Despite constant harassment of the nurses, no one would tell me what had happened to him, and we weren't allowed to see him until a doctor cleared him.

"Tell me what you saw again," I ordered Keith while I paced the waiting room. "From the beginning."

Keith held his stomach. If I had to guess, it had been hours since he'd last eaten. "Boyce convinced Simon to try one of the intermediate slopes so we could all do the trails together. Simon was falling behind. He's not very good on skis, so Abel doubled back to help him out. I was up ahead with Boyce, so I didn't see him crash. By the time I looked back, Simon was half-embedded in a tree. I knew it was bad, so I called 9-1-1 right away."

I sniffled, holding back tears. I should have answered my damn phone, but I'd been too busy with my own crap to worry about Simon. I'd taken him for granted.

I spotted a vending machine across the hall, walked over, and bought a candy bar and a bottle of water. I gave both to Keith, who ripped open the candy bar and tore into it with frightening speed.

"We've been fighting," I admitted in a thick voice. "Simon and me."

"I, uh, sensed something like that," Keith answered through a mouthful of chocolate and nougat. "I figured it wasn't my business."

I stubbornly wiped a tear before it could run down my cheek. "I wanted to spite him. That's why I didn't answer my phone. I wanted him to know what it was like to feel ignored."

Keith tentatively patted my hand. "If it makes you feel better, I don't think Simon was ignoring you on purpose. He talks about you non-stop while we're working. He's always trying to do what's best for you."

"You guys talk about me?"

"Simon talks," Keith corrected. "I listen and try to give him advice, but I'm not much of a relationship expert. I live with my mom, you know?"

That got a small chuckle out of me. "You're a good kid, Keith."

"You seem cool, too," he replied. "And Simon really cares about you. He's worried you're pulling away from him for a reason he doesn't know about. You should talk to him. If I've learned anything from TV and movies, it's that communication is the secret to a long, healthy relationship."

"I'll remember that. Thanks."

A doctor with a neatly-trimmed beard emerged from the double doors. "Mrs. York?" he asked me.

I stood up quickly. "It's Finch. Maxine Finch. I haven't changed my surname. Is Simon okay?"

"I'm Dr. Fitzgerald," he said, shaking my hand. "Simon was in rough shape, but he's stable. We got him into surgery as soon as he arrived at the hospital to repair torn ligaments in his leg and stabilize his knee. He has a concussion, but it should resolve itself with time. We're going to keep an eye on it while he's here, but he should be able to go home in a couple of days."

"He's going to be okay?" I clarified. "He'll be able to work?"

"With physical therapy, he should regain full use of his knee," Dr. Fitzgerald assured me.

"Can I see him?" I asked.

"Of course. He's asking for you. Follow me."

Keith respectfully remained in the waiting room as Fitzgerald led me past the nurses' desk and into the hospital hallways. I kept my eyes on the spot between Fitzgerald's shoulder blades. I hated hospitals more than I hated doctors' offices. The things that happened between these walls were just as horrifying as the things I'd seen at the Lodge lately. I didn't need more images of death stamped in my head. When Fitzgerald beckoned me into a room, I wasn't sure I wanted to see what was inside.

Simon lay in bed, his injured leg supported by a foam pillow. His head was bandaged, and the side of his face played host to several scratches and bruises. Worry clamped around my heart and squeezed tight, but when Simon saw me, he managed a weak smile.

"There she is," he muttered, reaching toward me. "Come here, baby."

"I'll give you a moment," Fitzgerald said and backed out of the room.

Slowly, I stepped toward Simon. Our fingers touched. Everything hit me at once. I could have lost him today. When I found it harder to get closer to him, he took me around the waist and pulled me onto the bed. I buried my face in his shoulder and cried.

"I'm okay," he whispered lovingly. "It's just a knee injury. They said I'll make a full recovery."

"What happened?" I said, lifting my eyes to look into his. I cupped his cheek. "Keith said you ran into a tree."

"It was a disaster from the start," he answered. "I shouldn't have agreed to go skiing with them, not when I'm so horrible at it. But Boyce bought me brand-new gear and insisted—"

"He bought gear for you? I thought you were going to rent it."

"His friend works at the shop there," Simon said, groaning as he readjusted his position on the pillows. "Boyce insisted."

"So, we're in more debt to him."

Simon shot me a look. "Please don't start."

"Fine. Please tell me what happened."

"We started on the easy hill," Simon began. "I mostly kept up with them, but Boyce and his friends were bored. They wanted to try a more advanced route. Keith and I were going to stay behind, but Boyce convinced us we could do it, so we took the chair lift farther up the mountain." He winced, either from the memory or his injuries. "I didn't feel comfortable with the new route. The sign said it was for 'advanced-intermediate skiers,' whatever that's supposed to mean. But I was afraid Boyce might go back on his word to invest in the Lodge if I didn't ski down with them."

"Oh, honey." I smoothed his hair away from his bandaged forehead. "You didn't have to do that. We can make it without Boyce."

"I'm scared we can't," he admitted. "That's why I followed them down the hill. Keith was doing okay. He managed to keep pace with Boyce. I didn't rush anything. I went slowly."

"And then?"

"I guess I wasn't going fast enough to impress the rest of the Club," he said tersely. "Abel, one of the other guys in the Club, waited for me to catch up. He started giving me pointers on how to go faster without falling over. It worked. We started catching up with the rest of the club. Then I guess we got our signals crossed because Abel cut in front of me. I veered off to avoid colliding with him, lost control of the skis, and slammed into a tree."

"Abel cut you off?"

"Yeah, we were cutting curves. That's what you do on steep hills like that."

"But Abel should have left enough space not to put you in danger," I said. "Every good skier knows to give others around them enough room to maneuver."

"What, you think he did it on purpose?"

I shrugged. "It sounds like this whole thing was a set-up. You told Boyce you weren't a good skier, but he made you go on the advanced slope anyway. Then this Abel guy convinces you to move faster when you weren't ready for it? I'm starting to think they were in on it together, probably because Boyce wants the Lodge, and if you aren't around—"

Simon groaned, but it wasn't out of pain. "Give it a rest, Max! Do you really think they were plotting to kill me today so Boyce could buy the Lodge? First of all, that's ridiculous. Secondly, they'd have to murder you, too, because we own it together. And third, if Boyce wanted the Lodge so badly, he would have bought it off the bank to begin with."

"You heard the bank guy," I insisted. "He said other people had offers on the Lodge, but he liked us best. What if Boyce did try to buy it, but we got it instead?"

"Stop," Simon said. "I don't want to hear this anymore."

"I don't like them," I told him. "Boyce or any of his friends. I don't trust them."

"Yeah, well, I don't trust Lily."

I stared at him. "What are you talking about?"

His hard eyes bore into mine. "Keith called you right after he called 9-1-1. I heard him dial. Why didn't you answer? Why did it take you so long to get here?"

"This hospital is sixty miles away from Silver Creek.

"It's ten o'clock at night," he shot back. "I crashed around four in the afternoon. You're telling me it took you six hours to drive sixty miles?"

Furious that he had backed me into a corner, I replied, "Fine, I was with Lily. Does that make you happy?"

"No," he spat. "Because it means you prioritized some girl you hardly know over your husband."

"That wasn't it—"

"She's the reason you're sick," he went on, hardly listening to me. "The weakness you're feeling, the hallucinations. They're because of her!"

With as much condescension as possible, I said, "Hallucinations aren't contagious, Simon."

He slammed his fist on the blanket, and I leaped up from the bed. "Damn it, Max! You know what I mean."

I trembled from head to toe, but I couldn't figure out if I was mad or scared. "Actually, I don't."

"It's her fault," he said weakly. With so much emotion running between us, he was running out of steam. "It all started that night you accidentally ended up in her bed. I don't know what she's doing to you, but it's not good, Max. You shouldn't trust her. You can't…"

His eyelids floated shut, and he pressed a button near the edge of the bed. From the fluid bag above his head, a clear liquid made its way through the tubing and into the needle taped to the inside of Simon's arm. Within a minute, he was asleep.

*a*s Keith drove me back to the Lodge, I was filled with weird relief. Simon would be spending the night and the next day at the hospital to make sure his concussion didn't worsen, so I'd be all alone at home. I fiddled with a piece of thread unraveling from the truck's passenger seat. Keith noticed my nervousness.

"Simon will pull through," he said, misinterpreting my anxious movements. "He'll be back on his feet in no time."

"I know. He's strong. He's come back from worse things than this."

Keith shot me a sidelong glance. "Like what?"

"If he hasn't told you himself, it's best if I don't fill you in," I explained. "What happened to Simon was incredibly personal."

"No wonder you two make such a good couple," Keith said casually. "From what I've heard, you've both been through hell. Now you have each other to rely on."

I wasn't sure that was the case anymore, but I didn't

want to give that impression to Keith. "Simon's always had my back," I said, staring wistfully through the window. "And I've always had his."

"You never disagree?"

I let out a short laugh. "We disagree plenty. Usually, we try to see the fight from the other person's perspective to work things out."

"And you always work everything out?"

I side-eyed Keith. "Are you asking about Simon and me or for future reference. Is there a girl you've got your eye on?"

He blushed and ducked his head. The glow of the intersection lights cast red shadows across his ill-defined cheeks. "No. Definitely not."

"That sounds like a lie." I nudged him with my elbow. "Who is she? Tell me. Tell me!"

The light turned green, and Keith batted my hand away. "No distracting the driver!"

I retreated, laughing, and Keith stepped on the gas pedal. We were almost to Silver Creek. The city lights were long gone, but the warm golden glow up ahead signified the small town was close by.

As we drove through town, people waved to Keith, spotting his familiar truck. Before long, I realized they were waving to me, too. With a smile, I returned the greetings.

"One of the locals now, huh?" Keith asked. "They like you."

"We've barely talked to anyone," I said. "We haven't had the time. Simon's been working. I've been sick. I feel bad they don't really know anything about us."

"Everyone here understands how busy you are," Keith told me. "When you have time, you'll get to know the town. Don't worry."

We passed through the town square and came out on the other end. The turn toward the Lodge approached, and I released a heavy sigh.

"You gonna be okay by yourself tonight?" Keith asked. "I can stick around if you want. Make sure nothing goes bump in the night."

I half-grinned, thinking Keith had no idea what he was in for if he *did* stay. "That's okay, Keith. Thank you for offering."

"Sure thing. Here you go."

We pulled into the lot in front of the Lodge. He reached across me to manually unlock the door, and I caught a whiff of cologne. Who wore cologne to go skiing?

"Should I come by tomorrow?" he asked. "Simon had a plan for the work that needs to be done, but I'm not sure what was next. I can work on some other projects if you like."

"Take the day off," I said, sliding out of the truck. My boots crunched into the snow. "I'll give you an update at the end of the day when I pick up Simon from the hospital."

Keith saluted me. "Yes, ma'am."

Like a gentleman, he waited until I had reached the front porch and unlocked the door before driving away. His mother must have taught him that trick.

The Lodge didn't seem half as terrifying as it did before. Now, it just felt empty. Without carpets, wallboards, fresh paint, or furniture, the Lodge was bare. More than ever, it seemed like the appropriate place for ghosts to linger.

Lily, for once, did not appear on the steps. Where did she go when I wasn't around? Did she exist without someone to interact with her?

Something—or someone—caught my eye on the second-floor balcony. I didn't look up right away, studying the apparition without moving my head. All I saw was a silvery figure of a stooped man. He seemed rather solid, except around the edges, where his outline blurred like traffic lights through the windshield on a rainy day. My gut told me this was the same man I'd seen walking through the Lodge as if he owned the place.

I gathered my wits and looked up. As soon as my eyes reached the place where the man stood, he vanished. He could have been a trick of the light.

I shed my boots, gloves, hat, and coat, casting off the weight of the day. A sense of peace settled in my chest. I was oddly calm, given the circumstances. In the bathroom that worked, I drew a warm bath and lit a few candles. While I bathed and relaxed, the plucking of classical guitar strings floated through the air. I didn't notice the music right away, too entranced by the lavender bubbles and dancing candlelight. When it came to my attention, I sat up and listened closely.

"Clair de Lune." It was a piano piece, but whoever played it now had reworked it to fit the guitar. It was just as beautiful as the original, perhaps more so because the player's talent shown through in every note.

As quietly as possible, I lifted myself from the tub. Water dripped from my legs, pooling on the unfinished floor as I wrapped myself in a robe. I hurriedly dried off, stepped into a pair of waiting slippers, and peeked into the corridor.

The music came from beyond the lobby, in one of the rooms we hadn't spent much time in yet. I followed the lilting guitar medley through the dining area and recreation room. The last room at the back of the house was a quaint hall for hosting events. Like those in the presidential suite, the sweeping windows presented an unfiltered view of the woods and mountains behind the Lodge.

I edged inside, rolling my feet from heels to toes to keep my footsteps as silent as possible. At the opposite end of the room, a woman sat in a rusty folding chair with her back to me. She was less solid than the man I'd seen on the stairs. If I squinted, I could see right through her body. The guitar on her lap had the same effect.

In the reflection of the window, I watched her fingers fly over the fretboard. She was completely absorbed in the song, eyes closed and left ear tilted down to catch every sound from the instrument. I held my breath, amazed, as she expertly plucked the guitar. Not a single note wrong or wasted.

When she finished, I resisted the urge to applaud. The woman remained in playing position as the last notes resonated through the hall as if she were savoring the sound of the final chord. Then she slowly opened her eyes and looked up, her gaze connecting with mine in the window's reflection.

"Sorry, I—" I began.

With a startled gasp, she disappeared, guitar and all. The folding chair wobbled and fell over as if someone had hastily vacated it. The air warmed considerably. I hadn't noticed how cold it was in the hall until the woman was gone.

Tentatively, I walked across the hall and set the folding chair upright. The rusted metal was freezing to touch. I sat down and looked out on the Lodge's backyard. From here, the ugly, dead tree loomed over the left side of the property. Something clicked in my head.

LATER, I snuggled beneath several layers of blankets and willed myself to go to sleep. It was different without Simon. I missed his warmth, smell, and general presence. Aside from the night he'd spent on the couch, we hadn't slept apart in a number of years. I wasn't used to reaching out and feeling a cold, empty space next to me. To make up for it, I rolled to the middle of the air mattress and stretched out as far as possible. It was freeing to have so much space, but I ultimately ended up curled in a tight ball. Some habits were hard to break.

I thought of Simon, glaring at me from his hospital bed. He'd pushed that button for morphine without hesitation, almost as if he hadn't considered fighting the pain. Like he *wanted* the drugs and knew his injury was the perfect excuse to use them. Despite my thicket of blankets, I shuddered. Ever since I'd met Simon, I feared one thing: that he would turn into his brother, Casey.

I drifted off to sleep. When I woke again, it was because of that magnetic pull I'd felt a few times before. This time, it didn't alarm me so much, though I cautioned myself before getting out of bed. The way Lily spoke of the "energy" in the house made it sound unpredictable and self-serving. The last time I'd let it led me wherever it wanted me to go, I ended up falling off the roof.

Like last time, a curious mental fog separated me from the rest of the world. It was almost like I was looking at the Lodge through a thin veil, one that painted a different reality over what was actually in front of me. As I got to my feet, I turned on a flashlight and shone it around the room. The beam cut through some of the fog but didn't dismiss the spell laid over the Lodge. I gasped aloud as the gutted room transform into a fully-furnished excerpt from the seventies' version of the Lodge.

Drapes covered the windows. Green and pink wallpaper clashed with the ornate, cherrywood furniture. A shag carpet coated the floor. When I stepped forward, the dusty fibers tickled between my toes. This was what the Lodge looked like many years ago.

The "energy" didn't let me stop and stare for long. It tugged at my legs and forced me into the hallway. I didn't have time to put on my slippers. My bare feet grew cold as I went out into the lobby and stared, open-mouthed at the changed room. The reception area was completely different, with a front desk that blended in with the wood paneling on the walls. An immense book lay open. When I approached it, I saw it was handwritten records of everyone who stayed at the Lodge during that time. No computers for easy record-keeping.

One name jumped out at me: Christine Higgins. Everything else on the list was blurry like those details weren't important. The energy pulled on me again and led me toward the stairs. I kept my hand on the banister as I went up, not trusting myself to stay balanced against the invisible force.

As I passed the balcony that looked over the lobby, I caught another glimpse of the same man from earlier. He looked younger now. His hands were folded neatly as he leaned on the railing and observed the lobby from above. I found I could only see him if I didn't look straight at him. As soon as I tried, he became invisible.

The energy wasn't showing me this man, though. It kept pulling me down the hall toward the presidential suite. We stopped short of the biggest bedroom, and the door to my left swung open slowly.

It was the same room as last time. I looked in from the doorway and recognized the shape of it, including the window that led out to the roof. Like the rest of the Lodge, it was decorated in a seventies style. Clearly, people had been here recently. The covers on the bed lay on the floor in a messy pile, like they'd been yanked off. Two suitcases lined the wall. One was neatly packed with a woman's folded clothes. The other looked as if someone had dropped a live grenade in it.

On the bedside table, a lit cigarette smoldered in an ashtray. A guitar lay face down on the orange carpet, the neck splintered from the body. Small circular burns decorated the body of the instrument like someone had taken the cigarette and intentionally held the hot end against the delicate wood.

A draft entered the room from the open window and curled around my bare feet. I approached the window and looked out. This time, I saw something. The same woman from the hall, the one who'd been playing guitar, stood on the edge of the roof. She gazed longingly up at the dead white tree and fiddled with something in her grasp: a length of rope.

As I did two nights ago, I ducked through the window and climbed out onto the roof. The woman shaped the rope into a rough noose and tossed one end over the sturdiest branch of the tree. Once it was secure, she looped the other end around her neck.

"Wait!" I yelled, sliding across the icy roof as I tried to reach her. The cold pierced the bottom of my feet like sharp splinters. "Please, stop!"

I expected her to disappear like she did before. I *hoped* she would, so I wouldn't have to see what came next. But the woman remained where she was, her toes hanging off the edge of the roof as she contemplated whether or not to kill herself.

"Christine?" I said in a soft voice, slowing my pace as I grew closer to her. "Are you Christine Higgins?"

The woman turned toward me. Her face contorted with pain. Tear tracks stained her cheeks. Her eyes were swollen and red. A ring of bruises encircled her neck—ten small, finger-sized bruises. Someone had tried to strangle her long before she decided to strangle herself.

"You can't stop this," she said in a voice as musically pleasing as her guitar playing. "No one can. It's already happened."

"But you shouldn't have to relive it," I replied quietly. "It's not right."

Was that a flash of hope in her sad eyes?

"Who are you?" she asked.

"I'm Max."

"You can see me," she said pensively. "Not many people can."

"You wanted me to." I took another step toward her.

The more I focused on her, the more she seemed to solidify. She wasn't like Lily, who could fool almost anyone into thinking she was alive, but it was a start.

"You brought me out here before to show me how you died."

Christine's lower lip trembled. "I just need someone to see me."

"I see you," I assured her, reaching my hand out. "I see you, Christine."

When her skin touched mine, I expected to feel a human hand. Though I saw our hands touching, I felt nothing. It was like she wasn't even there. Then again, I supposed she wasn't.

Difficult though it was to hang onto nothing, I led Christine a few steps away from the edge of the roof. The noose vanished from around her neck.

"Thank you," she said gratefully. "I've never walked away before."

"I heard you playing guitar earlier," I told her. "My husband has wanted to learn 'Clair de Lune' on guitar for years, but he could never figure out how to transpose it properly. You did it beautifully."

Though she was dead, she blushed. "Goodness, you really think so?"

"I know so."

Her joy faded quickly. "My husband ruined my guitar."

I pointed at the open window behind us. "That was your room?"

"Yes."

"Did something happen in there?"

Christine's chin wobbled as she struggled to keep her tears at bay. "No, no. Nothing else happened. It was an accident."

I gently cupped Christine's elbow. Perhaps she could feel it, even if I couldn't. "You can tell me. It's already happened, remember?"

"He was upset again," she began wobbly. "He's always upset about something. I do a lot of things wrong. He said I packed his suitcase incorrectly. He likes me to pack it by outfit rather than separating it into articles of clothing." She sniffed heavily. "I told him I couldn't fit everything in if I had to organize it that way, but he wouldn't listen."

"You packed it the way it would fit?"

She nodded. "For the first two nights, he didn't say anything. I thought he didn't notice or mind. On the third night, he couldn't find a shirt he was looking for. He took it out on me. I was napping in the bed, and he yanked the mattress out from under me. He threw my guitar—I was supposed to perform in the hall that night—and burned it with his cigarette. Then he—he grabbed me—"

She motioned to her neck but was unable to put the action into words. Her eyes filled with tears again.

"He hurt you," I finished for her, leaving the unpleasant details out. "What happened next?"

"Someone knocked on the door, so he stopped," Christine said. "I couldn't speak. He had damaged my vocal cords. I had to call the front desk and tell them I was too sick to perform. That night, I told him not to bother trying to kill me again. I said I'd do it myself. Then I marched out onto the roof, tied myself to that tree, and stepped off. I don't think he expected me to go through with it."

"But why did you do it?" I asked. "There are other ways to get out of an unhappy marriage. Why didn't you report him to the police?"

"Honey, there are a million reasons why I didn't leave him before," Christine said, though she did not seem to be patronizing me. "Least of all because people frowned upon divorced women quite a bit back then. I killed myself because he finally took the last piece of me: my music. It was everything to me. Without it, I no longer felt human. I saw no point in remaining alive in a world that had no meaning."

I swallowed a large lump in my throat. Never once had I thought about committing suicide, but Christine talked about it with reverence. "I'm sorry you felt that way."

She looked across the roof at the moon. "It's a lovely night. It would have been a shame to ruin it by repeating the past."

"Can you stop?" I asked. "Do you have to keep doing this?"

"I don't know," she whispered. "I can't seem to stop."

"What happened to your husband?" I said. "After you stepped off the roof? Do you know?"

Christine hugged herself as if she could feel the chilly breeze drifting through the trees. My feet were practically frozen to the rooftop.

"I thought it hadn't worked." Christine gazed blankly into the distance, lost in thought. "One moment, I was hanging from the tree. The next, I was back on the roof, watching him shouting and sobbing from the window. I looked over the edge and saw my body. The police came and found me. They saw the bruises on my neck and arrested my husband. I'm not sure what happened after that. All I know is I've been stuck at this lodge for over forty years, stepping off this roof over and over again."

"Go inside," I ordered gently. I guided her toward the open window, but without a real body to maneuver, all I could do was fan her spirit away from the edge of the roof. "You don't have to keep doing this to yourself."

Christine stepped through the window and into the room. I followed and found that the room was no longer destroyed. The bed was made, and only one suitcase—the neatly packed one—rested on the floor. Her guitar leaned against the wall in one piece. It was like Christine's husband was never there.

"Goodness," she said, looking around. "This place is quite nice when it's all cleaned up, isn't it?"

"It is," I agreed. "You can switch rooms, too, if you'd like. And I plan on cutting that tree down eventually."

"Are you the new protector?" she asked out of the blue.

I recalled what Lily had said earlier, something about the ghosts of the Silver Creek Lodge needing protection. Was that my responsibility?

"Maybe," I answered Christine. "We'll see how it goes. Have a good night."

"Are you leaving?"

"I'll be right downstairs," I assured her. "You can come to see me any time you like."

For the first time, she seemed happy. She sat on the bed and bounced to test the softness of the mattress. Then she flopped back, spread her arms wide, and let out a small squeak of joy. With a smile, I retreated from her room to let her enjoy her newfound freedom.

At the end of the corridor, I ran into Lily. Though she looked to be in good spirits, she seemed weaker than usual.

"Taking my advice, I see?" she said, and her voice was definitely hoarse. "Getting to know the other residents?"

"I stopped her from jumping." I couldn't help but let my chest puff with pride. "Maybe this won't be so bad after all."

Lily lost her balance, almost falling down the rest of the steps.

"Whoa!" I grabbed her by the arms and hugged her

183

close. Though her regular warmth was present, something was missing between us. "Are you okay?"

She nodded weakly. "The energy here ebbs and flows. If other people are using it copiously, I can't get enough. That's why I get sick."

"Is that why *I've* been sick?"

"Most likely." Lily clung to me as we made our way to the first floor. "You can learn to control it, though. We don't have a choice."

"This is more complicated than I thought it would be," I admitted. "Where's the science behind it all?"

"Maybe you can find out."

We made it back to my room. The facade had been lifted. There were no more seventies decorations or furniture around. The air mattress looked lonely in the middle of the barren room. The thought of climbing in alone made me sad.

"Will you stay with me tonight?" I asked Lily.

"Of course."

13

*I*n the morning, Lily was gone, but there was a dent in Simon's pillow and the sheets were warm as if someone had just gotten up. I rolled out of bed, stretched, and checked outside. The sun was out, and some of the snow on the ground was melting. It was a nice morning for a jog, so that's what I decided to do.

I put on my running gear, made sure to wear a scarf to protect my mouth, and took a quick lap through the nearby woods. When I returned to the Lodge, cold and out of breath, my phone buzzed in my pocket. Though I didn't recognize the number, I answered anyway.

"Hello?"

"Hi, is this Maxine?"

"Yes, this is she."

"This is Dr. Fitzgerald," a warm voice replied. "I'm calling on behalf of your husband, Simon."

I tensed. "Is everything okay?"

"Everything's great," he assured me. "He's doing well.

We're going to run a few more tests today to make sure his concussion hasn't progressed in any alarming fashion. As long as nothing changes, you can pick him up later this evening."

"Thank you so much," I said.

"Would you like to speak to him?"

I hesitated, but Dr. Fitzgerald had already handed the phone over.

I heard Simon mutter something before he said, "Hey, Max?"

"Hi," I said. "Are you doing okay?"

"The doctor said I'm fine. Are you going to pick me up?"

"Later tonight."

Simon groaned. "Can't you come now? I don't want to do all these extra tests. I feel fine."

"I'd feel better if you do the tests," I told him. "What if you come home and something goes wrong?"

"Fine," he said shortly. "Never mind. See you later—"

"Simon, come on—"

He hung up on me. Frustration almost convinced me to hurl the phone across the snowy yard and into one of the hot springs. I curled my fingers tighter around the phone then slipped it into my pocket to prevent myself from doing something stupid.

The hot springs steamed and bubbled. I watched them from a safe distance. I couldn't look at the heated pools without reliving yesterday's incident. Though I knew the truth now, it didn't change the things I'd seen. Somehow, what had happened in the hot springs affected me more than seeing Christine on the roof. Being naked had a way of making the most invincible people seem vulnerable.

If Lily were around, she would tell me to face my fears and confront whatever waited for me in the hot springs. If I didn't do it now, it would come back to haunt me later. Literally.

With short steps, I walked closer to the hot springs. Remembering Lily's advice, I tried to keep an open mind. It wasn't her I'd seen under the water. Someone else had died here, and like Christine Higgens, they also had a reason for accidentally torturing me.

As I neared the deepest pool, a figure shimmered into existence. I hid behind the corner of the Lodge and watched. He was a short, squat man with a square face and a neatly combed mustache. Most of his rotund body was hidden beneath the water's surface, except for his shoulders and head. He flicked bubbles with obvious glee. He sighed heavily and let his head rest back on the land.

As I was about to step out from behind my hiding place to introduce myself, the man began to cough. He pounded himself on the chest as if to dislodge something. His face turned red then purple. He gasped and wheezed for breath. Then his head sank below the pool's surface.

I darted over and looked into the springs. The man stared back at me, his pudgy fingers opening and closing as he fought for whatever life he could cling to. I thought of the hands clamped around my ankles yesterday. This man needed a lifeline.

I lay on my stomach near the pool, rolled up my sleeve, and plunged my hand into the water. I fumbled around, feeling nothing, then touched the man's clammy palm. I clasped his hand and pulled him upward with all my might.

His head broke the surface, and he launched himself out of the pool. With his face pressed to the dead grass, he heaved for air. I thumped him on the back to help dislodge water from his lungs.

"Earl?" he asked hoarsely without turning his head. "Is that you?"

"Uh, no," I answered. "I'm Max."

The man rolled over, and his eyes went wide with surprise. "Shit, are you kidding me?"

"I beg your pardon?"

He scrambled to his feet and covered himself with a towel that appeared out of nowhere. His round belly spilled over his short swim trunks. "Of all the people that coulda pulled me out of there, it's gotta be a gal that looks like you. Christ, that's embarrassing. Where's Earl?"

"The former owner? He passed away."

"That explains it." The man wiped water from what little hair remained on his head. "Where'd you come from?"

"We moved in last month," I explained, wondering if I'd ever get accustomed to speaking so casually to someone who didn't have a heartbeat. "We're renovating the Lodge. What about you?"

"Jersey," the man grunted. "I'm Walter. Walter Briggs."

I gestured to the hot springs. "Does that keep happening to you?"

"Every damn day," Walter replied grumpily. "Until Earl started pulling me out."

"Earl pulled you out?"

"Yeah, I started expecting him. Then he disappeared, and I thought I was doomed until you showed up." He dropped the towel around his butt and flossed it back and forth to dry off his swim trunks. "Thanks again for the save."

"What happened to you before you went under?" I asked. "You looked like you were choking."

"Heart attack," Walter answered casually. "A guy like me really should have been watching my cholesterol levels, but what can I say? I was a big fan of cheeseburgers. Bit me in the ass, didn't it? No one pulled me out when it counted."

"You mean when you were alive?"

He raised an eyebrow. "Not exactly well-practiced with tact, are you?"

I grimaced. "Sorry about that. I'm new to all of this."

Walter smiled wryly. "Don't worry. You'll get the hang of it. And yeah, about twelve years ago, I came to Silver Creek to get a big job done. Celebrated with a nice dunk in the hot springs. Didn't expect to die there. That's for damn sure."

"No one saw you go under?"

"Nope," he said. "I was here during the off-season. The place was pretty empty. Earl feels bad, but it wasn't his fault. He had other things on his mind."

I stomped my feet to warm them. "What do you do for work?"

189

"I build safes," Walter answered. "Not sure why Earl wanted one here, but—"

"Whoa, back up." I put my hands up to silence him. "Did you say you built a safe on this property? In the Lodge?"

"Yes, ma'am," he replied. "First floor, in one of the back rooms. It's a thing of beauty. Still there if you want to check it out."

"Why did you build it?" I asked.

Walter looked at me like I was crazy. "Honey, someone hired me to do it."

"No, I meant what was the safe for?" I clarified. "What did Earl intend to put in it?"

"No idea," he answered. "It wasn't any of my business. All I know is he wanted a safe built into the foundation of the house. I obliged."

"It's locked," I told him. "We tried everything and can't get in. We called a professional and everything—"

Walter released a big belly laugh and patted himself on the back. "I did my job well then, huh? I used to advertise my safes as uncrackable. Whatever you put in there is safe from every person on this earth. Except me, of course."

"Are you saying you can get into the safe here? Without the combination."

"Sure, sweetheart."

"No strings attached?" I clarified.

He gestured to the hot springs. "As far as I'm concerned, we're already square. Let's go see my finest piece of work, shall we?"

Walter hung the towel around his neck and walked

right through the wall of the Lodge. I rolled my eyes and used the actual door to follow. When we met in the smallest room on the first floor, Walter had swapped his swim trunks for a pair of khaki pants and a polo shirt with the name of his company embroidered on the front.

We hadn't done anything to cover the safe door. The wall around it was ripped away, and the cold, metal door took up most of the space like a weird decoration. Each time I passed by this room, a strange vibe radiated out to meet me and sent shivers up and down my spine. At some point, I started avoiding the safe.

Walter squinted at the spinning dial on the safe door, but when he attempted to grasp it, his fingers melted right through. "Ah, hell. It's not my lucky day."

"You can't do it?" I asked.

"I can't touch it," he corrected. "That's not to say I can't do it. I built a back way into all these safes. I don't need a combination. Come here. I'll show you what to do."

Goose bumps crept up my arms as I stepped between Walter and the safe. Energy pulsed from the other side and washed over me like a series of small sonic waves.

"Do you feel that?" I muttered to Walter.

"We all feel it." He put his hands on my shoulder and squared me off against the safe like he was the referee of a wrestling match. "Okay. Do exactly as I say. You can't mess this up."

"Is it wired to explode if I do it wrong?"

"No, it just won't open." Walter chuckled at his joke. "All right, see that little tab beneath the dial?"

I ran my fingers around the dial and located a tiny

piece of metal that didn't fit smoothly into the rest of the locking mechanism. Were it not for Walter, I would never have known it was there.

"Got it?" Walter said. "Now wiggle your fingernail under the tab and pry it up."

I did as he said. With some fine finagling, the tab popped loose. I took a firm hold of the end and pried it from beneath the dial. A long, thin piece of metal—like a sturdier sewing needle—came out in my hands.

"Excellent," Walter said, beaming. "That was step one."

"How many steps are there?"

"About ten more before we can get in there," he answered. When he spotted my aghast expression, he shrugged. "What? I had to make sure no one else would figure out how to open it."

After several additional puzzles—the strangest of which included tapping on the safe door in a specific rhythmic manner—Walter finally asked me to input a combination and spin the dial.

"Zero, six, zero, seven, sixty-seven," he said.

I lifted an eyebrow. "Not exactly the hardest code to crack."

"It's my birthday," he said. "Besides, no one ever got in, did they?"

I couldn't argue with him there. What with all the shenanigans required to bypass the owner's combination, I doubted anyone but the person who installed the safe—Earl, according to Walter—had been inside.

I listened to each click of the dial as I spun it to the correct numbers. When I got to the last seven and pressed the dial inward, a satisfying clunk echoed from behind the locking mechanism. Walter lifted his arms in triumph.

"There you have it, girlie," he said.

I made to pull the door open, but Walter stepped between me and the unlocked dial. A gust of freezing cold air made my hair stand on end as he seized my arms and pulled me away.

"Whoa, what do you think you're doing?" he demanded, his face scrunched in a way that didn't suit his happy-go-lucky attitude.

I shrugged off his chilly grip. "Opening the safe."

"Give a guy a warning," he said. "I told you I'd help open it, not stick around to see what's inside."

"Are you scared?"

"Hell yeah," he replied. "And I'm not ashamed to admit it."

"I thought you didn't know what was in the safe," I said.

Walter faded, his figure shimmering at the edges. "Sometimes, it's better to stay ignorant."

He vanished completely, and the warmth returned to the room. I faced the safe again, staring at the unlocked dial. With a quick spin, I could make sure no one opened it. I could stay ignorant like Walter advised.

A whisper tickled my neck. It crept along my skin and crawled into my ears. Like before, I couldn't understand a word, but I did comprehend the intention of the speaker. It was a request: *open the safe.*

I grasped the bulky metal handle and pulled. The door swung open. My pupils dilated, fighting to see inside.

With no windows, the room inside the safe was utterly dark.

I grabbed a flashlight and switched it on. From a safe distance, I shined the beam into the mouth of the secret room. As my nerves stood at attention, I highlighted old wallpaper, moldy carpeting, and a single wooden desk: the remnants of the old Lodge.

When nothing threatening barged out of the darkness, I stepped closer and peered inside. The room was mostly empty. If I wanted an explanation for the odd pulses of energy I'd felt through the door, I was out of luck.

I lifted my foot over the lip of the door and stepped inside. The smell was odd, like rusted metal and dirt. It reminded me of Lily, though not as pleasant. I couldn't find a light switch, but I did locate a box of matches on a shelf and several tall candles placed around the room. One by one, I lit the candles until a fluttering yellow glow filled the room.

I switched off the flashlight and spun on the spot. The room was just a room. It didn't hold any fantastic secrets or piles of money. Disappointment and annoyance fought for dominance in my head. We could've used a pile of cash.

I almost left, bored with the place already, but something caught my eye. A piece of paper stuck out from one of the desk drawers. I pulled open the drawer and found several rolls of thick glossy maps. I unfurled the first one and laid it flat on the desk's surface, but as soon as I let go of the corners, it sprang back to its original shape.

Four heavy paperweights, each cast out of iron in the

shape of the earth, rested nearby. I set one on each corner of the map to hold it in place and bent over to examine it. This one was a regular map of the world, but someone had drawn across it with a permanent marker. Strange lines covered the map, weaving in and out of each, intersecting at certain points. No matter how long I squinted at them, I couldn't make sense of the lines. They weren't coordinates or fault lines or anything else I could think of that someone might mark on a map. It was almost as if they'd been drawn at random.

Near the points where certain lines intersected, the mapmaker had included additional markers in red pen. The map was dotted all over with these, but there was no key to explain what they signified. Looking for an explanation, I took another map from the drawer and unrolled it.

This map covered Europe. More strange lines and red dots decorated the various countries. Some red markers had been drawn larger than others as if to symbolize something of greater importance. Again, there was no key.

One by one, I unrolled the rest of the maps. By my count, there were thirty-seven from all around the world. Each one focused on a different part of the earth. The United Kingdom had three maps all to itself as if the map owner was particularly interested in the subject there. When I unrolled the last map, I recognized the outline of the location.

"Silver Creek," I muttered to myself, tracing the drawn lines.

The final map, unlike the others, featured a single asterisk, drawn over the intersection of two lines. I leaned closer, squinting at the unlabeled land. The asterisk was scribbled right on the spot where the Lodge sat. In minuscule handwriting, someone had written "ley lines" beside the Lodge's location.

ARMED with the single map of Silver Creek, I drove into town. The library was Silver Creek's pride and joy. It was one of the largest buildings in town and loomed over the smaller shops and restaurants along Main Street. I had never been inside before, but when I caught sight of the high ceiling and soaring shelves, I regretted not having come in sooner.

I approached the front desk. The librarian was an older man with jowls, wearing a brown woolen vest with a nametag pinned to it: Charles. Though the library had a computer to organize everything, the librarian recorded the dates of recently returned books by hand.

"Hello, miss," he said in a gravelly voice. "Can I help you find something?"

"Yes, I'm looking for some information on ley lines."

Charles chuckled as if enjoying a private joke. "You too, eh? Follow me."

He set aside his pen and led me deeper into the library. I couldn't help but stare upwards. The shelves went so high that it seemed impossible to reach the books up there without a crane.

"This is an impressive library for such a small town," I

commented. "How does Silver Creek afford to keep up a place like this?"

"It's privately funded," Charles said. "When Silver Creek was founded, the first families who settled here came from highly-educated backgrounds. They built this library themselves."

"Wow," I muttered, overwhelmed by the sheer amount of knowledge around me. "I wasn't expecting this."

"No one ever does."

Charles ducked into an alcove, and we emerged in a small cave made of books. A plush leather chair stood in one corner, along with a side table to rest your coffee on if you had it. This section of the library looked like someone's private office. All that was missing was a desk and a fireplace.

"All the books on pseudoscience are in here," Charles said. He pointed to a stuffed shelf. "Ley lines over there."

"I'm sorry. Pseudo-what?"

"Pseudoscience," he repeated, eyebrows scrunched in confusion. "Don't you know what you're researching?"

"Not really," I admitted. "That's why I'm researching it."

Charles pulled a few old volumes from the shelves. "If you want to be a ley hunter, start with these. It'll give you the lay of the land. No pun intended. Once you're finished with those, I've got some old documents about Silver Creek you might be interested in. I keep 'em in a humidity-controlled environment so they don't get damaged. Let me know if you want to see them."

I accepted the stack of books, unsure of what I'd

gotten myself into. "Thanks for all your help. Do you know a lot about ley lines?"

"It's a bunch of blather if you ask me," he replied. "Happy coincidences. But who am I to stop people from following their dreams of hunting down magical places? Enjoy the books. I'll be at the front desk if you need me."

As Charles left, I settled in the leather armchair and opened the first book titled *The Lure of Ley Lines.* Within minutes, I was completely absorbed.

WHEN I EMERGED from the library's cave, it was with an arm full of additional books on ley lines and a wealth of fresh understanding.

"Did you find what you needed?" Charles asked.

"Yes, and I'd like to see those documents you were talking about sometime."

He scanned the books to check them out. "I'd be happy to show them to you, but they can't be checked out. Would you like to come back tomorrow?"

"Absolutely."

I zipped up my coat, balanced my books, and waved goodbye to Charles. Outside, it had begun to snow great big flakes. I leaned into the wind, determined not to drop any of my new research material. As I fumbled for my keys, voices floated across the parking lot.

"I warned you," a young boy called. "I told you not to talk about my mom like that!"

I squinted through the flurry and spotted a pack of teenagers in the alleyway between the library and the courthouse. Bubbles, once more, was in the center. Hastily, I tossed the books into the passenger seat and closed the car.

"Your mom's a—"

I came up being Bubbles and gently put my hand over her mouth. "Insults are for the petty," I announced to the young teenagers. "Personally, I refuse to put up with them. Everyone, on your way."

The boy who Bubbles kept bothering glared at me. "Why do you always stick up for her? She's a jerk. No one in school likes her. She's the one who always picks fights. Not us."

Bubbles jerked free of my hand and said, "I do not!"

"Yes, you do," another kid added. "All the teachers know you're a troublemaker. That's why you're in detention all the time."

"That's enough," I said. "I'll handle Bubbles. The rest of you should get home before you catch pneumonia."

Grumbling, the teenagers went on their way. Bubbles tried to pull out of my grip, but I held her fast. I sank to my knees to be on her eye level.

"Is it true?" I asked her. "Are you the bully?"

Bubbles refused to meet my gaze. As she turned her head, I caught sight of a pattern of bruises around her neck. At first, I thought they were from the last time she picked a fight, but these were fresh. A memory flashed: Christine Higgen's neck was covered in the same kind of bruises from when her husband tried to strangle her.

"Bubbles, where did you get these?" I murmured, pulling her scarf down to get a better look.

"Don't!" She smacked my hand away, her lower lip trembling as she held back tears.

"No," I said firmly. "Who did this to you? There's no way it was those kids—" The truth hit me like a brick to the face. "This is why you pick fights, isn't it? To cover up the bruises you already have." I gently tugged Bubbles closer. "Honey, who's hurting you?"

14

*B*efore I could get an answer, Bubbles slipped from my grasp, shedding her coat like a snakeskin. Ten seconds later, she was halfway across the parking lot, leaving me with nothing but her empty, expensive winter coat.

"Go home!" I shouted after her, though I doubted she could hear me over the whistling wind. Shaking my head, I folded up her coat and went back to my car. I'd give it to her the next time I saw her in town.

As I drove home, I considered stopping at the local police station to report Bubbles's injuries, but instinct told me not to. Bubbles needed help, but I wasn't sure telling the cops was the best way to give it to her. She was hiding the fact that she was being abused, and one of her parents or guardians was probably the culprit. Now that I thought about it, I'd never seen Bubbles out and about with family. All I knew about her was that she was a big *Rebel Queen* fan.

Lily was waiting for me when I got back to the Lodge. She lingered on the porch steps and gazed at the ground as if wondering whether or not she could step farther from the building without disappearing.

"Hey there," I called as I got my books out of the front seat. "Haven't seen you around today?"

"Other people were taking up the energy." She nodded at the stack of books. "I'm guessing you know something about that?"

"Come inside. I want to share what I learned."

I left Bubbles's coat in the car and stored my worry for her in a different compartment of my brain. Inside, I dumped the books on the kitchen table and put on a pot of coffee while I talked to Lily.

"Do you know what ley lines are?" I asked her.

She shook her head. "No idea."

I opened the first book I'd read to the introduction. "Some people believe these lines of energy crisscross over the earth, connecting important sites like Stonehenge and the Pyramids." I rolled out one of the maps I'd taken from the safe room and traced one of the lines. "See these red dots? Each one symbolizes a special place, like a monument or an ancient site. If you notice, you can draw straight lines through the dots."

Lily studied the map. "So what? That could be a coincidence. Humans are built to notice patterns."

"That's what Charles—the librarian—said, too," I replied. "But I'm not so sure. Look at this." I rolled out the map of Silver Creek and pointed to the asterisk. "When two ley lines intersect, it makes that place more powerful. Look at what's under the asterisk."

She leaned closer for a better look. "It's the Lodge."

"I think this building is positioned right over two intersecting ley lines," I said excitedly. "I think that's why you, Christine, Walter, and whoever else is stuck here. It's something to do with the energy of the ley lines."

Lily wrinkled her nose. "I don't know, Max. Doesn't this seem a little preposterous to you?"

"Are you kidding?" I asked her. "I'm talking to a dead woman, and you think magical lines of energy are preposterous?"

She released a quick laugh. "You have a point there. Where did you find these maps anyway?"

"They were hidden in the safe room."

Her face paled. "You went in there?"

"Yeah, Walter helped me open it. He's the one that built the door. Why?"

She stood up and paced across the kitchen, kneading her temples. "You shouldn't have opened that door, Max. There's a reason Earl blocked it off."

"Walter wouldn't go in either," I said uneasily. "He was scared of that room. Why?"

Lily pressed her lips together.

"What happened in there?"

"I don't know," she whispered. "But I do know I don't ever want to go back in that room."

"Go back? You'd been in there before?"

She placed her palms on either side of her head and

squeezed like she was trying to compress her entire brain. "I don't know. I don't know!"

Gently, I took her hands away from her head and gathered them in mine. I tipped her chin up to look at me. "Hey, everything's going to be okay. I'll figure it out."

"Can you promise you won't go back in that room?"

"I'll keep it closed for now," I offered. "But, I need to figure out whatever happened in there."

Lily's breath shuddered, but she seemed to calm down. The shrill ring of my phone interrupted the comforting moment between us. I answered quickly.

"Hello?"

"Hi, Ms. Finch," said Dr. Fitzgerald. "Simon is looking good. He's ready to go home. You can come pick him up as soon as possible."

"Thanks, Doc," I replied. "I'll be there when I can."

As I hung up, Lily sniffled. "You have to go?"

"I have to get Simon," I sighed. "Can you hold down the fort?"

"Like I have a choice."

SIMON WAS up and about when I arrived at the hospital. My heart jumped with glee at the sight of him on his feet, even if he needed crutches to get around on his injured knee. When he saw me come in, his bruised face turned up in half a smile. Momentarily, we forgot about our dumb arguments. We were together again, he was safe, and that was all that mattered.

Carefully, to not hurt him, I leaned against his chest

and wrapped my arms loosely around his waist. He rested his chin on top of my head. I inhaled his familiar smell and almost cried with relief.

"I missed you," he murmured into my hair.

I squeezed him tighter, and he released a short grunt. "Sorry!" I said, pulling away. "Let's get you out of here."

To Simon's chagrin, hospital policy said he had to leave in a wheelchair. I helped him into his coat and boots then wheeled him out to the parking lot. He hopped into the car without a problem. If his knee was bothering him, he didn't show it, but Simon had always been a silent sufferer. He powered through pain, sometimes to the point of recklessness.

"I called Keith already," he said as we drove back to Silver Creek. "He's ready to start working again tomorrow. I think I can keep to our original schedule, especially if Boyce comes through with his construction crew."

My grasp on the steering wheel tightened. "I'm still not sure I want to get Boyce involved. Isn't there anyone else in town who might want to invest?"

Simon tried to hide his scowl by turning toward the window, but I saw his reflection in my side mirror. "No, there isn't. It's a small town, Max. I don't know why you're so against Boyce."

"Really? Because I feel like I've told you a hundred times," I snapped. "He's too interested in the Lodge. He's going to want more control."

"So we give him more control! Do you want to succeed or not?"

"I want to run my own business without some random rich guy getting in the way—"

"He's not some random rich guy. He's the mayor of the town."

"*Unofficial* mayor."

"Whatever, it doesn't matter."

"It does matter—"

A deer stepped in front of the car. I screamed and jerked the wheel. The car plowed into a snowbank on the side of the road, and the deer bounded off into the dark forest.

I gave myself exactly ten seconds to get my emotions together. Then I turned to Simon. "Are you okay? Are you hurt?"

He groped for my hand over the center console. I held his tightly.

"I'm okay," he said. "You?"

"Just startled."

"How's the car?"

I got out and checked the front bumper. Thankfully, we hadn't hit any hidden barricades or swerved into a ditch. The car was fine, just covered in thick snow.

"We're good," I told Simon, getting back in. "Though it might take a push to get back on the road."

With one hand on the back of Simon's seat, I put the car in reverse and eased on the gas pedal. The car groaned as it struggled to dislodge itself from the snowdrift. I gave it more gas—still nothing.

"Come on, baby," I said, patting the dashboard. "I don't want to push."

As Simon braced himself, I stomped on the gas. The car lurched out of the snowdrift and slid back onto the road. A pair of headlights shone through the back windshield. Quickly, I switched into first gear and sped up. The headlights backed off.

Simon squeezed my thigh. "Let's try to make the rest of the night uneventful, huh?"

IT WAS one thing to try. It was another to actually succeed. The Lodge was about the worst place to house anyone coming home from the hospital. Without a real bed, comfort always seemed just out of reach. The kitchen had a working stove, but soup didn't taste as good when you had to eat it out of a paper bowl or slurp it from a coffee mug.

I layered the air mattress with extra blankets to make it softer while the tub in the working bathroom filled with hot water. Simon pulled off his shirt by himself, but I helped wriggle his pants off over the bulky brace around his knee. He held onto my shoulder and balanced on one leg as I eased him into the tub.

He was so tall that his knees stuck out of the water. I washed his hair for him and soaped his back. He got the rest without issue. We didn't talk, but that was for the best. We couldn't speak without arguing.

When he was clean, he stepped into a fresh pair of boxers and fell into bed. I played with his hair while his eyes drifted shut.

"Baby?" he mumbled sleepily. "Can you get me those painkillers from my bag? My knee hurts."

I fetched the plastic bag the doctor had sent home with Simon and fished around for the bottle of medications. When I read the label, I winced—Vicodin.

"This is a strong dose," I told Simon. "I can get you some Advil if you'd prefer."

He held out his hand for the bottle. "My knee really hurts. I'd rather take the painkillers."

I didn't give him the pills. "Simon, I'm not sure it's a good idea—"

"Are you the doctor?" he asked sharply. "I'm in pain. I want the painkillers. Why are you hounding me about this?"

The contempt in his voice took me by surprise. He never spoke to me that way, not even when he was angry.

"I'm hounding you," I began shakily, "because you made me promise to stop you if I thought you were going to do something stupid. Like drink or take drugs you don't need. Being completely sober was *your* idea, remember?"

"I'm not Casey," he shot back. "I can control myself. Plus, it's not cocaine. It's for my knee. I'm not going to suddenly become an addict because I take a dose of Vicodin."

He snatched the bottle out of my hand, uncapped it, and popped a pill into his mouth. Before I could protest, he swallowed it dry.

"In case you forgot," he said. "*I'm* not the one who died of an overdose."

"Simon, I know that. I just—"

"Please go away. I'm too tired to fight."

I got up to leave, defeated once more, but I paused in the doorway. "Ever since we got here, you've dismissed my concerns. You refuse to listen to me. You push me away. I'm tired of pretending like nothing's wrong. I know we're in a difficult situation. I know I've done and said some things that were hurtful to you. I'm sorry about that, but I can't keep doing this with you. Please figure out what's bothering you so we can talk about it together. Because if we don't talk soon, I'll wonder why we bothered getting married."

IN THE MORNING, I checked on Simon once, while he was still sleeping, to make sure he was okay, but let him do his own thing otherwise. When he got up, he avoided me like the plague. At breakfast, I noticed he skipped the Vicodin and took Advil instead. Maybe something I said last night actually resonated with him.

He hopped around on his good leg like a baby bird with a broken wing and refused to ask for help. When he reached for a coffee cup, the crutch slipped out from under him and knocked his arm out of place. The mug went flying and shattered on the floor. I stood from the table to help sweep the fragments.

"I got it," he said and grabbed the broom before me.

"Are you working today?" I asked.

He grunted his acknowledgment. Giving me the

complete silent treatment would have been slightly too immature for his tastes. Slightly.

"Well, take it easy," I advised him, pretending our discussion last night had never happened. The ball was in his court. At some point, he'd have to get over himself. "I don't want to have to drive you back to the hospital."

"Uh-huh."

I rolled my eyes and grabbed my coat. "Okay, see you."

He found his voice. "You're going somewhere?"

"Into town," I said, getting my coat on. "I'm doing some research. For *Rebel Queen*."

"Oh." There was a note of inquiry in his tone, but he didn't follow up with a question. "Okay."

In the car, I let out a forceful breath but refused to get upset. Regardless of Simon, I had other things to do. First off, I wanted to get back to the library and check out Charles's documents.

"You're back," said the librarian when I arrived. "I wasn't expecting you so soon."

"Can I have a look at those papers you told me about?"

"Sure thing."

He led me to a room that didn't match the cozy scholarly vibe of the rest of the library. It was a white, sterile room with glass walls and shelves. Inside, the air felt oddly stagnant. Cautiously, Charles removed a single leather-bound journal from the shelf.

"This was written around the time Silver Creek was founded," he said, placing the journal on a stand for me to read. "Be gentle with it. The pages are fragile. This particular founder was a hunter of ley lines. He came here looking for an intersection."

I played dumb. "An intersection?"

"Yes, where two ley lines cross, it's said to hold great power," Charles explained. "People who believe in such power would harness the energy for their own means for rituals and the like."

I hadn't read about any rituals yet. Did that mean someone was holding court in the safe room at the Lodge?

"I thought you didn't know much about ley lines," I said to Charles.

"I'm a librarian, sweetheart. I know a little about everything."

When Charles left, I buried my nose in the journal. The first several chapters were all about the founder's relocation to Silver Creek. According to his autobiography, he was born in Scotland and sailed to America. His interest in ley lines began in his home country, but his sole purpose of traveling to the States was to find an unclaimed plot of land where two lines intersected.

I'm getting close, one passage read. *I can feel the energy rising. It makes my skin crawl, in a good way. The hair on my arm stands on end as the energy pulses through me. I've never felt anything like this before.*

I recalled standing outside the safe before Walter helped me open it, feeling the same pulse of energy as the founder described. The passage picked up in a new paragraph:

It's here! In the middle of the woods! I've pinpointed the precise location of the intersection. I can feel where the pulse is strongest. My God, the things I can accomplish with this energy will be endless, but I must protect this land. I must claim it and declare it and its powers to be mine. But how shall I ensure no one questions my claim to it?

I skipped a few pages and discovered the answer. The founder told no one about the ley line intersection and declared the land as the perfect place for his home. He built a log cabin, one that eventually became the foundation for the Lodge. The founder had included a blueprint of the original building. As I studied it, I recognized the shape. It matched the part of the Lodge hidden behind Walter's safe.

The founder wrote in first person, so I had no idea who the journal belonged to until I flipped to the last page and saw a final signature scribbled in hasty cursive: *Emory Driscoll.*

My stomach catapulted. Were Emory and Boyce related? I gently closed the journal, placed it back where it belonged, and made my way out to the checkout desk.

"Charles?" I asked softly. "The journal you showed me belonged to someone named Emory Driscoll. Is that—?"

"Boyce's great uncle," Charles answered. "Yes, indeed."

"Does that mean Boyce knows about the ley lines?"

Charles's lips turned up in a knowing smile. "What ley lines?"

As I left the library, my head whirled with the possibilities. No wonder Boyce wanted to acquire the Lodge so desperately. His family had built it. He knew what lay beneath the foundation of the building. That's why he played stupid when we showed him the safe.

Thinking of Boyce must have conjured him out of thin air. From my car, stopped at the main light in town, I spotted his unmistakable designer coat and coiffed salt-and-pepper hair from behind. He waited outside the market and tapped his foot impatiently while he took a call on his phone. He rapped on the window of the market and beckoned to someone inside. The door opened and out came—

"Bubbles," I sighed.

She carried a see-through, plastic grocery bag that contained a single box of tampons. With her head dipped low, she approached Boyce. He put a hand on the back of her neck and guided her up the street as if he were carrying a cat by the scruff of the neck.

Hatred bubbled in my veins. When the light turned green, I had half a mind to hit the gas and run over Boyce. As I passed them, I looked in my side mirror and caught sight of Bubbles. She was close to tears, clutching the bag of tampons close to her chest as Boyce shoved her along. The bruises around her eye hadn't healed yet, but the fingerprints on her neck were hidden by a thick knitted scarf.

When it came down to it, we hardly knew anything about Boyce. He was the "unofficial mayor" of Silver Creek. He had money and a vested interest in the Lodge. He possibly knew about the lines, and from the looks of things, he was also Bubbles's father. When I added it all up, I didn't like the equation's end result.

"Simon!" I called into the Lodge when I arrived home. "We are *not,* under any circumstances, going into business with Boyce. You have no idea what I just found out about him—"

Keith popped out from behind the new support beams he was installing along the banister of the staircase. "Hey, Max!"

"Hi, Keith," I said, tightening my lips. "I didn't realize you'd be back working so soon. Is Simon around?"

"He's in the kitchen," he answered. "What did you find out about Boyce?"

"Oh, nothing," I said, pretending to be unbothered as I hung up my coat and took off my snowy boots by the door. "Don't worry about it."

Keith set aside a screwdriver and turned his attention to me. "Why don't you want to go into business with Boyce?"

"Don't worry, Keith," I said casually. "You won't be out of a job. We'll find a way to pay you."

"I'm not worried about that." He drew out a hammer and tapped it against his palm. "If you don't go into business with Boyce, it'll be a big mistake."

"Thanks for your advice, but this is something for Simon and me to discuss."

Keith pushed his tongue into his cheek. "Simon wants

Boyce to invest. You're the only one who thinks it's a bad idea."

I took a step back, startled by his accusatory tone. "I'm sorry, are you married to Simon?"

"No, I—"

"Then this isn't your decision," I finished. "I like you, Keith, but you need to mind your own business. Boyce isn't the great man you think he is."

"I know *exactly* what kind of man Boyce is," he said defiantly.

"Did you know Bubbles was his daughter?"

"Yes."

"Have you ever noticed the bruises she's always sporting?"

He shrugged. "She gets in a lot of fights with other kids."

"To cover up what's actually happening at home," I told him. "He's abusing her. You still think he's a good man?"

Keith's jaw unhinged, and he didn't formulate a response. My blood boiling, I left him that way to let the news sink in and went to find Simon.

At first glance, Simon didn't appear to be in the kitchen. I released a sigh of frustration. This wouldn't be an easy conversation, and I wasn't in the mood to chase Simon around the Lodge. As I turned to leave, a small whimper echoed from the corner.

Simon huddled in a ball behind the kitchen table, his good leg tucked as close to his chest as possible. The other stuck straight out in front of him. His crutches lay askew. The whites of his eyes shone, and he trembled violently.

"Simon!" I shoved the table out of the way and dropped to my knees. "What happened? Did you fall?"

His jaw chattered as he tried to speak. Tears ran down his cheeks.

"I saw…" he began.

"You saw what?" I asked softly. "What, honey?"

His finger lifted to point across the room. "I saw Casey."

15

---

*N*o matter how much I tugged at Simon's sleeves, he wouldn't uncurl himself. Finally, I sat next to him, wrapped my arms around him, and rested my head on his shoulder. Several minutes later, the tension in his body unwound. He let go of his knees, his breathing evened out, and he calmed slightly.

"Do you want to tell me what happened?" I asked softly.

Simon buried his face in my shoulder. "It was horrible."

"It's over," I whispered, stroking his hair. "It's gone. Everything's okay."

"I came in to make tea," Simon said hoarsely. "He was standing by the stove, staring at me. He had lesions all over his body. His skin was peeling off."

"Krokodil," I muttered and shook my head.

Also known as desomorphine, Krokodil had been a favorite drug of Simon's parents. It was highly addictive, and when it was illicitly produced, the drug contained toxic contaminants. When injected, Krokodil could damage skin, blood vessels, bone, and muscle, resulting in a zombie-like appearance of those who abused it. The last time we'd seen Casey alive, he was no more than a bag of bones held together by a few stray pieces of flesh. Since they had been identical twins, it was like seeing the devil's side of Simon.

"He begged me to save him," Simon murmured. A stray sob escaped from between his lips. "He said I owed him because I didn't save him the first time."

I took Simon's head between my hands and made him look at me. "Casey's death was not your fault. Neither was his addiction. He was a product of his environment."

"I should have done better," Simon said, crying freely. "I shouldn't have let him go out on his own—"

"He was a grown man who made his own choices," I replied. "He learned those behaviors from your parents. It was *not* your fault."

"I told him to leave," he said. "When he showed up at our house that night, looking for help, I told him to go and never come back. Then he walked into traffic."

I cradled Simon's head against my chest and rocked him until his sobs subsided. "You did everything you could for your brother. Addiction ruined his life, and he didn't want to live like that anymore."

His fingers clutched my waist. "Ever since we got to the Lodge, I've felt like he's been watching me. I've seen him out of the corner of my eye or watching me from the second-floor balcony. Now, he appears right in front of me. Is this what happened to you?"

"Yes," I replied. "Yes, the Lodge made me see things, too."

"It's contagious," he declared. "Whatever illness Lily brought with her."

"Lily's not sick," I said. "She's dead."

Simon finally looked at me. His eyes were red with tears. "What are you talking about?"

I adjusted my position so his weight wasn't so heavy across my legs. "I have to tell you something about the Lodge. I found out about these things called ley lines—"

"Ley lines? What are you talking—?"

"I'll explain if you don't interrupt me," I told him, and he fell quiet. "Ley lines are points of energy that extend all across the globe. When they intersect, the power produced is tenfold…"

So I shared the new knowledge I'd acquired with Simon. Once it was all out in the open—everything from the ley lines to the ghosts to Boyce's obsession with the Lodge—Simon's terror morphed into confusion.

"Are you sure?" he said when I had finished. "It seems a bit…"

"Ridiculous?" I asked. "I thought so, too, but can you think of a logical explanation for all of this?"

"No." He rubbed his temples. "What are we going to do about Bubbles? Do we need proof before we report it to the police?"

"I'm afraid if we report it, we'll make a bigger mess of it than it already is," I said. "Boyce could deny it."

"Besides, the police chief is a member of the Gentlemen's Club," Simon added. "Boyce probably has him in his pocket already."

"And if someone reports Boyce, he could come down harder on Bubbles," I said. "I don't want her to get hurt anymore, especially because of us."

"Then we need proof," he said. "We'll get it. Somehow. I won't let a kid suffer if we can stop it." A moment of silence passed while we both thought the same thing: Simon couldn't save his brother, but he would do his best to save Bubbles. The moment passed, and Simon asked, "So Lily is really dead?"

"I sure am." Lily appeared in the doorway of the kitchen. She looked at me. "You told him, huh?"

"He saw his brother," I explained. "His dead brother."

Lily gave an understanding nod. "I see. Wow, the two of you are both in tune with the energies here. That's pretty wild."

"Why?" Simon asked, suspicious.

"It's rare for it to affect someone so much," she explained. "Most people who have stayed here in the past ten years never realized they were rooming with ghosts. Maybe one or two had reactions and fled the scene."

Simon used the table to lever himself off the floor. "I need some time to process this. Where's Keith?"

"Fixing the banister."

"I'll get him to drive me into town. We can pick up more supplies."

"Don't mention Boyce to Keith," I advised Simon as I handed him his crutches. "The kid's obsessed with him."

Simon waved to acknowledge me. I waited until he and Keith left the Lodge before turning to Lily.

"I think he took that rather well," I said.

She appeared doubtful. "If you say so."

With a pop like a bursting bubble, she vanished. Whether she willed herself to appear and disappear randomly like that was a mystery. As more time passed and the energy from the ley lines grew wily, Lily seemed to have less power and control over her existence.

I let a sigh escape and poured a cup of tea from the kettle Simon had let boil over. Our lives were a mess of tangled lines and relationships. Every time I went looking for answers, I only got more questions.

As I went into the lobby to relax on the old leather sofa, I caught a glimpse of someone leaning on the railing up on the second floor. When I looked up, the fellow disappeared.

"Hey!" I called, changing direction. "Get back here!"

I started up the stairs, tea in hand and my eyes peeled for the elusive ghost. A flash of silver darted across the second floor.

"I just want to talk," I said as I reached the landing. "Please, come out."

The door to the presidential suite squeaked, and I spotted a boot disappearing inside. I headed down the corridor, knocked politely, and let myself in.

We hadn't been inside the presidential suite for weeks. Keith and Simon had made little progress in renovating it, simply because it was so large compared to the rest of the guest rooms. It was still bare. No carpeting, wallboard, or furniture to complete it, but the view from the high windows made the room attractive regardless.

Out on the balcony, a man stood in the same position as I'd seen him on the stairs. He rested his elbow on the railing, crossed one foot behind the other, and gazed off into the distance, seemingly lost in thought. As quietly as possible, I went out to meet him.

"Hello there," he said before I could greet him. "You found me at last."

Tentatively, to not spook him, I joined him at the balcony's edge. "You've been hiding from me."

"Not hiding," he corrected. "Watching. Waiting."

In this form, he looked to be in his mid-forties. He wore thick-rimmed, tortoiseshell glasses and a hand-knit-ted, red sweater. He would look right at home resting on the leather sofa downstairs, next to the fire, with a thick book and perhaps an old pipe to smoke.

"So you bought my lodge, eh?" he asked.

"Your lodge?" I said. "Are you Earl?"

He nodded solemnly and extended his hand. "Earl Driscoll. Pleased to officially meet you."

I shook his ghostly hand. Like Lily, he was solid and warm. His surname registered with me a half-second later. "Did you say *Driscoll?* As in Boyce?"

A sneer lifted Earl's upper lip. "It's bad enough you have to bring that man around my property. You have to mention his name to me, too?"

"I'm sorry, but—the two of you are related?"

"He's my nephew. Little bastard."

The snow piled on the railing melted against my skin,

but I paid it no mind. "Does this have something to do with the ley lines?"

Earl's gaze sharply snapped to mine. "You figure that out, too, huh? Guess I didn't do my job as well as I was supposed to."

"Lily asked me to look into the energy in the Lodge," I explained. "It was affecting all of us too much to ignore it. Can you please explain what all of this means?"

Earl sighed, turned around, and rested his elbows against the balcony. With a sad smile, he regarded the Lodge. "This place has history. Do you know it?"

"Emory Driscoll built it when he discovered the ley line intersection," I reported like a child presenting a homework assignment. "To prevent anyone else from discovering the ley lines."

"Emory Driscoll was my father," Earl said. "He came to Silver Creek for the sole purpose of discovering those ley lines. When he realized how much power they brought to the land—"

"He wanted it all for himself?" I asked wryly.

Earl lifted an eyebrow. "He knew someone *else* might use that power incorrectly. You see, my father had a way with nature, and ley lines are a form of natural energy. My father interacted with the lines' energy the way any gardener tends his plants. He cultivated the power of the ley lines, fed and fertilized it. In return, the energy favored him. Within a year, his wealth doubled. In five, he had more money than he could ever hope to spend in his lifetime. He used it to build up the town of Silver Creek and donated much to charity."

"But someone discovered the ley lines eventually, right?" I asked. "Didn't anyone notice your father's sudden success?"

"His brother did," Earl answered. "Benjamin Driscoll was the walking definition of greed. He refused to work or contribute to society, and yet he believed himself deserving of money and power. When my father grew wealthy, Benjamin grew jealous. He came to Silver Creek and demanded Emory share his secrets."

"What did Emory do?" I asked. The wind picked up. I began to shiver, but Earl's story held me captive.

"He refused to acknowledge a secret," Earl replied. "He told Benjamin that his wealth was a result of luck and street smarts."

"I guess Benjamin didn't buy that?"

Earl shook his head. "He felt the energy of the ley lines, even if he didn't quite know what they were. He knew my father's power came from the land, so he became determined to claim it for himself."

"He tried to oust his brother," I guessed.

"He tried to kill his brother," Earl rectified. "One night, while Emory was sleeping, Benjamin snuck into his room with a knife and stabbed him. Thankfully, Emory was expecting a betrayal of some sort and managed to roll out of the way. Benjamin only nicked his arm. He had the scar for the rest of his life."

My teeth chattered. "What happened after? Did they fight?"

"Emory had the energy of the ley lines on his side," Earl explained. "He used this power to drive Benjamin from Silver Creek. He forced Benjamin to forget about our side of the family. For years, the ley lines were safe."

"And then?" I prompted, reading the sad look on Earl's face.

"Benjamin had a son, then a grandson," he replied. "The grandson bore all the same traits as Benjamin. He was greedy and privileged and thought the world should hand him whatever he wanted on a silver platter."

"Boyce," I said darkly.

"When Boyce arrived in Silver Creek over ten years ago, I was the keeper and protector of the Lodge and the ley lines," Earl said, his chest puffing proudly. "My father had passed and assigned the responsibility to me. With my wife, we nursed the energy as he had, and we too lived in beautiful comfort." Earl deflated as the next thought crossed his mind. "I didn't know who Boyce was at first. He was careful not to share his last name with me, and he showed no interest in the Lodge or the ley lines. He was simply another guest, come to stay for the winter. He had little money and could only afford the smallest room at the rear of the Lodge."

"The one positioned right over the intersection," I said.

Earl nodded. "One night, Boyce performed a brutal ritual. He forced the ley lines to feed him energy. When the ritual took, I felt it shake the earth. I woke in my bed, knowing something had gone terribly wrong. By the time I found Boyce, it was too late. He had abused the earth's energies, and the ley lines had little left to give. It wasn't until later that I uncovered all the horrible effects of his abhorrent ritual."

"Like trapping the spirits of those who died on the property?" I asked.

"Precisely," he said. "For years after Boyce's ritual, I tried to fix the problem, but the ley lines recovered at a glacial pace. Even now, they are unpredictable. The lines have regained some of their former strength, but it is not constant. Without that energy, I never discovered how to send these poor spirits through to the other side."

"Then you got stuck here yourself," I said. "What about your wife? Is she here, too?"

A cleft appeared in Earl's chin. "My wife didn't die on the property. She passed in the hospital. Even in death, we are not reunited."

"Oh, Earl."

He wiped invisible tears from his eyelashes. "It matters not. I *will* find a way to be with her again. I refuse to give up."

"I'll help," I offered. "I have no idea what I'm doing, but Lily says it's rare to find someone who feels the ley lines' power like I do. What can I do?"

"The best thing you can do to help is to keep Boyce off this land," he answered. "That man ruined everything. And if he gets the chance, he'll do it again."

"Again?" I repeated. "Why would he need to do it again?"

"The ritual he performed loses its effectiveness after a certain amount of time," Earl said. "He's losing money as we speak. He won't be able to turn a profit until he repeats the ritual."

"How do we stop him?" I asked.

"Keep the room locked," Earl advised. "I had Walter install that safe for the sole purpose of keeping Boyce out of there. If he finds a way to get in, he'll repeat his ritual for sure. Ever since I died, he's been trying to buy the Lodge, but there's still a bit of power in the ley lines. The energy sensed you and Simon would be better protectors, so it orchestrated your ownership of the Lodge."

I hugged myself tightly, unsure how to feel. According to Earl, it wasn't the bank that had decided we were the best owners for the Lodge. It was the ley lines. Was all of this predetermined?

"How did you figure out who Boyce was?" I asked. "How did he figure out who *you* were if Emory banished that side of the family from Silver Creek?"

"Before Emory used the ley lines to erase Benjamin's memory, effectively Benjamin kept a journal of his escapades," Earl explained. "Boyce, the snooping idiot, found them in his grandfather's things. That's how he learned about Silver Creek, me, and the ley lines. After the ritual, it became obvious to me who he was. I remembered what the land felt like when my father banished Benjamin. The land recognized Boyce before I did. The energy tried to warn me, but I didn't understand."

"What about this ritual?" I said. "Why was it so horrible? What could Boyce have done to affect the ley lines that much?"

"The ley lines favor those with good intention," Earl said. "It is why my father had so much prosperity here. People like Benjamin and Boyce would not have been able to harvest the energy as my father did. They needed rituals to use the energy, and such rituals are not good for the land or for the people who get in the way."

"What do you mean?"

The lines around Earl's mouth deepened. "How much do you know about your friend Lily?"

PERHAPS THE LEY lines sensed I was searching for Lily because they lent her the energy to appear. I found her in the lobby, lounging on the leather sofa and gazing longingly through the front windows. For the umpteenth time, I wondered how a ghost could have borrowed my clothes.

"I talked to Earl," I said.

She jumped a little, obviously not expecting me. "About time. I've been telling him to catch you up."

"Well, I understand that he wanted to make sure I was trustworthy first." I sat next to her and pulled a throw blanket across my lap. "He told me some things about you. Things about your accident."

A line appeared between her brows. "Like what?"

"You know these things already," I said. "But you've forgotten them to protect yourself. Are you sure you want me to tell you about it?"

She squeezed my knee. "I can handle it."

"Do you remember when we found you?" I asked her. "When you got out of the car, you said someone was chasing you. You begged us to hide you. Do you remember who was following you at all?"

Her brows scrunched together as she fought to recall

that night. She shook her head. "I don't remember anything. I just know I felt like I was in danger."

"You were," I said. "Because the Gentlemen's Club boxed you in on the main road and forced you to drive up toward the Lodge."

"The Gentlemen's Club?" she asked. "You mean, Boyce's fanboys?"

"The originals," I confirmed. "He gathered a group of followers when he first arrived in Silver Creek and shared the knowledge of the ley lines. He promised to share the wealth with them if they helped him complete a ritual to harness the energy of the land. Unfortunately, the ritual required a sacrifice: one pure soul to feed to the land."

Lily stared blankly at me. "I don't get it."

"You didn't die when you crashed your car, Lily," I told her. "The Gentlemen's Club pulled you out and took you to the Lodge, where Boyce was waiting for you. When the time was right, he and his Club murdered you and infused your blood with the power of the ley lines. Anyone who was anointed with it became wealthy and successful overnight."

Lily's lower lip trembled as she fought to control her reaction to this news. "No, that can't be right. I died in a car crash. I wasn't a sacrifice—"

"It's why you're stuck here," I said. "The place where you crashed your car isn't on the Lodge's property. You didn't die there. You died in the hidden room above the ley line intersection."

When Keith's truck rumbled into the front yard, Lily let out a scared squeak and disappeared once more. I looked outside and realized why. Keith and Simon had returned from town with a visitor in tow: none other than Boyce Driscoll himself.

As I spied from the window, Boyce was his usual charming self. He chuckled politely at something Keith said and clapped Simon on the back as if they were brothers. Simon, who was usually happy to entertain Boyce, now looked at him with contempt. He hid it well, lingering behind the older, well-dressed man so Boyce couldn't see the rage on Simon's face.

Earl appeared at the top of the stairs, fuming. "He's back again, eh? Tell him to fu—"

"I'll handle it," I promised Earl. "Go hide somewhere."

Earl stayed in place right until Boyce stepped onto the porch. As Boyce's boot crossed the threshold, Earl vanished in the same manner as Lily had.

"Maxine!" Boyce cooed, spreading his arms wide. "It's good to see you. I spotted Simon and Keith in town and decided to check up on the two of you. I do believe it's my fault for getting Simon into such a predicament."

I clenched my teeth and smiled. "Well, he *did* tell you he wasn't very good and skiing. I heard you made him try a more difficult slope anyway."

"He was doing so well!"

Once more, Boyce thumped Simon on the back. A muscle in Simon's jaw jumped like he was holding back a yelp of pain. My face grew hot. More than ever, I wanted to punch Boyce in the face and show him what it felt like to be at the other end of a fist.

"I never thought he'd run into a tree," Boyce continued

and let out another one of his stupid chuckles. "He gave it the ol' college try."

"Did you want something?" I asked with forced politeness, and Keith caught wind of my edgy tone and shot me a warning look. "I'm afraid we're tight on timeline today."

"Of course you are. I won't intrude for long." He took a small envelope from his pocket and presented it to me with a flourish. "Take this as an apology. You are cordially invited to the first annual Silver Creek Winter Gala."

I pulled a fancy silver invitation from the envelope. "It's next week already?"

"A bit last minute, I know," Boyce said. "But all this holiday cheer got me in the mood to do something good. All the proceeds from the gala go to less fortunate families. You must come."

I glanced at Simon, who shook his head.

"We'll be there," I said.

16

*T*hat night, Lily, Simon, and I found ourselves sitting together in the living room. A box of half-eaten pizza lay open on the floor. Lily and I lounged on the couch, while Simon rested on the floor in front of me. He laid his head against my knees, often reaching back to squeeze my calves or feet as if to make sure I was still there.

We didn't talk much. We ate in relative silence, aside from the pizza-chewing and soda-slurping. It was almost like we didn't need to speak. Everyone knew what everyone else was thinking: what were we supposed to do next?

On the one hand, it was good to have everything out in the open. With a fresh understanding of the situation, we could cope with it better. Plus, lying to and fighting with Simon had taken so much out of me. Now that we were on the same side, we could get back to normal.

I caressed his hair, absentmindedly pulling each curl

and watching it spring back into place. For the first time in weeks, the lines on his face weren't etched so deeply. His eyes sleepily drifted shut as he leaned against me and enjoyed the feel of my fingers through his hair. I touched his neck and felt his pulse fluttering beneath my finger-tips. This simple contact reminded me of everything Simon and I had been through together and why I'd chosen him to be my partner for the rest of my life.

Next to me, Lily snuggled with a fluffy throw pillow that had appeared out of nowhere. She hugged it to her chest and wore a crocheted blanket around her shoulders like a cape. Her energy waxed and waned with the power of the ley lines, which resulted in her sporadic comings and goings. Sometimes, she only appeared for a few seconds. Other times, she managed to stick it out for a while longer. Tonight, the ley lines had given her enough energy to spend a good thirty minutes with us so far. There was a price, though; her skin was pale and drawn. She appeared sickly, as she did when we first happened upon her.

All wrapped up in blankets and pillows, Lily looked far younger than her age. Her wide-eyed gaze, small frame, and childlike innocence reminded me of Bubbles. They both needed help, and Simon and I were the only ones who could give it to them.

Bubbles was an entirely new problem. My heart ached for her in ways I couldn't describe. I recalled our first conversation and how floored I was that someone in the tiny town of Silver Creek happened to be a *Rebel Queen* fan. With her help, I had made the first steps toward progress on plotting volume three of my comic book series. Bubbles, more than anyone else, had made an impact on me. All I wanted was to give her the same courtesy. First, I had to figure out how to do it.

"Snow," Lily murmured.

Simon and I drew our attention out of our heads and looked toward the windows. Sure enough, big flakes of snow serenely floated from the sky and alighted on the ground outside. They perched on the porch railing and the roof of the car like tiny, perfect birds. Before long, too much snow had fallen to see the individual flakes.

No matter how many times the weather turned cold enough to snow, I never tired of it. Yes, it was freezing outside. Yes, the sky stayed a depressing shade of gray. But there was something about snow that comforted me. It was quiet and calm. It covered everything with a blanket of comfort.

I imagined what the Lodge might look like in six months or a year if everything went according to plan. This lobby would be the coziest place to watch the snowfall. Guests could read or relax by the fire, drink hot chocolate from the kitchen, and enjoy the smell of whatever our chef was cooking up that day in the kitchen. The Lodge itself would be beautiful, the type of place no one would want to leave.

"What are you thinking about?" Simon asked.

I hadn't realized he'd been looking at me. My eyebrows and mouth were set in determination. "I want to take down Boyce Driscoll."

Lily drew her toes closer to her body and tucked them

under the blanket. "A few people have tried. None have succeeded."

"They didn't know what we know about him," I said. "He's a killer, a child abuser, a thief, and an extortionist. I want to put him in jail. Everyone in Silver Creek would be better off without him. He's dangerous."

"He's the biggest contributor to the community," Simon pointed out. "This town runs because of his money. I want to get rid of him as much as you do, but no one will support us. No one will *believe* us. Either that, or they'll be too scared to oust him."

I crossed my arms and sank into the couch cushions. "He can't be allowed to do what he did and face no consequences. It's wrong."

"There *is* one thing you might be able to do," Lily said in a small voice.

Simon and I swiveled to look at her.

"Yes?" I prompted when she didn't spit it out right away.

Lily trembled and clutched her pillow tighter. "The energy of this land is fickle, but it favors those who nourish it."

I nodded. "Earl said the same thing. He compared himself and his father to gardeners, and the ley lines rewarded them for it."

"Likewise, the energy resents people who try to use it for personal gain," Lily said. "Every time Boyce sets foot on this land, I can feel the ley lines throbbing. The land wants him gone, too."

"Why isn't he smote when he steps on the property

then?" I asked, wishing the ley lines had the power to jettison Boyce across the country and into the next dimension.

"Because the land needs a vessel for its energy," Lily explained. "Someone to control it."

"Are we meant to have a wizards' duel with Boyce then?" Simon asked, dryly.

"Something of the sort," Lily said. "You could lure Boyce here, get him in the room above the intersection, and use the power of the ley lines to get rid of him. The land hates him so much that no one would ever hear of him again."

"That would certainly solve our problems," I muttered.

"But how does it work?" Simon asked. "If we use the land's energy, are we killing him? If he dies, it doesn't make us any better than him. Besides, you said yourself the land doesn't like when people use its energy to further their agenda."

"Loopholes," Lily replied. "If you get rid of Boyce, the ley lines can fully recover from the damage he did to them ten years ago. The land will reward you for banishing him, and your business here at the Lodge will thrive, as it did for Earl and his father."

"What's the catch?" Simon asked, wryly. "It can't be that easy."

Lily nervously chewed her lip. "You won't know if the ley lines are going to take your side until you get in the safe room with Boyce."

"There it is," Simon said.

"What are our chances?" I asked Lily.

"I can help you," she said. "The spirits in this house are fueled by the ley lines. You've already made friends with some of them. We can guide the land's energy, convince it to side with you."

Simon made an uncomfortable noise in the back of his throat. "This sounds dicey at best and incredibly dangerous at worst."

"I'll do it," I declared. "Someone has to take up Earl's legacy. The land trusted us enough to let us buy the Lodge. It will trust us enough to get rid of Boyce."

FOR THE FIRST time in weeks, Simon and I slept entwined. My legs rested over his hips. His arms encircled my shoulders. Our fingers locked together. Our body heat kept us so warm that we kicked off the covers—anything to stay together.

"I owe you an apology," Simon murmured.

I startled. I thought he was asleep.

"I'm sorry for the way I've been acting," he continued. "I thought you were making the wrong choices for no reason. I should have believed you when you told me letting Boyce invest was a bad idea. I'm sorry for blaming Lily for driving a wedge between us. I'm sorry for—"

"Hey." I caught his chin and placed a soft kiss on his lips. "I know, baby. I made mistakes, too. I should have been more honest with you about the Lodge and how it's been making me feel. I'm sorry, too."

He lightly traced the outline of my collarbone. "When

you stepped off the roof that day… what really happened?"

"A woman named Christine Higgins hung herself from that tree," I said, shuddering at the thought of it. "Her husband had been abusing her. That night, the energy made me feel like stepping off the roof—like she did— would solve all my problems. Like freedom was only one step away."

"But you're not suicidal?"

"No, baby."

He pressed his forehead against mine and cupped my neck. "I love you so much. I can't lose you."

"You won't."

"What if this thing with Boyce goes wrong?" he asked. "What if the ley lines won't cooperate with us?"

I pushed his curls away from his eyes. "Then we'll take comfort in knowing we tried everything we could to make things right."

MUCH OF THE next week passed without incident. With Lily's help, Simon drove off additional sightings of his dead brother. Throughout the day, I spotted Simon sitting quietly in a corner with his eyes closed. The combination of Lily's influence and this meditation tactic seemed to work; he had no further run-ins with nightmarish ghosts.

Additionally, his knee recovery was off to a good start. Three times a week, I drove Simon into town for physical therapy. It gave us both a break from the building energy at the Lodge. While Simon did his therapy, I worked on *Rebel Queen: Volume Three* in the nearby cafe.

For a reason I couldn't explain, my writer's block had resolved itself. I knew exactly what I wanted to do with the Queen's character, what decisions she should make, and how they would impact her. All thanks to one person.

"Bubbles!"

I waved across the cafe when I saw the pre-teen come in. When she spotted me, she smiled softly. For once, she didn't appear to have any fresh bruises. She held up a finger for me to wait and ordered at the counter. Then she came over to my table.

"Can I sit here?" she asked, clambering into the booth before I could give her an answer.

"Of course." I cleared my drawings and materials from her side of the table. "I have your coat in my car, by the way. Don't let me forget to give it to you on the way out."

Bubbles's smile faded slightly. The last time we'd seen each other, she'd run away because I'd figured out what was happening at her home. Hopefully, her joining me meant she was willing to let me help her.

"I have a bunch of coats like that one," she said. Sure enough, she wore a similar coat today, though the sleeves were shorter as if it was last year's style. She rifled through my half-completed drawings and notes for my storylines. "Are you writing?"

"I sure am," I said, beaming. "You inspired me."

"Me?"

"Yes, you." I prodded her with the butt end of a marker. "You were the one who made me realize why I

239

liked writing *Rebel Queen* to begin with, *and* you reminded me of all the important themes in the story."

Bubbles blushed and tucked her chin into her chest. "I was just telling you what I liked about your series. You're the one who wrote it."

"But you're the reader I've always dreamed of," I said. "I started drawing and writing stories because it was an outlet for all the hard things I couldn't process. But the reason I decided to publish my stories was to help other people. If the Queen inspired one other person to live more authentically, I considered my job a success."

"Do you think I'm authentic?" Bubbles asked.

"You are so much more than authentic," I assured her. "You're brave. Strong. Crafty. Stubborn. That's not always a bad thing," I added in response to the questioning look on her face. "Stubborn means resilient. You always bounce back."

She blushed again. "I never stood up for myself until I started reading your comic books," she said. "If it weren't for the Queen, I feel like I'd be much worse off."

I studied her over the lip of my coffee cup. "How are you doing? I haven't seen you picking any fights recently. Did you give that up?"

She scratched the scab on her ear that was almost healed. "Temporarily," she said quietly. "I haven't needed to pick any fights."

"You mean you haven't needed to cover up any bruises from home," I corrected her.

"You can't tell anyone," she hissed across the table.

"He'll get mad if you do. My mom tried to go to the police years ago. He almost killed her."

I swallowed hard and tried not to let the pain I felt for Bubbles show in my expression. "He hurts your Mom, too?"

Bubbles glanced around at the empty cafe before nodding. "He won't let us leave. He makes Mom feel guilty for thinking about it. He hits me when I stand up for us, which I've been doing more often."

"No one else in town knows about this?" I asked in a hushed tone. "Surely, someone else must have noticed all your bruises. Your mom must look injured, too."

"He mostly hurts her where people can't see," Bubbles explained. "And she doesn't go into town often. He won't let her work. He says her job is to stay home and take care of him."

I pinched my lip between my teeth, holding back rage. "Your father is the kind of man the Queen would hunt and kill."

"Why do you think I like your books so much?" she asked dryly. "If I had the Queen's powers, I would have rescued my mom already."

"Don't worry," I told her. "I have a plan."

Her eyes widened. "You can't do anything rash. He'll find a way to hurt you. Please, Max. Don't be stupid."

I leaned over the table and beckoned her closer. "Think of me as your Rebel Queen, Bubbles. I'll vanquish the villain."

I winked at her.

. . .

SIMON REFUSED to let his knee injury stop him from working on the Lodge. With Keith's help, he installed new flooring, put up wallboard, painted, and repaired whatever he could. He hobbled around one-legged, using whatever was around to prop himself up, from his crutches to broken furniture to the new toilets we hadn't had time to install in the rooms yet. When I wasn't writing volume three, I spent most of my time helping Simon "fix" things. He wasn't fooled.

"You don't have to babysit me," he said one day when I followed him into the kitchen. He hopped to the sink and filled a cup with water. "The therapist said I could work as long as I don't put too much weight on the knee."

"I know," I said. "I'm not babysitting. I'm helping you renovate."

"You missed the nail and hit your thumb with the hammer six times already," he said. "Because you were too busy watching me make sure I'm not hurting myself."

I hid my bruised thumb behind my back. "I'm *not* watching you."

"Then stop trying to help." He kissed my temple to offset the brusque order. "You're distracting me. Besides, I've got Keith. He handles what I can't."

Keith worked overtime every day. He arrived at dawn and stayed well past dusk to help us with the renovations. Despite our uncomfortable stand-off last week regarding Boyce, his pleasant manner had returned. He was all smiles, and he often arrived with fresh coffee and breakfast sandwiches for all of us in the mornings.

"Hiya, Max," he said at the end of one day, bounding

into the lobby with a handful of pretzels while I worked on *Rebel Queen.* He peered over my shoulder at the half-finished pages. "Wow, that's really coming along. Great job."

"Thanks, Keith." I closed my portfolio and set it aside, away from his prying eyes. "Hey, what do you like to do for fun around here? Once the Lodge is finished and we're not constantly working, I'd like to spend more time in the town."

He popped a pretzel into his mouth and chewed loudly. "Hmm, there's not much to do here except ski, hike, or camp. Silver Creek is super outdoorsy. In the summer, it's all about river rafting and trail biking."

"That sounds fun," I said. "What about groups I could join? I wouldn't mind getting to know some new people. You and Simon have the Gentlemen's Club. Is there an equivalent for the women in Silver Creek?"

"Totally!" he said, spraying me with pretzel crumbs. "Boyce's wife, Marcy, leads a book club. I think they meet up once a month at Boyce's house."

"Great! How do I join?"

Keith threw a pretzel in the air and caught it with his mouth. "Marcy will be at the gala tomorrow night. Introduce yourself to her and let her know you're interested in the book club. You'll be a shoo-in."

"The gala is tomorrow night already?"

"Yup." He bounced on his toes. "I got a new suit and everything. I'm so excited. Aren't you?"

I faked a smile. "*So* excited."

Simon hopped in on his crutches. "You getting out of here, Keith?"

"I was going to finish the molding in that second-floor bathroom," Keith said, mouth still full of snacks.

Simon waved him off. "It's late. Go home. We can finish it next week. Enjoy your weekend."

Keith put on his coat and hat. "I'll see you two at the gala, right? It's going to be huge. You can't miss it."

"We won't," I promised.

Keith waved goodbye and headed out. His headlights drew white beams against the dark trees. Simon plopped down next to me on the couch.

"I've never seen a dude so excited to wear a tux and go to a ball," he said.

"Something tells me he's excited for more than the gala," I muttered darkly. I stood up to watch Keith's truck roll out of the parking lot. I wondered if he would go straight home or not. "Hey, Simon? We're all out of hot chocolate mix. Do you mind if I pick some up in town?"

He lifted his head from the couch. "Right now?"

I slipped my arms into my coat without waiting for his answer. "Yeah, I'm really craving it. You'll be okay by yourself for an hour, right?"

"Sure, I'll be fine. Do you want me to go with you, though? It's dark out. The streets are icy."

"Don't worry," I said. "I'll manage. You relax. I made your favorite bolognese sauce. It's waiting for you in the kitchen." With that, I placed a kiss on his forehead, put on my boots, and headed out into the cold night.

. . .

As MUCH AS I loved snow, I hated driving in it. It piled up in the corners of the windshield, blocked the side mirrors, and transformed the winding, single-lane road that led to and from the Lodge into an icy death trap. My blood drummed as I inched downhill, squinting over the dashboard to see through the flurries. When I passed the dented tree that marked the spot where Lily crashed her car all those years ago, a shudder started at the top of my head and made its way all the way down to my toes.

Keith's truck was too big for him to maneuver it any faster down the hill, so I caught up with him with relative ease on the main road. I stayed a few car lengths back, so he wouldn't suspect I was following him. As I suspected, he didn't head toward his mother's cute house in the nearby neighborhood. Rather, he turned in the opposite direction, toward a part of town I had yet to visit.

A few minutes later, he pulled into the parking lot of a small, ugly bar. With a tin roof, shabby walls, and garish neon signs advertising the various beers sold there, the bar didn't appear particularly inviting. Almost all pick-up trucks were parked outside, and most of them had some sort of camouflage accessory. If I had to guess, this bar catered to the hunting crowd.

Keith got out of his truck and jogged inside, blowing warm air into his hands. I parked my car around the side of the bar and followed him in.

Surprisingly, the inside of the bar was rather cheerful. Christmas lights were strung across the ceiling. A few windowsills sported Menorahs and dreidels as if the owners wanted to make sure everyone felt at home this holiday. The place was warm and smelled like cinnamon, not at all the beer and cigarettes vibe I was expecting.

I stayed hidden behind a crowded high-top as Keith shook off his coat and sat in a shadowy booth toward the back of the bar. One person was already there, nursing a goblet of dark beer. When he leaned forward, the light overhead illuminated his face.

"Boyce," I muttered. "Of course."

With my hat on and my hood up, I casually made my way across the bar. Keeping my face out of Boyce and Keith's view, I hopped onto an empty barstool adjacent to their booth. As I ordered a beer, their voices floated out to meet me.

"Well?" Boyce asked. "Is everything in place?"

"I got the safe combination," Keith said, pulling a tattered piece of paper from his pocket. "The stupid old man wrote it down and kept it hidden under a floorboard."

Boyce accepted the paper. "You've certainly earned your place amongst the Gentlemen's Club, Keith. To think, I didn't believe you had the stones. What of the Lodge's residents?"

"They're coming to the gala," Keith replied. "We'll get Max alone and bring her to you at the Lodge around midnight, while everyone is distracted by the final auction."

"I'll finally be able to complete the ritual," Boyce said. "With that insufferable Max as a sacrifice."

17

"*A*re you sure that's what he said?"

Simon paced back and forth. The crutches clanked against the new flooring with each of Simon's steps. He wasn't pleased to find out I'd followed Keith instead of buying hot chocolate, but he'd quickly gotten over it when I gave him the info.

"I'm positive," I said. "The gala is just a distraction for the rest of the town. Boyce plans on kidnapping me and using me for his next ritual. Tomorrow night."

Simon's left crutch got caught on the corner of the sofa. He stumbled, and I put a hand on his chest to steady him. "I can't believe this," he muttered, finally sitting down. "This is what we get for risking it all. Move to a town and get sacrificed for some bizarre human ritual."

"You're safe," I reminded him. "They don't want you."

Lily, who'd been popping in and out of the conversation as much as the Lodge's energy would allow, appeared by the fireplace. "It's because Max is more in tune with the land. Boyce can feel it when he interacts with you. If he sacrifices someone who's close to the land, it will improve his outcome."

"What about you?" I asked her. "What tie did you have to this land?"

"I was born here," she revealed. "In the room above the intersection before Earl closed it off. I'm tied to this land more than anyone else. Except maybe Earl and Emory. Boyce must have found out who I was and decided I was the perfect target."

"Well, he's not getting Max," Simon said ferociously. "I'll shoot him before he lays a hand on her."

"Let's not be rash." I rested my hand on his knee. "We have to look at this in a positive way. At least we know what Boyce is planning. We can come up with our own plan."

"Our own plan?" Simon repeated. "We're not schemers, Max. We're artists."

"Art requires creativity," I told him. "We're nothing if not creative. If you think about it, this is kind of perfect. Where does Boyce want to do the ritual? In the safe room. Where did Lily suggest we should banish him with the power of the ley lines?"

Simon lifted an eyebrow. "I hope you're not suggesting what I think you're suggesting."

"Let him kidnap me," I proposed with a shrug that looked more nonchalant than I felt. "He'll take me into the safe room, thinking he's in the clear for the ritual. Then Lily and the other spirits will join us, and we'll take him out instead."

"No way," Simon said. "I'm not letting some lunatic drag you from a party and do whatever he wants with you."

"It's a trick," I reminded him. "Boyce will think he's winning. He'll think he's getting his way. Then we'll take him by surprise and save the day."

Simon shook his head. "Nope. If I can't guarantee your safety, I'm not agreeing to it."

"Tomorrow's the winter solstice," Lily interjected. "And it's a full moon. No wonder Boyce planned his party then."

"What does that have to do with anything?" Simon asked.

Before Lily could reply, she disappeared with a slight *pop!* A second later, she reappeared on the stairs, looking nauseous.

"Ugh," she groaned. "It's getting worse." She came down the stairs and laid next to me on the couch. "Remember the energies here are all-natural. They come from the earth and the land. The Winter Solstice marks the shortest day of the year. Many people believed it was good luck when the solstice coincided with the full moon. It gives the land extra power."

"So Boyce is going to be super-powered?" Simon said. "Then we're *definitely* not participating in this craziness. We'll get out of town tonight, lay low in Breckenridge or something. When this blows over and it's safe, we'll come back."

"Safe for how long?" I asked. "Boyce will just try again next month."

Simon threw up his arms. "Then we'll leave! We'll move again. Get out of here and let someone else figure all of this out."

Lily vanished again. This time, she seemed to do it willingly.

I took Simon's hand. "Do you remember why you wanted to move here? You were so excited to have a place of your own. To renovate the Lodge and make this into the ultimate honeymoon destination."

"I changed my mind when the ghosts and murderers came out of the woodwork," he grumbled.

"We can get rid of the murderer," I said. "And we can help the ghosts. This place is magical. I feel it. You feel it. We can't give it up so easily. We can't betray Lily and Earl and the other people who are trapped here. We can't let Boyce keep doing what he's doing."

Simon's lip curled at the mention of Boyce's name. "I do hate that guy."

"Then let's make sure he gets what he deserves," I said. "That way, Bubbles and the rest of Silver Creek will be safe."

He touched my cheek. "You really want to do this?"

"I'm always writing about strong characters overcoming the worst of the worst," I told him. "It's time I started doing that in my own life, too."

Simon nodded. "Well said, my Queen."

THE ONLY CLOTHING I had fancy enough for Boyce Driscoll's Winter Charity Gala was the racy red dress I'd worn to Christian and Sienna's wedding. When the time came to put it on, Simon let out a low whistle.

"I forgot how good you look in that dress," he murmured into my neck, pulling me close.

As he zipped the dress for me, his fingers drew a swift line up the middle of my back. Warmth grew in my stomach and spread outward. The magnetic pull—now familiar to me—persuaded me to turn around and face Simon. I laced my arms around his neck and kissed him deeply.

"Wow," he said, breathless when I pulled away. "What was that for?"

"I felt like it."

Another kiss later, and the zipper of my dress came undone again.

"You have the pepper spray, right?"

"Strapped to my thigh like a sexy spy with a Glock."

"You are definitely sexy," Simon replied. "But can you get to it if Boyce overpowers you?"

I lifted the fabric around my thigh. The slit went high enough to give me easy access to the small can tucked into my garter. Simon's breath whooshed out of his lungs at the sight of my smooth skin.

"Easy access," I said, demonstrating how I would grab the pepper spray quickly if I needed it. "See?"

"Okay, put it away before I have to take you to bed again," Simon said, chuckling.

I let the dress fall back into place. No one would be

able to see the pepper spray unless they stuck their head under my skirt, at which point I would have a very different problem.

"Ready, lovebirds?" Lily asked. As usual, she had graced the staircase with her ethereal presence. When she saw us dressed in our best duds, she beamed proudly. "I didn't think Simon owned anything other than flannel shirts and worn-out jeans."

Simon adjusted his three-piece suit so the vest sat neatly beneath the jacket. Like me, he decided to wear the same outfit he'd worn to his best friend's wedding. The suit's velvet green fabric complemented my red dress quite nicely. Together, we looked like a walking Christmas commercial.

"Very funny," Simon said to Lily. "It's not fair to judge when I haven't had an opportunity to dress up yet. This knee brace doesn't do me any favors, though."

Over his slacks, he'd position the bulky metal knee brace that would help him walk without his crutches. He wasn't pleased with the idea of not being mobile while I was in potential danger.

"You look great." Lily straightened Simon's lapels and plucked a stray thread from my neckline. "Everything's going to go according to plan tonight."

"Can I get that in writing?" Simon teased.

Her eyes twinkled in response. If she wasn't dead, I might have been nervous that she and Simon were catching feelings for one another. As it was, I was happy they were getting along again.

"We'll be here to protect Max," Lily assured Simon. "I

filled everyone in, and we're all on high alert. When Boyce gets here, we'll be ready."

Lily's words were no joke. When we got in the car and drove away, I glanced back at the Lodge. The windows were lined with a row of pale, ghostly faces.

Simon looked in the rear view mirror and shuddered. "I don't think I've ever seen anything that creepy."

"They want to protect us," I reminded him. "They're on our side."

"Still."

NEITHER ONE OF us had been to Boyce's estate before. Like the Lodge, it was set apart from the rest of Silver Creek, about fifteen minutes away from the town's center. Unlike the Lodge, an actual road led through the woods towards the estate. Stylistic street lamps lined the way; each one wore a glistening white hat of snow.

"It's really coming down," Simon said, leaning closer to the steering wheel and squinting through the windshield. "Did the weather report mention a store like this—whoa!"

Out of nowhere, we hit traffic. A line of cars curved toward the estate, their brake lights glowing in the flurry. By the looks of things, Boyce had invited the entire town to this so-called gala.

Slowly but surely, we inched toward a huge wrought-iron gate. The name *Driscoll* had been twisted into the metal so everyone knew who owned the massive plot of land and the buildings upon it. The snow made it difficult to see much else. As we followed the line of cars up a mile-long cobblestone driveway, we got our first view of the house.

It was enormous, easily wider than two football fields end to end. The manor resembled an English country house, as if Boyce had gone abroad, pointed to the largest estate he'd seen, and asked his architects to duplicate it. The house, the garden, and the land looked like something right out of a Jane Austen novel. I practically expected Mr. Darcy to come marching from the foyer.

"Who needs this much space?" Simon muttered. "What could you possibly do with all the rooms in a house like this?"

"Half the town must work here to keep it clean," I added.

"Did Bubbles tell you it was like this?"

"She hasn't said anything about her house." I craned my neck to see the roof of the manor. "Good God, it has a rooftop bar."

"I can't imagine growing up in a place like this," Simon said. "It makes me mad. People are living on the streets with nothing, but Boyce has this whole place to himself. It's disgusting."

"People with money tend to only care about keeping it," I commented. "Not benefiting other people."

"Your parents had money," Simon reminded me. "You're the most generous person I know."

"I wouldn't go that far. My parents were comfortable middle class." I gestured to the elaborate circular driveway that took us closer to the front door. "This is way beyond the kind of money we had."

"Still," Simon said. "Your family was willing to give it away."

At a snail's pace, we finally reached the front of the ridiculous manor. A valet opened our doors and took Simon's place in the driver's seat.

"Where are you parking it?" Simon asked.

"Around the side of the manor, sir," replied the valet, pointing to the far edge of the property. "Don't worry. When you need it, we'll go get it for you."

Simon couldn't make a fuss without alerting others to our plan for the evening, but it would be mighty inconvenient to wait for a valet to get the car when Simon might have to make a quick getaway later.

"Can you park it there instead?" Simon indicated a patch of gravel that was unoccupied. "I don't mean to be a bother, but my knee is quite sore. If I have to leave early, I don't want to wait for a valet."

The valet nodded. "Of course, sir."

As the driver pulled the car into Simon's preferred space, I linked my arm through Simon's. "Nice job, baby," I murmured to him. "You sounded like a real snob."

He grinned. "Just trying to fit in."

As if the party wasn't ostentatious enough, a glorious red carpet led from the driveway all the way inside the house. We joined the crowd heading in. I recognized a few familiar faces: the baristas from the cafe, Charles, the librarian, and the doctor who'd diagnosed me with post-traumatic stress disorder. No one wanted to miss out on Boyce's lavish party.

The cause for the event was not advertised. No charities were invited to attend the "charity gala," yet the guests did not bat an eyelash as they signed up for raffle tickets and looked at items for auction. The grand prize was a trip for two to the Bahamas, and it was to be auctioned off right at midnight. Shortly before, we expected Boyce to make his move on me.

After we checked our coats and moved deeper into the main area of the house, we spotted Keith in his brand-new suit.

"Act normal," Simon muttered in my ear as he guided me across the gilded marble floor. "We've got to sell this."

"I'm gonna kill him," I whispered back. A second later, I pasted on a bright smile. "Hi, Keith! Wow, look at those slick threads."

Keith kissed me on both cheeks. "Thanks, Max. You both look great. What do you think of Boyce's house?" He spread his arms and beamed as if the house belonged to him.

"It's big," Simon said.

"Very big," I added.

Keith grabbed two flutes of champagne from a passing waiter and handed them to us. Simon shook his head, and Keith kept the second glass for himself. He gazed at the detailed ceiling high above us.

"Boyce said if I play my cards right, I might be able to afford a place like this someday," he said.

"If you play your cards right, huh?" I asked through clenched teeth. "What does that mean?"

He shrugged. "You know. Go back to school, get an education, find a good job. That kind of thing."

"It's harder than it sounds," Simon advised him. "People don't often find jobs *this* good."

"Boyce has an opportunity lined up for me," Keith said, puffing out his chest. "Once I'm finished at the Lodge, he's going to train me to work for his company."

"What exactly does his company do?" I asked.

Keith was saved from answering when a thin woman in a silver dress politely tapped my shoulder.

"Excuse me?" she said. "Are you Maxine Finch?"

"I certainly am."

The woman's eyes glistened with moisture like she was on the verge of tears. "I'm Elizabeth's mother. She's told me so much about you."

"I'm sorry. Whose mother?"

She pointed across the room. Bubbles, wearing a pink dress with a poufy skirt that did not suit her personality whatsoever, sat on the edge of an indoor fountain and dangled her feet over the rushing water. She seemed to be wondering whether or not to kick her gaudy pink shoes into the pool.

"Oh, Bubbles!" I said, turning back to the woman. "You must be Marcy!"

"Yes, I'm sorry." She clutched my arm, almost too tightly, and pulled me apart from Simon. "She told me how inspiring your comic books have been for her. I started reading them myself. What a story!" She blinked and wiped her eyes. "Goodness, forgive me. I've been so tired, arranging the details of this party. I guess it's finally getting to me."

"You should sit."

I guided her to a nearby chair. From a nearby station, I filled a glass with cold cucumber water and handed it to her. She drank gratefully. Simon lingered a few feet away, keeping up his conversation with Keith without letting me out of his sight.

"Thank you," Marcy sighed. "I'm already exhausted and the night hasn't even begun! I don't have the energy to be the perfect hostess."

As Marcy hydrated, I looked her up and down. Her skin hugged her bones tightly. She had little muscle mass as if stress had forced her to skip one too many meals. Her dress went all the way down to her ankles, and it was long-sleeved. Any bruises or marks would be hidden by the fabric.

"Stay here with me," I offered, pulling another chair closer to Marcy's. "Pretend we're deep in conversation. No one will interrupt us."

She laughed lightly and patted my knee. "I wish I could, but I'm the auctioneer tonight. People will literally be interrupting me all night."

"Where's Boyce?" I asked. "Can't he take over for you?"

Her face darkened, but she rearranged her slanted eyebrows and thin lips into a convincing smile, and I had to wonder if I'd imagined her previous expression. "Boyce likes to make an entrance once everyone is here. Then he likes to stay in the crowd to interact with the locals." She checked her watch. "Actually, he should be coming down any minute now."

"I'm not in a rush to see him," I said, perhaps more darkly than I meant to. "I'm comfortable talking to you.

Why don't I see you in town more often? Seems like everyone in Silver Creek is always out and about except for you."

"I like to keep to myself." She avoided my gaze while she replied as if she knew I'd sense she was lying if she looked me in the eye. "Besides, Boyce likes the house to be arranged in a certain way when he gets home."

"Bubbles mentioned something like that."

Her eyes snapped to mine. "What do you mean?"

"Well, I noticed she was getting hurt, and—"

Marcy shot up from her chair. "Stay out of our business," she hissed. "You don't know what you're talking about."

"I'm trying to help you—"

"Don't!" she spat. "My life is not the subject of gossip and speculation. Stop talking to my daughter if you're going to fill her head with stories and impossibilities."

She stalked off. Simon excused himself from his conversation with Keith and walked over.

"What was that all about?" he asked out of the corner of his mouth as he watched Marcy greet other guests.

"She's scared," I said. "I told her I know about Boyce's abuse."

"Was that wise?" Simon asked. "After all, we are going to try and kill her husband tonight."

I elbowed him in the gut. "We're not killing anyone. We're banishing him."

"My point is we're relying on some unknown magical energy to do this so-called banishing," he reminded me.

"We don't know what's going to happen, so maybe we shouldn't agitate his wife."

"I didn't mean to. I just wanted her to know she's not alone."

A spotlight clicked on, and the crowd turned to face its point of focus. At the top of an elegant staircase, Boyce stepped into the golden glow. The crowd applauded and cheered as he descended like a princess ready to be presented for her arranged marriage. He shook hands and kissed babies and acted like he was God. Meanwhile, the crowd believed him.

"So glad you could make it," he said to Simon and me when he eventually reached us. "Tonight is an important night for us."

"I'm sure it is," I replied. "Which charities are you supporting again, Boyce? Any that I've heard of?"

"All the donations we receive tonight will go toward improving the town," he said vaguely. "You'll see soon enough."

"Can't wait," I said acerbically.

THE EVENING PROGRESSED without much interest. For the locals, the charity gala was an excuse to dress up, eat expensive food, and pretend their lives were more interesting than they actually were. For the first time since we had moved to Silver Creek, I spoke to the other people who lived there for more than five minutes.

"The schools here are fantastic," a woman named Rooney told me. "I have a twelve-year-old and a fifteen-year-old, and they're both in the top twenty percent of the national average. They're practically getting a private education at a public school. Silver Creek is an excellent place to raise children."

"I can't get pregnant," I said, but for once, the statement wasn't accompanied by a pang of sadness. "But we might adopt."

"You should," Rooney encouraged. "There are so many children in this world who deserve a loving home. We adopted our youngest because my first pregnancy was so difficult. I wouldn't do it any other way."

I smiled as happiness radiated through me. If we got through the night, I'd bring up the adoption discussion to Simon again.

The night wore on. Marcy auctioned off various prizes, including new washer and dryer sets, fancy coffee makers, valuable antique books, and a set of crystals said to bring luck to the beholder.

"Sold!" Marcy cried, pointing to me at the back of the crowd. "To the woman in the back with the stunning red dress for two hundred dollars."

"Why the hell would you buy that?" Simon muttered in my ear as I grinned triumphantly.

"Weren't you listening?" I asked. "Marcy said the crystals belonged to the founder of Silver Creek. That means Boyce probably stole them from Emory or Earl. It's only right for us to return them to their rightful owners."

"Whatever you say," Simon replied. "I'll be back. I need the bathroom."

"Go quickly," I said. "It's almost midnight."

As Simon vanished amongst the locals, Boyce stepped up to the microphone on the auction stage. At once, the lights dimmed and the crowd grew quiet.

"Good evening, Silver Creek," he boomed. "Thank you all for coming out to this little gathering of mine. As promised, tonight's main prize is an all-inclusive trip to the Bahamas! Let's start the bidding at five hundred dollars."

Someone raised their hand, and the final auction began. Confused, I checked the clock. It was almost exactly midnight, but Boyce hadn't made any attempt to subdue me. Why would he busy himself with the auction when he should be on his way to the Lodge to start the ritual?

I scanned the room. Most everyone was infatuated with the bidding war, but two people were missing: Simon and Keith.

The hair rose on the back of my neck. The inaudible whispers tickled my ear.

They took Simon instead.

18

"*M*ax! Hey, Max, wait up!"

I pushed my way through the crowd and ignored the voice, but Bubbles caught up to me. As I suspected she might, she'd swapped her pink heels for a pair of black combat boots. She grabbed my hand.

"Bubbles, I can't talk right now," I said, rushing for the door. "I think Simon's in trouble."

She held on tightly. "I know. I saw Keith bash him on the head as he was coming out of the bathroom. That's why I came to find you?"

"What? Oh, God. I have to get home."

I bypassed the coatroom and burst outside. Snow whirled wildly around me. My dress whipped against my skin. The storm had worsened. I couldn't make out the end of the driveway.

The same valet who had parked our car approached me. He wore a thick-hooded parka to keep himself safe from the cold. "Ma'am, what are you doing out here without a coat? You'll freeze!"

"I need my keys," I barked. "Now!"

He opened the case that held all the keys and quickly located mine. I snatched it out of his grasp and made a run for the car. Halfway there, I realized Bubbles was still attached to me.

"Go back inside," I ordered her. I turned her by the shoulders to face the door, but she stubbornly pivoted back around. "Keith's dangerous. He might hurt Simon."

"I'm not letting you go alone," she said.

"Bubbles, you don't understand what's happening."

"It's something to do with my dad," she guessed. "Isn't it?"

My hesitation served as an answer.

"I knew it," Bubbles said. "Let me come with you. I can help."

"No, you can't," I told her firmly. "This is for the adults to handle. You'll be safer here."

"You said I was as strong as the Queen!"

"For a kid!" I shot back.

Her bottom lip wobbled, and her eyes filled with tears. My panic was coloring my tone and affecting Bubbles. I took her hands in mine. We both shivered. The cold was no joke.

"If anything happened to you, I would never forgive myself," I said to her. "I've already lost enough people in my life. I need you to stay where it's safe. Do you understand?"

Dubbles nodded and wiped her eyes on the hem of her dress. "Are you going to be okay?"

"I'll figure it out."

The valet shuffled over. "Miss, I really don't think you should be driving in this weather. The roads are blocked already. I called a snowplow so people can get home from the party tonight, but until it gets here, you should stay inside—"

"It's an emergency," I said. "I'll be fine."

I got into the car, switched on the ignition, and turned on the heat. The valet shrugged and returned to his place by an electric warmer. I backed out of the spot.

A loud slam sounded. The car thumped. I hit the brakes.

I rolled down the window and stuck out my head. "Did I just hit something?" I yelled to the valet.

He was already distracted by his phone, but he got up to check around my tires. "I don't see anything," he said. "You're clear."

Carefully, I let off the brake. The car rolled forward without issue. I released a sigh of relief and slowly made my way off Boyce's property.

The snowstorm was the worst one I'd seen in Silver Creek. It didn't come down in cute flurries. The flakes blew sideways, gathering on the windshield in huge piles no matter how fast the wiper blades flashed across the glass.

The tires slipped and slid over the fresh snow and the ice beneath it. I gripped the steering wheel so tightly that my knuckles ached. Boyce's stupid street lamps didn't help. Instead of illuminating the road, they backlit the snow, causing a glare that was nearly impossible to see through.

When I made it to the main road, the conditions weren't much better. The car's back end slid out when I pulled out of the woods. I whipped the steering wheel in the opposite direction to get the vehicle back on track. After a scary moment, during which I had no control over the car, the tires found traction again.

The closer I got to the Lodge, the more I felt the pull bringing me home. It was as if the land's energy wrapped tendrils around my every limb and wrenched me toward it. My whole body shook. How much of a head start had Keith gotten with Simon?

I pressed harder on the gas, and the tires spun on a patch of ice, sending the car into another miniature tailspin. My heart pounded as I coasted off the road, doing my best to keep the vehicle moving in as straight a path as possible. Once more, I regained control and pulled back onto the road. Fortunately, no one was on the road. Everyone was at Boyce's dumb party. I wondered who had bid the highest on the trip to the Bahamas. Anything was better than thinking about what was happening to Simon right now.

The snow was so thick that I almost missed the turn to the Lodge. I pumped the brakes and steered up the winding road. The trees kept most of the snow off the dirt road, so I picked up my speed. At the second to last corner, where the bent tree marked the place of Lily's almost death, I realized too late that I was driving too fast.

I stomped on the brakes and jerked the wheel to the right, careening toward the sharp bend in the road. It wasn't enough. The car spun, and the wheels locked. I screamed as I skidded off the road.

Crash!

The car slammed into a thick tree trunk. The driver's side door crumped. The seatbelt cut into my neck as the impact slammed me against the ruined door. A sickening crack split the air as my wrist smashed against the dashboard. The side airbag exploded, then the front one followed.

The car settled. Shattered glass from the driver's side window tinkled against the asphalt outside. Smoke hissed from under the hood. The airbags deflated, leaking fluid across the seat. I sat, stunned, as my body settled like the car. I performed a mental checklist.

My head was clear. That was good. Head injuries meant trouble. My left side ached, but I hoped it was just bruised. If I had internal injuries, I wouldn't know until I started vomiting blood, by which time, it would be too late.

My wrist, unfortunately, was ruined. It hung at a disgusting angle from my arm. The bones didn't line up normally at all. On the upside, all the adrenaline running through me meant I couldn't feel much pain.

The smell of gas permeated the car. Not good. With a groan, I hauled myself across the center console and kicked open the functioning door. I rolled out of the car and collapsed in the snow. As I caught my breath, the trunk sprang open, and someone climbed out.

ALEXANDRIA CLARKE

"Are you kidding me?" I gasped as Bubbles stumbled toward me. "What are you doing here?"

"I hopped into your trunk before the valet could see." She fell into the snow next to me. A trail of blood leaked from an unseen gash near her scalp. "I didn't think you'd be driving like a maniac."

"Damn it, Bubbles. Let me see your head."

She leaned forward, and I pushed her hair aside to look at the wound. In the pale light of the moon filtering through the trees, I could hardly see.

"It's not bad," I said. "It's just a shallow cut. You won't need stitches or anything, but I'm still getting you to the hospital in case you have some injury I can't see."

Black smoke billowed from beneath the hood of the car. I tugged Bubbles to her feet with my good hand and forced her up the road.

"We have to get away from the car," I said, keeping her in front of me. "There's a gas leak."

My head swam as I pushed Bubbles up the incline. All I could think about was getting to Simon, but as the cold pressed against us, my body began to fight against me.

"Are you okay?" Bubbles asked.

"Sure, kid."

I wasn't. I shivered violently, unable to regulate my internal temperature without a coat to keep me warm. As the shock wore off, the pain set in. I noticed chemical burns on my arms where the liquid from the airbags had gotten on me. Each time I took a breath in, a sharp pain shot through my left side, no doubt a sign of one or more broken ribs. My wrist was numb, and I worried that the

268

nerves had been severed. If that were the case, I might never be able to draw again.

Bubbles acted as my willpower. Whenever I wanted to give up, sit down, and let the snow cover me until I disappeared, she spoke up. She pushed me forward.

"One more step," she'd say. "Just take one more step. I can almost see the Lodge."

The acrid stench of smoke followed us. As we cleared the last bend in the road, a huge explosion echoed behind us. Fire billowed into the sky. The gas leak caught. The heat of it wafted through the trees, warming our backs. I was oddly grateful for the raging flames.

Bubbles trembled in fear as she looked back. Her eyes reflected the spreading flames. I turned her around and clutched her tightly to my side.

"One more step," I muttered. "I can almost see the Lodge."

This time, it wasn't a lie to make the walk less painful. As we neared the end of the dirt road, the Lodge finally came into view. As I stepped over the property line, a huge jolt of energy coursed through me. My head cleared, my skin warmed, and my wrist stopped throbbing.

Lily appeared at my side. Bubbles screamed.

"It's okay!" I told Bubbles. "She's a friend."

"She's dead!" Bubbles yelled.

"She's quick," Lily added. She knelt to look Bubbles in the eye. "I may be dead, but you don't need to fear me."

Though tremors rocked Bubbles's body, she nodded her assent. Lily rose to her feet.

"You need to come inside," Lily said. "Keith's here with

Simon. He's setting up the ritual so Boyce can complete it as soon as he arrives. We're doing what we can to stop him, but it's not enough. The land's energy is hiding. It knows Boyce is coming."

"Is Simon okay?" I asked, shuffling along beside Lily.

"He's hurt," Lily answered. "He has a huge lump on his head, which could be dangerous, considering he's still recovering from his last concussion."

"Damn it. Where is he?"

"Keith's got him tied up in the kitchen."

"I'm gonna kill him," I muttered for the second time that night.

With Bubbles and Lily flanking me, I punched through the front door of the Lodge. As I stepped inside, another jolt of energy washed over me. The power of the ley lines wasn't hiding underground; it was hiding in me. With each passing second, I felt stronger and stronger.

Bubbles gasped and pointed down. "Ew!"

I looked at my wrist. The bones appeared to be mending themselves. They moved beneath the skin, twisting and turning until they landed in the right places. It hurt, but not as bad as it should have. When the bones stilled, I experimentally made a fist and flexed my wrist.

"It's fixed," I said incredulously.

"Not my head," Bubbles said, feeling for the cut near her scalp. Her fingers came away bloody. "It's only happening to you."

"The land trusts Max," Lily said. "It's chosen you. We all have."

When I looked up, the room was full of ghosts. Many

of them I'd never met before, but I recognized Christine, Walter, and Earl, who all stood at the forefront of the group. The others crowded behind them, their faces set in determination. They were ready for all of this to be over.

"I'll do whatever I can to make this up to you," I promised them. "If you stand behind me, I'll make sure no one ever takes advantage of the power on this land again. I will free you all from whatever bonds are keeping you here."

There were no cheers like when Boyce introduced himself at his own party. Instead, the ghosts gave me their best looks of grim satisfaction.

"We're here for you," Earl said. "Get rid of that bastard, once and for all."

"I'll do my best." I planted Bubbles on the couch. "Stay here."

I left the ghosts to formulate a plan and rushed into the kitchen. Simon was tied to an aluminum folding chair with the rope we used to secure loads to Keith's pickup truck. Plastic zip ties cut red lines around his wrists. His head lolled limply on his neck. A bulbous lump on his forehead had already begun to bruise. His eyelids fluttered. He was awake, but barely.

"Simon!" I rushed to his side and gently moved his head in a more comfortable position. "Baby, it's me. I'm here."

He groaned. "Max?"

"Shh, everything's going to be all right."

I grabbed a pair of kitchen scissors from the drawer and cut the zip ties around his wrists. When it came to the ropes, the scissors proved useless. I fought to untangle Simon from the chair, but Keith's knots were impossible to pull free.

A gun cocked. I froze.

"I wouldn't do that if I were you."

Keith stood in the doorway between the kitchen and the lobby. He pointed a loaded shotgun at my head.

I raised my hands and slowly got to my feet. "Keith, you don't know what you're doing. You're making a mistake."

"I know exactly what I'm doing," he replied. "I'm earning my spot in the Gentlemen's Club. After Boyce's ritual, I'm going to be rich. I'll be able to buy my mom a nice big house, one that isn't tainted with the memories of my father."

"Were you planning this all along?" I asked him. The more he talked, the less likely he'd be to shoot. "Ever since we asked you to work for us?"

"Not at the beginning," he replied. "I needed work, and renovating the Lodge was a good opportunity, especially since you two were willing to pay me in cash. I've been trying to get in with the Gentlemen's Club for years, but Boyce never paid me a lick of attention. When he learned I was working for you, I finally had something to give him."

"You said you'd spy on us in return for a spot in the club."

"It's not personal," he assured me. He adjusted his boots against the new flooring to get better leverage. "I don't think you and Simon are bad people. You don't deserve any of this, but when it comes down to it, I have to look out for my mother and myself."

"And you think being one of Boyce's sycophants is going to help your family?" I asked. "Boyce doesn't care about you, Keith. You said it yourself."

Keith's eyes flickered nervously. "The guys in the club have everything they want, and they get it from Boyce."

"Boyce isn't sharing half of the money he's made in the last decade. Look at the house he lives in." I stepped closer to Keith, putting myself between the muzzle of the gun and Simon's chest. "He used you, Keith. He only needed you to get inside the Lodge. He won't honor your agreement afterward."

"You're wrong," Keith said. "He promised me."

"Do you know what this ritual of his does?" I asked. "Do you know about the ley lines?"

He nodded confidently. "Boyce told me everything."

"Everything?" I repeated. "Did he tell you the energy below us will be ruined for another ten years if he completes the ritual? Or that he killed Lily and used her blood to anoint his followers? Is that what you want to do, Keith? Wear my blood in exchange for your success? What would your mother think of that?"

Keith frantically shook his head. The mouth of the shotgun jiggled. "You're wrong. Boyce isn't a killer. He'd be in prison if he were."

"He murderer Lily," I said. "And he plans to kill me tonight."

"No," Keith said. "Lily's alive. I saw her the other day."

Lily popped into existence right beside Keith. "Guess again, bozo."

Keith yelped, and my nerves skyrocketed as the shotgun aimed wildly around the room. "Jesus! How did you do that?"

Lily disappeared and reappeared in front of Keith's gun. She stuck a finger in each of the barrels. "I'm dead. That's why I'm not afraid of your silly weapon."

"This is crazy," Keith said, the whites of eyes showing as Lily vanished once more. "We're not supposed to kill anyone. He said to capture one of you and bring you back here. He needs an owner of the land to complete the ritual."

"He needs someone connected to the energy here," I corrected. "Someone with a strong bond to the land. What did you think a sacrifice meant, Keith?"

His face turned red as he sputtered. "I don't know! I thought it was metaphorical. I'm not here to kill anyone!"

Swiftly, I stepped forward, grabbed the barrel of the shotgun, and wrenched the whole thing out of his grasp. He didn't fight me. As soon as the gun left his hands, he sank into the chair next to Simon's and covered his face with his hands.

"I'm so stupid," he muttered. "I should have known better. I should have listened to Mom."

I emptied the rounds from the shotgun and set them on the table next to Keith. "It's not entirely your fault. Boyce is an annoyingly good manipulator."

Keith looked up at me with red eyes. "You don't hate me?"

"That depends on whether Simon recovers from whatever you bashed against his head," I said. "And on how you choose to act for the remainder of the evening."

Keith had enough decency to look properly ashamed as he examined Simon's wound. "It was a vase. I think he'll be okay. I didn't hit him that hard."

Simon stirred as if he sensed we were talking about him. My heart stopped as he slowly lifted his hand… and smacked Keith across the face.

"Stupid," Simon said weakly. "Stupid, stupid, stupid."

Keith's embarrassed blush renewed itself. "I know. I'm sorry. I had no idea he was planning to kill one of you! I'm not a murderer! I don't want to spend my life in jail."

"You could still benefit from the power of the ley lines," I said. "If you work with us."

"It doesn't matter anymore," Keith said, clutching his hair and pulling it away from his scalp. "I don't deserve it. I'm surprised you haven't shot me already."

"We're not like Boyce," I informed him. "We aren't killers. Besides, it's easy to play the bad guy when you think you're getting something out of it."

Keith's eyes glistened. "I don't want to be a part of a group that hurts people to get ahead."

"I wish you'd decided that an hour ago," Simon muttered. "Before you broke a vase over my head."

"I'm sorry," Keith said again. "I'll do whatever you want me to. I won't participate in Boyce's crazy ritual."

I regarded Keith's pleading look and jerked my head toward the lobby. "Go out front and keep watch for the

Gentlemen's Club. I assume we should be expecting them shortly?"

"In ten minutes or so." Keith wiped his eyes and stood up. "I'll yell when I see them."

When he was gone, I dampened a paper towel and wiped the dried blood off Simon's forehead. He hissed as I blotted around the swollen lump.

"Do you think he's telling the truth?" Simon asked. "Keith?"

"He's not smart enough to come up with a double-agent plan," I replied quietly. "Keith is a simple kid. All he wants is a good life and to take care of his mom. He thought teaming up with Boyce would help him get it."

"What if he goes back to Boyce's side?" he said. "We can't trust him to help us."

"Keith's not a killer," I said. "He folded like paper as soon as we told him Boyce's real plan. I doubt he'll switch sides again, not unless he wants to spend the rest of his life in jail."

"Boyce evaded prison," Simon muttered murderously.

"Trust me," I said. "I saw the look on Keith's face. He doesn't want to be like Boyce, despite years of thinking otherwise."

Simon tested the lump on his head and flinched. "What are we supposed to do now?"

"We stick to the original plan," I told him. "When Boyce gets here, we'll lure him into the safe room and let the ley lines do their thing."

"What if it doesn't work?" Simon whispered.

I pressed a kiss to the uninjured side of his forehead. "It will work. It has to."

Keith skidded into the kitchen. "Look alive! I just saw headlights coming up the driveway."

"This is it," I said. "Let's move Simon to a safe place. Keith, follow my lead. Where's Bubbles?"

I checked the lobby, but the younger girl was nowhere to be found. As I passed the front door, someone kicked in. I leaped out of the way.

Boyce strolled in, flanked by five members of the Gentlemen's Club. He dragged Bubbles by the ear.

"Good evening, Maxine," he said, throwing Bubbles to the floor; the girl cried and shook at her father's feet. "You left the party so early. I thought I'd come thank you in person for attending and for ensuring another ten years of my success."

19

I didn't dare take my eyes off Boyce and his thugs as I helped Bubbles off the floor. She ran behind me and hugged my waist, sobbing against my back.

"How generous of you," I said to Boyce, baring my teeth. "I'm afraid we don't require your hospitality, though. You can leave now."

He barked a laugh and stepped farther into the Lodge. Intent on protecting Bubbles, I hurriedly backed up, keeping the girl with me. The other five men came through the doorway as well. Unlike Boyce, they weren't reveling in our fear. In fact, they looked rather unsure of their purpose.

"Nice try." Boyce plucked off his gloves, finger by finger. "Maxine, do you know who built this beautiful Lodge?"

"Emory Driscoll," I answered. "Your great-uncle."

He tipped his hat. "I see you did your research. In that

case, you should already know that I am the rightful heir to this land. After all, I am the only remaining member of the Driscoll family."

"Because you killed Earl," I snapped.

Boyce placed his hand over his heart and gasped. "Of course I didn't! You think I would murder my uncle?"

"He was the only person standing between you and the energy on this land," I said. "If you didn't kill him, why did he die so suddenly?"

"He was old," Boyce said dismissively. "And he had a heart condition. I don't control other people's bodies, Maxine. That's just ridiculous."

"Regardless, the Lodge and the land don't belong to you," I spat. "Simon and I are the rightful owners of this property now."

Boyce's smile wavered. "I put an enormous bid on this place. It should have been mine."

"But it's not," I said. "You don't belong here. You never will, not unless you can learn to respect the land and its power."

He lifted a finger to wag in my face. "Do not lecture me about respect. I am the mayor of this town—"

"Unofficial mayor," I said. "If the Silver Creek locals knew about what you've done here, you wouldn't be any kind of authority figure in this town at all."

"I built this town from the ground up," he snarled.

"Emory and Earl built this town," I said. "All you did was bribe people into thinking you were a decent person."

"Enough!" Boyce said. "It doesn't matter whose name

is on the paperwork here. At the end of the night, you'll be dead, and I'll be richer."

He lunged toward me. I dodged his outstretched hand and shoved Bubbles out of Boyce's reach.

"Bubbles, run!" I told the girl as one of Boyce's henchman grabbed me and painfully pulled my arms behind my back. "Find a place to hide!"

Another man tried to push past me to catch Bubbles, but I stomped on his foot as he passed. He yelped, cradling his foot as Bubbles fled.

"Spread out," Boyce ordered his men. "Search the place. Find my daughter and bring her to me. Where is that buffoon Keith? He was supposed to lock down the husband. You—" He jabbed his finger at the man holding me. "Bring her with me."

The man shoved me forward, following Boyce as he headed toward the safe room. The other four men split up to obey Boyce's instructions.

"I'm Max," I said cheerfully to the man who forced me down the hallway. "What's your name?"

"Harry," he grunted.

"Nice to meet you, Harry. What do you do for a living?"

"I'm a bank manager."

"Ah, no doubt Boyce's bank manager?"

Harry nodded, thoroughly confused as to why I was talking to him so casually.

"How many crimes have you committed?" I asked. "Specifically, crimes that worked to Boyce's advantage?"

Harry wasn't so keen to answer that question. I heard his teeth clench together.

"I'm just curious," I continued. "Because it seems like Boyce is really the only one benefitting from this absurd ritual. I mean, is your house as big as his?"

"Shut up," Boyce hissed. He reached the last room in the hallway and kicked open the door. "Don't listen to her, Harry. She doesn't know what she's talking about?"

"Don't I?" I said. "All I'm saying is I doubt *you* live in a mansion like Boyce's. Am I right, Harry?"

Boyce punched me in the stomach. I doubled over, coughing and gagging. It was a good thing I hadn't eaten any of the lush hors d'oeuvres at Boyce's party because he would have seen them again on his expensive shoes.

"Get her inside, Harry."

For the shortest second, Harry hesitated.

"*Inside,* Harry," Boyce hissed.

Harry shoved me over the threshold and into the small storage room. As we faced the safe door, energy thrummed in my body. It seemed to live just below the surface of my skin. I half-expected to start glowing golden rays of sunlight, as the power made me feel warm and invincible.

Boyce drew a piece of paper from his pocket. When he unfolded it, I caught sight of the complicated set of numbers that were the key to opening the safe. He wouldn't need Walter's secret back way in to unlock the door. Earl's old combination would do the trick just fine.

Boyce spun the dial, reading the numbers off the paper to himself as he did so. When he plugged in the last digit, the lock clicked out of place. Boyce grinned and tucked the paper away.

"It's lovely not having to break in," he said and yanked open the door.

A gust of musty-smelling air wafted out of the room. With it came another wave of power, though it seemed I was the only one who could feel it. Boyce and Harry were unaffected as my skin and scalp tingled.

Boyce peered into the gloomy darkness. "This place could use some touching up, eh?"

He pulled a lighter from his pocket and lit the tall candles stationed around the room. As the glittering fire illuminated the damp walls, Boyce took a deep breath.

"Smells like someone pissed in here," he observed.

"Classy," I commented.

He beckoned me forward. "Ladies first."

"I'm a feminist," I said. "I believe in equal rights. You can head in first."

He snapped his fingers, and Harry shoved me into the dark room. I screamed out loud as the energy in my body tripled, infusing itself in every one of my nerves. It felt like someone had lit me on fire.

Apparently, Harry thought so, too. He hissed and dropped me as if my skin had burned him. I fell to my hands and knees as energy coursed through me, shaking as I fought to breathe through the weird fog that clouded my mind.

"Subdue her, Harry!" Boyce ordered.

"Sorry, Boyce. She's red-hot. Look."

Harry knelt beside me and pointed to my arms. The

fine hairs stood on end as if responding to a call to arms. Boyce's lip curled.

"Goddammit," he said. "She's charged."

"What the hell does that mean?" I gasped. The pain had started to fade, leaving me with a strangely satisfying feeling of fullness.

Boyce rolled his eyes and didn't bother to answer. "Don't let her leave this room, Harry. I'll be back with the things I need for the ritual."

Boyce left. The heavy safe door thudded behind him, and my heart dropped as I heard the dial spin.

"What's the point of ordering you to keep me here if he was going to lock us both in any way?" I muttered.

Harry's breathing quickened. "What did you say?"

I jerked my chin toward the safe door. "Didn't you hear the lock engage?"

"No." Harry pushed himself to his feet and attempted to open the safe door. It didn't give. "No! Are you kidding me, Boyce?"

"Guess he doesn't trust you that much, eh?" I gazed around at the candles. "No ventilation in here. Hopefully, he comes back."

Harry banged on the safe, no doubt injuring his hand against the thick metal. "Boyce! Hey, Boyce! You locked us in here."

"He did it on purpose." I leaned against the wall and let the energy flow through every vein. If I breathed deeply, I felt able to control the power that flowed through me. "Face it, Harry. Boyce doesn't care if you're claustrophobic. He's only doing this to benefit himself."

Harry paced from one end to the other, running his fingers through what little hair he had left. "I didn't want to be a part of this. Boyce approached me with a business proposition years ago. I had no idea we were going to be doing this weird voodoo shit."

"It's not voodoo," I assured him. "But you're on the right track."

"The other guys don't like it, either," Harry continued. "Boyce is so cryptic. He never tells you exactly what he's planning. Like tonight? None of expected to come here and attack you. Do I look like a thug?"

In his designer suit that was a bit too tight around his beer belly, he most certainly did not. None of Boyce's men looked as though they belonged in a secret cult.

"Since your self-esteem appears to be low today, I'm going to say no," I told him.

He stopped pacing to stare at me. "How can you be so calm? Do you know what Boyce is planning to do with you?"

"He wants to kill me," I answered nonchalantly. "He thinks I'm the key to another decade of success in Silver Creek."

"It's nuts," Harry said. "He tried to explain all this earth energy crap to us. I mean, is it even real?"

"Like being charged?"

"Exactly!"

I tilted my head to get a better look at Harry from my low seat on the ground. "What exactly did Boyce mean by that, if you don't mind my asking?"

Harry threw his hands into the air and resumed

pacing. "I don't know. He said you'd be more dangerous if you were 'charged.'" He used his fingers to put air quotes around the word. "He said if you learned that you were a conductor of the energy here, it would allow you to take control of the ritual. He's terrified of that."

I clamped my lip between my teeth, determined to keep my expression unreadable. "Harry, look at me."

He caught my eye.

"Breathe," I instructed.

Harry closed his eyes and took one calming breath. "It smells like smoke in here," he muttered.

"Don't worry," I said. "Boyce will be back before either one of us dies of oxygen deprivation. He needs me for this stupid ritual. Here's the thing. Do you want to sink to his level? Do you want to become a killer, without even reaping the same benefits as Boyce? As it is, you only get his scraps."

Harry's throat bobbed as he swallowed his nerves. "I don't know what I'm doing here, Max. My wife lost her job. Our twin boys are starting college next year, and we can't afford to send them to the schools they want to go to. I had to take a second mortgage out on our house. We're hemorrhaging money."

"I understand," I said. "This lodge and this land are all Simon and I have. We put our entire savings into it. If we fail to get this business off the ground, we'll be homeless."

Harry blinked tears out of his eyes. "What are we supposed to do?"

"You could complete the ritual," I said. He raised his eyebrows in surprise. "You could kill my husband and me.

You could go along with Boyce's scheme and hope something good comes out of whatever crazy magic he's talking about."

Harry buried his head in his hands.

"Or," I continued, "you could help me turn this thing around. Boyce isn't the god of Silver Creek. The town and your family can thrive without him. If we banish Boyce from the land, we can share the earth's energy."

"It's real?" he asked, peeking out from behind his fingers. "This so-called energy?"

"That's what you felt when you dropped me earlier," I said. "That energy isn't in the land anymore. It's in me. Boyce won't be able to control it unless he kills me first, and I sure as hell am not planning to die tonight."

"Will you help me?" he asked. "When all of this is over, if there's a way to fix things, will you help me support my family?"

"I'll do my best to make sure your boys get to go to whatever college they want," I assured him, "while you and your wife can keep your house."

Harry whirled around as the safe dial spun again, signaling Boyce's return. My heart sank as Harry waited impatiently for the door to open. Maybe I hadn't gotten through to him.

The safe opened, and light spilled in. Boyce's ugly leather loafer lifted itself over the lip.

"Harry, take this for me—"

Before Boyce could complete his order, Harry swung. His meaty fist connected with Boyce's fleshy face. Boyce yelled and clutched his nose. Blood flowed freely from his nostrils.

"Run!" Harry shouted at me.

I scrambled to my feet and shoved past Boyce to get out of the safe. He made a blind grab for me, catching my arm, but I thrust my palm into his already-injured nose. He screamed in agony and let go.

"You bitch!" he roared.

I made a run for it, crashing into the wall in the hallway as my heels slid across the new wood floors. Behind me, Harry and Boyce threw punches at each other. Clearly, neither one of them had trained in boxing before. The fight quickly grew wild and dangerous.

I skidded to a stop as another one of Boyce's henchmen appeared at the end of the corridor. He was much larger than Harry. I had two options: charge him or turn around and make a break for the emergency exit at the back of the Lodge.

I charged. It was the only way to find out where Simon, Keith, and Bubbles had gone. The man's eyes widened as I thundered toward him like he wasn't expecting me to attack. Too late, I realized he'd taken the shotgun from the kitchen table and reloaded it.

Boom!

I hit the deck. The bullets slammed against the wall, ruining the fresh coat of paint.

"You asshole!" I yelled. "We just renovated!"

I got to my feet as the man cocked the gun to try again. As he closed one eye and looked over the muzzle, I felt a flash of energy to my right.

Lily appeared out of nowhere. She grabbed the barrel of the gun and twisted it upward, bending the metal as easily as she would a Twizzler. The man fired. The bullets got stuck in the ruined barrel, and the recoil forced the butt of the gun into the man's chest.

Already fazed, the man stumbled backward. Earl appeared behind him and made a gesture like clapping his hands over the man's ears. His hands sunk through the man's head. With a stunned look, the man fell backward and collapsed onto the floor, totally unconscious.

"Is he dead?" I gasped.

"Just unaware," Earl said. He stared at his hands. "I had no idea I could do that."

A roar echoed through the lobby, and another member of the Gentlemen's Club vaulted the couch to get to me. He wrapped his hands around my throat and yanked me across his body. I bit his hand, but he held on fast.

Christine Higgins solidified before me.

"Not today, dick!"

She swung at the man's head as if to slap him across the face. Like Earl's victim, the man went limp as soon as the ghost touched him. I rolled off of him, gasping for air.

Panting, Christine planted her hands on her hips. "That felt *good.*"

"Thank you," I told the ghost trio. "Have you seen the others?"

"Keith locked himself and Simon in the kitchen pantry," Lily reported. "He has the door barred. No one's found them yet. They're safe for now."

"What about Bubbles?"

"We haven't seen her," Earl said. "Neither have Boyce's men. She must have found somewhere to bunker down, too."

"You can't—I don't know—sense her or something?"

Lily shook her head. "It doesn't work that way."

"You have to go back," Earl added. "You have to get Boyce in that room. It's the only way you'll be able to banish him."

I shook my head. "I have to find Bubbles. She could be in trouble."

"Max!" Lily called after me as I ran past them and into the next section of the Lodge. "It's not safe! Boyce still has three other guys on the property."

"Two," I corrected her. "Harry's on our side now. He's distracting Boyce as we speak."

I stumbled into the recreation room. The long, wide hall didn't have many places for Bubbles to hide. I checked a broom closet and behind a wall of fitness supplies to no avail.

"Bubbles?" I called softly. "It's Max."

Out of nowhere, a hairy fist swung out of the darkness. I wasn't quick enough to avoid it, and the first two knuckles connected with my top lip. My front tooth dropped out. I spat it on the floor with a mouthful of blood.

A man, the size of a truck, stepped out of the shadows and cracked his knuckles. I recognized him from town: Gary Hills. He owned the only weight-lifting gym in Silver Creek, and the guys who worked out there were roid-raging muscle buffs. Gary was their king.

"Boyce said it might come to this," Gary drawled. "I can't say I'm disappointed. The other Club members are weak. They didn't want to hit a woman, but I'm not above it. You like pain, Ms. Finch?"

"About as much as I like you," I retorted.

Gary swung again. This time, I had no problem ducking under the blow. Gary was strong, but he wasn't fast. Weight-lifters didn't have the kind of mobility for a chase. That gave me the advantage.

"I'd love to stay and chat, Gary," I said as I faked one way and darted the other. When Gary spun around, I jabbed my fingers into both his eye sockets. "But I've gotta run."

Gary howled and covered his eyes. For good measure, I kicked him in the balls. He crumpled to the floor. I sprinted out of the recreation room.

I checked the event hall next. Nothing. I peered through the windows to see into the woods behind the Lodge. The snowstorm raged on. I hoped Bubbles was smart enough to stay inside rather than risk running through the freezing cold. Ironically, she was safer with her father than she would be out there.

In the kitchen, I knocked on the pantry door. "Simon, Keith! It's me."

"Max?" Keith asked in a trembling voice. "Are you okay? Is it over?"

"It's not over," I said. "But I'm all right. What about you guys?"

"Simon keeps trying to go to sleep," Keith said through the door. "Max, I'm afraid I really hurt him."

My chest tightened. I leaned my head against the wall. "Wake him up. Keith, I swear. You *have* to keep him awake. Do you understand me?"

"Yes."

"Call 9-1-1," I ordered. "We're going to need help after this. Have you seen Bubbles?"

"No, I had to hide Simon. She's not with you?"

"It's okay. I'll find her. Stay hidden until this is over, or the ambulance shows up, okay?"

In a very small voice, he replied, "Okay."

It took all of my willpower to turn away from the pantry. My heart ached for Simon and Keith. For Harry and the other desperate men Boyce had taken advantage of.

"You're right," I muttered to Earl and Lily. "I have to stop Boyce first."

"We're with you," Lily said.

"Every step of the way," Earl added.

We headed back toward the first-floor hallway. In the lobby, we found Boyce's last man standing over the unconscious body of his comrade. When we walked in, his eyes flickered to the ghosts at my side. He could see them. He lifted his hands above his head.

"Whatever this is," he said, backing toward the door. "I want no part in it. It's was never my intention to raise the dead."

"Get out," I snarled.

The man stumbled out of the Lodge, got into his car, and drove away. I kicked off my heels and moved silently through the hall. The Lodge was quiet. Had Harry and Boyce beat each other to death?

I got my answer as I peeked into the smallest room. Harry lay unconscious on the ground. Blood poured from an ugly gash in his midsection. Pity and sadness tasted bitter on my tongue as I leaned down and pressed my fingers to his neck. I felt a pulse, slow but steady. He was alive.

"On your feet."

I froze as Boyce emerged from the safe room. Harry had gotten in a few more choice shots before he'd lost consciousness. Along with his broken nose, Boyce also sported a black eye and a kink in his right arm that was altogether not normal. He brandished a knife in his uninjured left hand.

I lifted my hands to show him I was unarmed. "He needs help, Boyce. He's going to die if that wound keeps bleeding."

"I don't care," Boyce snapped. "Get in here."

"Boyce, I—"

Roughly, he yanked Bubbles into my sightline from where she'd been cowering in the safe room. He put the knife to her throat.

"Don't!"

Boyce bared his teeth. "Get in here, or the girl dies."

"Your daughter?" I said. "You would kill your daughter?"

Bubbles trembled in her father's grasp as the knife pressed against her skin. A droplet of blood dribbled down her neck.

"I'll say it was an accident," Boyce said. His eyes were bloodshot, and his voice shook with rage. "They'll believe me. The whole town loves me. I am a god!"

My jaw clenched. "You are nothing more than a desperate boy with a Napoleon complex."

"I'll kill her," he whispered darkly. "Last chance."

"Please, Max," Bubbles said.

I stepped swiftly inside the chamber. Boyce pushed Bubbles aside and slammed the door shut, once more confining us all inside the candlelit room without any ventilation.

We circled the room, keeping the large desk between us. Bubbles huddled in a corner, her knees curled up to her chest.

"This isn't going to go your way," I told Boyce. "I'm charged. You know it; I know it. The land knows it. You can't win."

"You have no idea how to wield that power," Boyce hissed. "It'll eat you alive if you try to use it. I'm the only one who's strong enough."

"Somehow, I doubt that."

He threw the knife at me. I dodged out of the way, but the blade clipped my shoulder and opened a shallow cut. Boyce lunged across the chamber and caught hold of my dress. He yanked me to the floor and crawled on top of me.

"It's mine," he spat, holding me down. "I won't have this power taken away from me. Not again. I belong here." He reached for the fallen knife and brought it to my neck.

ALEXANDRIA CLARKE

"No need for fancy rituals tonight. All I want is your blood."

I struggled against him, bucking my hips to throw him off, but he weighed twice as much as I did. No matter what I did, I couldn't dislodge him.

"Finally," Boyce whispered and pressed the blade against my throat.

Bubbles came out of nowhere. She swung a heavy silver candlestick like a baseball bat. The makeshift weapon crashed into Boyce's temple, and he keeled over. I scrambled out from under his weight.

"*That's* what it feels like!" Bubbles spat breathlessly at her father. "How do you like it?"

Boyce surged to his knees, but the blow to his head had thrown off his balance. He toppled over again. "You—you can't—"

I stood over Boyce. "I can do whatever I want. This is *my* land."

The power in my body reached its peak. I lifted my chin and spread my arms, letting it flow through every part of me. The candles flickered in response to the rising energy.

Every person who had ever died at the Lodge appeared in the chamber. Lily and Earl were in the front lines as the ghosts closed in around Boyce. He looked around in horror.

"Do you see them, Boyce?" I thundered. My voice resonated through the chamber as if I spoke from the top of a mountain. "You subjected them to this fate. Now, they will deliver yours."

The ghosts encircled Boyce, chanting unintelligibly as they blocked him from view. The earth's energy whipped my hair around my face and flung the fabric of my dress around. Bubbles clung to my waist, and we watched the spirits descend on Boyce. The power of the ley lines burned my skin, wanting to get out. I let out a scream.

"Stay with me!" Bubbles shouted over the whirling wind. "Max, stay with me!"

I focused on her little face—those bright, determined eyes shining through everything else. The entire chamber seemed to spin with the intensity of the ghosts' vengeance.

When the wind grew to a mind-numbing roar, and I thought my skin might tear from my body, and I couldn't take anymore, everything stopped. The chamber was still. The ghosts had disappeared.

And Boyce was gone.

20

TWO YEARS LATER

For the first time since we opened the Silver Creek Lodge, we were completely booked. As Christmas approached, everyone wanted to visit Silver Creek for a taste of the small-town holiday season. Even better, a recent storm had dumped several feet of snow on the nearby slopes. Avid skiers called constantly, hoping for a place to stay while they carved fresh lines on the mountain. Every room at the Lodge was accounted for, including the presidential suite. As I checked in on the happy couple who'd booked it, snow fell past the windows.

"Alrighty, you're all set." I handed over a set of keys and smiled. "Upstairs. Last door at the end of the hall. Do you need someone to help you with your bags?"

"Yes, please," the woman replied. "My husband's back isn't what it used to be."

The older man huffed. "I am perfectly healthy!"

"Sure, dear."

Chuckling, I called, "Keith!"

He came in from outside with an armful of firewood. He stomped the snow off his boots. "What can I do for you, Max?"

"Help Mr. and Mrs. Borden with their bags, please," I said. "I'll take care of the fire."

Keith set the wood in a crate by the hearth and beamed at the Bordens. "I'll be happy to take your luggage up for you. Shall we?"

"What a handsome young man," Mrs. Borden said as Keith shouldered their bags. She leaned over the check-in desk. "This place is gorgeous. I already feel like I'm in heaven!"

"That's our goal," I said. "To make sure you have the best stay possible."

The woman shivered happily. "There's something in the air here. I can't explain it! Oh, goodness me. My husband's going up to the room on his own. Excuse me!"

She pranced off to follow her husband and Keith upstairs. I laughed and shook my head. By the fireplace, I opened the grate that kept the ashes from flying into the lobby and added another piece of wood. The fire tickled the fresh wood. I calmly withdrew my hand as the warmth grew. I no longer panicked at the sight of a flame.

"Excuse me, ma'am?" a familiar voice said. "We're checking in. I believe you have the best room in the house set aside for us."

My face split into a wide grin as I spun around and saw Sienna behind me. I threw my arms around her and spun her around. She squealed with joy.

"Careful, careful!" she chided. When I set her down, she rubbed her belly. "This little one makes me nauseous, and I refuse to throw up anywhere in this beautiful place."

"I still can't believe you're pregnant." I knelt and made kissy noises at Sienna's stomach. "Hello, little girl! It's your Auntie Max. I can't wait to meet you!"

"Will you stand up? You look insane." She pulled me to my feet. "By the way, it's a boy."

"No!"

"You're disappointed."

"It's fine," I grumbled. "I just wanted our daughter to be best friends with yours."

"Lily can be best friends with a boy!"

"I suppose," I said. "Where's Christian?"

Sienna jerked her thumb over her shoulder. "He was supposed to be bringing the bags in from the car. I don't know what's taking so long."

I peeked out the window. The parking lot was full of snow-covered cars. I spotted Christian's lanky form right away. "Ah. That's why. Simon found him."

Sienna joined me. When she spotted Simon and the baby cradled in his arms, she let out a gasp. "Is that Lily? She's gotten so big!"

"She's growing like a weed," I said. "I can't believe she's only a year old."

Christian completely ignored the baggage in the back of their car in favor of gently poking Lily's stomach to make her laugh. The baby babbled and cooed in Simon's arm, trying to catch Christian's fingers. She was thoroughly protected by a fat, baby-sized parka, a thick hat, and furry boots, but the snow was starting to come down hard.

I cracked open the window. "Hey! Will the two of you get in here before the baby freezes to death, please?"

"And get the luggage!" Sienna added. "Or you won't be getting in those hot springs with me tonight!"

We chuckled merrily as the boys jumped into action. With Simon's help, they emptied the car and brought everything inside. Sienna confiscated Lily from Simon's arms and held her up in the air.

"Hello, little baby," she said in a high-pitched voice. "Who loves you, Lily? Who's the best auntie in the world? I brought you presents."

"Now who looks insane?" I joked.

Lily blew a raspberry, spraying spit all over Sienna's face. She wrinkled her nose and handed me the baby. "You can have her back."

"Get used to it," I advised her as I balanced Lily on my hip. "I hear boys are worse."

"Sorry, we didn't get to pick the gender like you two did," Christian said. He gave me a one-armed hug. "Hi, Max. You look good."

Simon kissed my forehead as he dragged Sienna and Christian's bags farther inside. "That's the perk of adopting. You can pick the cutest one."

I smiled down at our baby. Her soft brown eyes lit up when she saw me, and she clapped her hands. Though it had only been six months since we'd adopted the orphaned girl from the Philippines, I felt as though I had given birth to her myself.

So much had changed in a short period of time. As the ley lines recovered from banishing Boyce from Silver Creek, the land and the Lodge thrived. With Keith's help, we finished renovating the Lodge in record time. We opened our doors in the summertime, six months after we had moved to Silver Creek. The grass grew greener than I'd ever seen before. The leaves on the trees seemed to whisper secrets to one another. The flowers we'd planted by the front windows bloomed into beautiful fireworks of color. When the weather was warm, several hummingbirds flitted around the garden. The few guests we had acquired gasped and pointed when they spotted their iridescent wings glittering in the sunlight.

When fall rolled around, the entire lodge changed color. Green and pink morphed to orange and brown. The land was no less beautiful as the air filled with chimney smoke and the crisp scent of freshly-fallen apples. More people flocked to Silver Creek to appreciate the autumnal colors, and our numbers began to grow.

When November rolled around again, we had broken even on the Lodge. At the end of the year, we turned a profit. Our financial advisor told us he'd never seen anyone turn a property around so quickly. He totaled the numbers six times to ensure he hadn't made a mistake.

Those who didn't know the secrets of Silver Creek Lodge would never fully understand where our luck came from. Simon and I, on the other hand, knew exactly why our business had been so successful from the start. Our connection with the land's energy meant everything to us.

I felt it every day, a subtle pulse beneath my feet that spread warmth and love throughout the entire property.

We never found out what happened to Boyce. After that night in the hidden chamber, he had simply vanished from existence. Some nights, when the wind was especially strong, I wondered if he was still out there. But then a comfortable warmth would blanket me in familiarity, and the whispers would start near my ears again. I was no longer scared of those voices. They belonged to Lily, Earl, Christine, Walter, and all the others who came before them.

When Simon finished bringing Sienna and Christian's bags to their room, Christian clapped Simon on the shoulders. "Let's hear it for my boy! He just told me the good news."

Simon blushed and nervously stroked his hair.

"What good news?" I asked, suspicious. "You didn't tell me anything."

"A producer from L.A. saw one of my videos on YouTube," Simon said. "He wants to produce an album for me, and he wants to record it live in Silver Creek. He says the falling snow and crackling fire will add a level of ambiance that listeners will die for."

"You got a record deal?" I said breathlessly.

"I got a record deal."

I squealed and threw my arms around Simon's neck, careful not to squish the baby as I hugged him. "I'm so proud of you. I knew you could do it!"

"Of course he could." Sienna ruffled Simon's curls. "Girls are swooning over your music videos. We all want a beautiful man to play guitar and sing to us in a snowy winter wonderland."

"Hey," Christian said, pouting. "What about me?"

"Realtors are hot, too, babe," Sienna said in an obligatory fashion.

Christian shrugged. "I'll take it."

I lightly smacked Simon's chest. "Why didn't you tell me earlier?"

"Because you got *your* big news today, too," he reminded me. "I didn't want to steal your thunder."

"You wouldn't have," I assured him. "Good news is meant to be enjoyed by all."

"Wait, what's your good news?" Sienna asked me. "Oh my god, are you adopting another baby?"

I laughed. "One is quite enough for now. Actually, it's about *Rebel Queen*. Volume three sold so well that they're going to reprint it. Also, a production company wants to turn it into a television show."

Sienna couldn't contain her excitement and yelled. Christian rushed to her side.

"Babe, are you okay?" he demanded.

"Am I okay? I'm great!" She danced around me like I was a goddess to worship and chanted, "My friends are famous. My friends are famous!" A second later, she burst into tears.

"I have no idea what's happening," Christian sighed.

"I'm just so happy," Sienna said thickly. She drew all three of us into a group hug. "You guys deserve the best life. I'm glad you're finally getting it."

Keith came down the stairs as we were all wrapped up

together. He awkwardly waited until our embrace naturally pulled apart.

"What's up, Keith?" I asked, wiping happy tears from my eyes.

He drew two envelopes from the back pocket of his jeans and handed one to me and the other to Sienna. "I wanted to invite you all to the first-ever, all-inclusive Holiday Ball, sponsored by the good people of the Silver Creek Community Club."

Since the Gentlemen's Club had been disbanded after Boyce's disappearance, Silver Creek needed a new group to support its welfare. Keith had stepped up to the plate and created the Community Club. The Club met at the library weekly. It was open for anyone to join, and the locals jumped at the opportunity to take the future of Silver Creek into their own hands. Despite Boyce's predictions that Silver Creek would fail without him, the town blossomed. Employment opportunities skyrocketed, the schools had new roofs installed to stop melted snow from leaking in, and the population had almost doubled in the last two years.

Best of all, Keith had learned the value of friendship and hard work. Instead of buying his mother a bigger house, he built an addition to hers. Simon helped, of course, and it became our tradition to go to Keith's house for Thanksgiving every year.

"We would be honored," I told Keith, holding the invitation against my heart.

"Free food?" Christian said. "I'm in."

Keith grinned. "Perfect. I'll be in the kitchen if anyone

needs me. Marcy's teaching Bubbles and me how to cook!"

As Keith disappeared through the swinging doors, Lily started fussing.

"That's her sleepy cry," Simon said. "I got her."

"Are you sure?" I asked. "I can put her down."

"You stay," he said, kissing my cheek. "Enjoy the day. The guests love having you around."

Simon made sure Lily's parka was zipped all the way up, tucked her against his chest, and headed outside again.

"Uh, where is he going?" Sienna asked. "Don't the two of you live here?"

"We built a cabin on the edge of the property," I said. "To separate home and work. It's perfect for the three of us."

"I want to see!" Sienna clung to my arm. "But Lily had the right idea. I need a nap first. Babe? Shall we check out our fancy room?"

Christian linked his arm through his wife's. "We shall."

"See you at dinner," I called as they headed upstairs.

I flinched as a huge crash echoed from the kitchen, followed by the sound of Keith swearing. I rushed into the back. A huge mixing bowl spun on the floor, spraying pasta sauce all over the room. Keith stood in the corner, covered in the stuff, while Bubbles and her mother attempted to tame the wayward bowl.

"What happened?" I asked, stepping aside to avoid getting pasta sauce on my pants.

"I'm sorry!" Keith said. "I didn't mean to."

"Just an accident," Marcy said.

In the years since Boyce's disappearance, she had gained a healthy amount of weight. It turned out she was an amazing chef, so amazing that we had hired her to work at the Lodge.

Her pink cheeks glowed as she smiled at Keith and patted him reassuringly on the shoulder. "We can always make more."

"Keith has butterfingers," Bubbles informed me. "He dropped the bowl while he was mixing the sauce."

Marcy lightly swatted Bubbles with a dishtowel. "Don't make him feel bad. He's learning. Come here, Keith. I'll teach you the easiest way to peel garlic."

"Can I borrow Bubbles for a minute?" I asked Marcy. "I'll have her back to you shortly."

"Keep her," Marcy joked.

Bubbles followed me out of the kitchen and down the first-floor corridor. I led her to the last room. It was bigger than before. We'd removed the massive safe door and included the secret room in the renovations. Simon and I concluded that the best way to hide the intersecting ley lines was in plain sight. No one would suspect that my work office was situated over one of the most powerful points on the earth.

I sat behind the desk and drew something out of the drawer. "I have an early Christmas present for you."

Bubbles, who had grown four inches since her four-teenth birthday, rewarded me with a wide grin. "What is it?"

I handed her the wrapped gift. She held it in her palms and pressed it to her chest.

"Is this what I think it is?" she asked.

"Open it and see."

She ripped the red-and-white paper off and squealed happily when she saw what was beneath it. "An advance copy of *Rebel Queen: Volume Four*!" She kissed the cover and spun around. "Thank you, thank you, thank you!"

As she suffocated me with a hug, I said, "You have to keep that to yourself. No posting spoilers online. No one knows you have it, and if my publisher finds out I gave it away before the release date, he'll kill me. Got it?"

She stuck out her pinky for me to shake. "I promise."

"Get out of here, punk."

As Bubbles pranced off, I shook my head and sighed. Sometimes, it was hard for me to believe my life right now was real. It all seemed too perfect. When that feeling hit me, I made a point to sit back and enjoy it.

I scooted my chair back and propped my feet up on the desk, facing the window so I could watch the snow lazily drift from the sky. A soft pulse of energy flowed up from the floor and warmed my body, a sweet reminder of more good things to come. In it, I felt the presence of Lily, Earl, and the other spirits who had helped us make this place beautiful again.

All was right with the Silver Creek Lodge.

Made in the USA
Columbia, SC
17 February 2025

54017107R00170